James Miller was born in Caithness in 1948, with an upbringing divided between a croft and a fishing village.

After studying at Aberdeen University, he taught in the Philippines, and then worked for the British Council in both London and Afghanistan; he now lives near Inverness.

His previous published work includes *Caithness* (Skelton & Shaw, 1979), *Portrait of Caithness and Sutherland* (Robert Hale, 1985), and a part of *A Fine White Stoor* appeared in an earlier form in *Dougie* (self-published, 1986).

A FINE WHITE STOOR

A FINE WHITE STOOR

JAMES MILLER

to Fiona
with best wishes
James Miller

BALNAIN

Text © James Miller 1992

Printed and bound in Britain by BPCC Wheatons, Exeter

The publisher gratefully acknowledges subsidy from the Scottish
Arts Council towards the publication of this volume.

Published in 1992 by
Balnain Books
Druim House,
LochLoy Road,
Nairn IV12 5LF

British Library Cataloguing in Publication Data
A catalogue record for this book is available from
the British Library

ISBN 0-872557-16-3

The work was completed in 1981 and any resemblance to events since then in Caithness is purely coincidental. Likewise, any readers who think they recognise the characters are mistaken; all the characters and events are fictitious.

The author is grateful to the Executors of the Estate of the late Sir Alexander Gray for permission to quote from the poem 'Scotland', from *Gossip*, published by Faber and Faber, 1928.

PART ONE

RAIN AND FROST

CHAPTER ONE

Dougie awoke as the alarm clock clattered into life and, as he stretched his hand to snap it into silence, he realised it was Hogmanay — the last day of the year.

It was dark everywhere in the room and everywhere outside, the curtains a black wall dividing two areas of darkness. In winter it was like that — you rose before the sun and went to bed long after it.

He found the switch and clicked light into the room. His clothes lay in an untidy pile on the chair, the dungarees draped like an empty man across the arms. He threw back the blankets and swung his legs to the floor, shivering a little in the chill air.

Dressed, he unlocked the door of the house. A stiff westerly breeze was rattling the skeletons of the raspberry bushes in the garden. He stepped up onto the hillock at the end of the house, turned his back on the wind and urinated into the gloom.

It looked like rain — great clouds massing there in the west against the lesser darkness of the sky. A faintness marked the east, the first note in a long, slow dawn.

He went back into the house and switched on the electric fire in the kitchen. His mother would light the peat fire later when she rose. While he waited for the electric kettle to boil, he spread butter thickly on a bannock and began to munch it. On the radio, a woman was giving tips for a new year party. His own bottle for the celebrations stood in its brown-paper wrapping on the sideboard, behind the clock and next to the bottles of sheep medicine.

He stood before the mirror and combed his hair, dragging the instrument through the brown, tousled mass. At the same time he felt his chin and decided to postpone shaving until the evening, before he went first-footing. The singing of the kettle reached a high note and then fell off as a stream of vapour belched across the table. He put half a spoonful of tea into a mug and poured on the boiling water.

The air in the byre was thick and heavy, and the amber light from the solitary cobwebbed bulb in the rafters made everything cosy. The cows struggled to their feet as he came in and closed the door behind him. Two cats, anticipating food, emerged from the straw. He bent and stroked one, and it purred and rubbed against his boots. He broke open a bale of hay and threw lumps of the compressed grass into each of the cows' hecks. As they chewed, he scraped away the sharn from their heels and heaped it in the drain that ran the length of the byre.

There were three cows, and two stirks who were both well grown now and likely to fetch a good price at the mart in a few months' time. His father had kept five cattle but Dougie had decided after the old man's death to invest more in sheep, animals more to his liking and less work too, all in all. But he kept three cows, as much as anything for the milk which he could sell to tourists in the summer, and for the subsidy. It took only a few minutes for him to fill his pail with warm frothing milk. He poured a skint into the cats' dish and clanked out of the byre into the grey morning.

His family had been in the croft for as long as anyone in the district could remember. Once, he had taken an interest in genealogy and had made extensive enquiries among the older men and women of the parish, but nobody could mind anything further back than his great grandfather who had fought in the Crimea, or was it India, and had come home with a limp he carried to the end of his days. Memories of old Dan'l were vague even for Isa, who was past ninety and still with a clear head. 'I mind him,' she had said, 'because I used to go to the hoose when I was just a bairn, and he would put us on the pony's back — a fine horsie it was, with four black feet and a long mane. Your great grandad had a whisker and he used to grab us bairns and rub his face against us. Oh we used to skirl. Now he got the croft fae his faither but that was before my time. I heard them speaking aboot it but I canna mind his name. Have ye no tried the kirk records?'

But the kirk records only went as far back as the beginning of the century; the minister said the older stuff had been lost in the fire when the vestry burned. That had been in 1898 and a terrible thing it had been; it had taken five years to have the damage repaired.

'Your grandfather now I mind fine,' Isa had said. 'It was him who took the Hill Park into grass and wi a spade too.'

The Hill Park had been a sloping waste of heather and peat hag but by his own efforts the grandfather had drained it and sown it until it became the meadow it now was, still prone to flooding but otherwise good pasture. Grandfather's picture still hung in the kitchen: the face was solemn, the eyes gazing off somewhere to the right under thick brows and a high forehead topped with a wave of swept-back hair. Dougie often stared at the face and imagined occasionally that the eyes moved with the hint of humour in them and that the corners of the mouth crinkled. An unkempt beard hid the chin but the upper lip was shaved clean. Dougie saw his grandfather as a man of vision; the eyes were looking beyond the croft to more patches of heather and rush which could become more hill parks. Isa said it had taken seven years of hard trauchle to bring in the acres and it seemed it had been too much for the man — not long after that he had died, falling in the stooks in the throes of a heart attack.

Dougie ducked inside the milkhouse and set the filled pail on the flagstone shelf. The squat chamber had a cool, creamy smell. He picked out two eggs from a basket and

13

took them into the house for his breakfast.

His mother was up and boiling the kettle for more tea. She was a short, slightly bent figure with grey, watery eyes set close together in a lined face, framed with a checked headscarf, which she always wore except when she went to town, when it was replaced by a hat. Her hands were fleshy and rough, the fingers a little stiff with arthritis.

'It looks like rain,' said Dougie, placing the eggs on the table.

'The forecast said it would be dry,' said his mother, taking the eggs and putting them in a pan on the cooker. 'They're aye wrong.'

He picked up a copy of the *Farmer's Weekly*, as she started to rake out the ashes from below the grate. The sky was bright now, yellowish gray in the east between the layers of cloud, and when she had finished with the ashes she rose to put off the kitchen light. The new day suffused the room and glinted on the brassware, the ornaments and the photographs.

As well as of his grandfather, there were pictures of other members of the family. His cousin Elsie and her husband lived in Canada now and sent long letters describing the good life they were leading, the big house, the two cars and the children's progress through school. Each Christmas they sent a card with their photo on it. Next to their latest one stood a faded brown picture of Dougie's Uncle Charlie, who had been killed at Ypres when he was nineteen. Stuck into a corner of the frame was a small blurred print of Dougie himself taken when he was ten; his mother had discovered the image at the bottom of an old tin box and had rescued it from oblivion.

The largest picture on the sideboard showed the face of Dougie's father. The mouth was open in a smile but Dougie thought it gave the man a vacant look, as if he had been persuaded to pose by a handful of beads like some native in a far-off colony. He had been a man with little imagination, substituting toil for ambition. Everybody said the brains of the grandfather had skipped a generation. The croft should of course have passed to Charlie, the eldest brother, but he, poor soul, had met his end in the trenches. The other brothers had done well in their trades and had long since gone south to Edinburgh or Glasgow. Only young Dan had been left to take over the croft and it had never for a moment entered the youngest son's head that he could have done something else for himself. He likewise could never conceive of the land and the house not passing to Dougie, nor of Dougie's possible wish to seek another source of livelihood.

Thus Dougie was groomed to be a crofter and was taken out of school at the earliest opportunity, three days after his fifteenth birthday, to drive the tractor, catch sheep and scythe thistles.

With the dawn, the wind freshened and blew in sharp, cutting gusts from the west. Dougie pulled his bonnet lower on his brow and strode quickly to the old stable to let the dog out. Bess heard his feet on the flags long before his hand reached for the sneck and, as soon as the door was open, she disappeared between his legs on her daily rampage around the croft, scattering the hens and barking and coming back to lie like a tense spring at her master's feet.

'Come on, ya daft bitch,' he said.

Then he got out the tractor and drove bales of hay down to the parks at the edge of the hill, rough pasture with tufts of wind-battered rushes in the hollows and whins to give some shelter to the flock. Here he had built a manger of net strung on posts. The net was coloured orange, grey, black and pink, made from pieces gleaned from the beach and wherever he could find them. He broke open the bales of hay and spread them in the net; and the sheep came down from the hill and out from the whins to feed, bleating and eyeing the dog. As they jostled at the fodder, he stood back to count them, and felt the first spits of rain on his face.

'Michty, what rain!'

Dan and his wife and young Dougie all scraped their

feet in turn on the wire mat and stepped into the house, acknowledging the greeting from Dan's wife's sister Bella.

Dougie had been warned to be on his best behaviour, as if he needed reminding, with his hair slicked down with oil the way it was and his neck near throttled in a tie. Bella was his mother's oldest sister and she was a widow; Dougie knew what the word meant but at the age of eight he was not quite sure why such a state should command such obeisance. After all, old Jeanie at the end of the loch was a widow but he never had his hair plastered to his head with oil when they went to visit her. Bella was educated, or so his mother said; maybe that was why.

Bella spoke in proper English and occasionally lapsed into dialect. She had been a teacher in Edinburgh and had married a headmaster, coming back to the parish after her man had died a few years into his retirement. Bella was in her sixties; she was also very religious and played the organ in the kirk.

They all took their coats off in the hall, as Bella called the porch, and shook them gently. Bowls of geraniums and maidenhair ferns watched them.

'And how are you all?' asked Bella when they were all ensconced in the ben room. Dougie was sitting up straight as he had been instructed.

'Fine, no reason til complain at all,' said Dan. 'How are you keeping yourself?' And so the conversation rambled on — what awful weather, the minister had gone to see his sister for the new year, Annag had a new hat, frost had nipped a rose bush in the corner of the garden, wasn't young Georgie MacDonald cheeky for answering back Mrs Gunn at the shop when she told him to keep his fingers off the liquorice unless he intended to buy it. Dougie saw it coming: 'I'm sure you don't behave like that, Douglas,' said Bella.

He blushed and his mother looked proud. His father took out his cigarettes and Bella set sail to the sideboard for an ashtray.

'And how are you doing at school?'

The hated question. What could you say in the presence

of your parents and an aunt who was a teacher and religious.

'He's at his lessons when he has to,' his mother answered for him.

'If he can count and sign his name, that'll do him fine,' said his father. 'Nobody needed Latin til follow a ploo.'

'That's a bit hard Daniel,' said Bella. 'Well, if you do your best, Douglas, we can't complain, can we?'

She smiled at him, and he blushed and murmured a weak affirmative. Despite her posh ways, he quite liked his aunt: the house was cosy and the sofa — not a couch — was comfortable, and she would slip him a shilling on their departure.

Eventually Bella moved to indicate the advent of the tea. This, in turn, gave Dan the cue to produce his bottle of whisky and to say, as he always did on these occasions, 'Ye'll tak a wee dram for the new year.' And, as always on these occasions, Bella shook her head and replied, 'Oh, just a wee droppie.' And out came four glasses, small ones, with pipers on their sides.

'Would you like a taste of sherry?' said Bella to her mother.

'Just a wee drop,' she replied, as usual.

'And for you, Douglas, I've got something very special,' went on Bella. 'The children in Edinburgh loved it but this is the first time I've made any here.'

From the innards of the sideboard she produced a lemonade bottle filled with a dull liquid. She poured some into a tumbler and handed it to him. It was green, a glimmering concoction that flickered in the light. What had happened to the sweet strawberry cordial of yester year and fond memory? Dougie held the tumbler between thumb and forefinger.

'It's ginger wine,' pronounced Bella in triumph.

'What do you say?' prompted his mother.

'Thanks,' he said. He put the glass to his lips. The first mouthful took the skin off his tongue and seared the inside of his nose. He swallowed and breathed flames.

Sweat broke out on his face. He stared, pop-eyed, at the fire, which seemed suddenly cold. He wanted to spit.

But his mother was going on about the ginger wine old Jamesina used to make and how grand it had been, and Bella was pouring a glass of whisky for his father. She gave Dan a glass for him to fill with his whisky for her and, while his father slowly uncorked his bottle, Dougie gently took another very small sip. He swept it around his mouth and mixed it with copious amounts of saliva before swallowing. Sensation was returning to his oral organs.

'Do you like that now, Douglas?' enquired Bella.

'Aye,' he whispered.

A plate of black bun and slices of cherry cake appeared, and he chewed away the fire. By the time the kettle had boiled, he had reduced the amount of ginger wine by one quarter. The table was laid with Bella's finest floral crockery, silver teaspoons and knives, butter, jam, marmalade, crowdie, bannocks, bread and cakes. By the time they were ready to sit at this feast, he had half of the ginger wine left. When the adults rose and turned away from him, he stretched his arm to a geranium pot and swiftly emptied the vile liquid onto the soil. Just in time.

'Would you like another glass, Douglas?'

'No thank you Auntie Bella.'

The road from the croft ran straight towards the village two miles away. The first stretch was rough stones interspersed with puddles which rose and spread in the wind to soften the earth and turn it into sticky mire. Beyond this, an asphalted road came in from the left and bore the tracks of vehicles like broad smears of paint. On either side lay bare fields, windblasted at this time of year with tufts of sheep wool fluttering on the barbed wire and stone dykes.

From the hillock at the end of the house, Dougie could see almost the entire stretch of road, except for a hollow with tangled hawthorn and a few bedraggled willows where it dipped to cross a burn. Now he could see a figure on a bicycle and, from the style of pedalling, the shape of the hunched shoulders and because there would only be one person who would be cycling to visit him at this time, he recognised Donald's Jamie.

The cyclist took several minutes to cover the last rough half mile, slowly avoiding the puddles and pushing against the stiff breeze scouring from the west. Still, for a man of seventy, he was doing well, thought Dougie. Bess rushed off, a barking arrow, to welcome the visitor.

'Ho, ho,' cried Donald's Jamie when he applied the brakes, Bess swirling round him and furiously wagging her tail.

'Aye, Jamie,' said Dougie. 'Sit doon, Bess.'

'That's a tough pedal wi that wind.' The old man's face gleamed with the exertion. He took out a handkerchief that looked as if it had been last used to clean a stove and blew his nose loudly. He was short and thickset, with a square face and a prominent nose laced with red veins. His flat bonnet was rammed tight over his forehead and now he eased it upward to reveal the weather mark where the white skin of his bald head began.

Dougie stood with his hands deep in his dungaree pockets. 'Micht be rain. How are ye the day?'

'Canna complain. All fine yoursels? I seed Geordie sorting his fence at the brig.'

'He said he was going to do that the other day.'

'All set for the night?'

'The bottle's ready.'

'I took back your drill.' Donald's Jamie fumbled inside his zipped-up blue anorak and brought out the tool he had borrowed several weeks before. From another pocket he removed a clutch of bits in a torn plastic bag.

'Ye could have waited for a better day,' said Dougie, though he knew that Donald's Jamie always settled his debts and returned loans at this time, so that he could start the new year a free man, as he termed it. Of course, it was fairly certain that he would be back within a couple of days to borrow the drill again, but that would be next year's obligation.

'I finished another creel last nicht,' said the old man proudly.

Before he had retired, Donald's Jamie had kept a boat and set lobster creels every summer. In winter he still made fishing gear which he sold to supplement his pension. Occasionally he wove nets for the crofters and farmers, who used them to secure grain stacks against the wind.

Dougie offered a cigarette and both men hunched to light up. At the first draw, Donald's Jamie burst into a fit of coughing. 'The ould wind's getting done,' he spluttered.

They moved into the lee of the tractor shed.

'I must take in a loads of neeps as long's it's dry,' said Dougie.

'Aye.'

'I mayna be so active the morn.'

Donald's Jamie wheezed with laughter at this reference to a future hangover. 'I'll away in and see your mother.' And he clumped out of sight around the house.

Dougie hitched the cart to the tractor and drove to the turnip field. Clouds were piling in from the west. The neeps were already plucked and cut free from earth and shaw, and lay in rows like dull, irregular bowls. With a greip it did not take long to fill the cart, or with sufficient to feed the cattle for a day or two. It was no use breaking your back for the sake of it.

'Ye're not working hard enough if ye're not sweating,' his father had said years ago to encourage his young son to drag and throw and push weights too much for a boy. In the pride of adolescence Dougie had slaved to match his father's strength until his body had grown stiff and sore. Now he was his own boss and only the hot summer sun stained his shirt with sweat.

A flock of lapwings wheeled over the moor and two crows flew swiftly down the hill to the sea. Drops of rain spotted the tractor with a darker grey as he drove back to the steading.

In the house, his mother and Donald's Jamie, still with

his bicycle clips on, were drinking tea.

'Jamie was saying that Jean at the shop is no well again,' said his mother, as he poured himself a cup.

'She's never well,' he grunted.

-Always the same, this endless merry-go-round of gossip. It's all they speak about — weather, illness, lack o illness, the price o paraffin, who's expecting, how long they've been married, Geordag's fences in a mess so that his sheep are never oot o Big Annag's land, the price o coal, Callum drunk again, Mary Ross's bad leg — is it enough to satisfy them, talk like this? They're no stupid yet they've let their brains rust in their heads as if they never needed to learn another thing as long's they live. Nobody seems interested in the things I'm interested in.

'Did you go to the pub last nicht?' asked Donald's Jamie.

'No,' said Dougie. 'I wanted to see something on the TV.'

Donald's Jamie sucked noisily at his tea. Then he rose and put his bonnet on his bald head. 'Weel, I'd better be going home or I'll get shot.'

'Tell Kathie I was asking for her and tell her I'll be doon some afternoon,' said Dougie's mother. 'Ye can take some eggs wi ye.'

'Oh no, no. The last time I did that I cracked the lot in my pocket. Thanks all the same.'

'Ye sure? Dougie can take them doon later on.'

'Aye,' said Dougie. 'I'll drop them off.'

'That'll do fine,' Donald's Jamie clumped out, speaking over his shoulder. 'The rain's no that heavy yet and wi this wind I'll get home before it thickens in.'

He took his bike from the wall and wheeled it to the edge of the road. 'Weel weel then,' he cried, throwing his leg in a stiff arc over the bar and wobbling off between the puddles.

Dougie watched him for a few moments and then went to unload the turnips. As he threw them into the old stable, he remembered a dream he had had a few nights before. It had been a strange fantasy, all the stranger for his having remembered it vividly. He had been crouching behind a drystone dyke, peering over the top across a clutter of fields and sheds. In the sky, planes, jet planes like those that screeched over the land when pilots were in training, hurtled this way and that. It was war. One plane dived towards the wall where he was crouching, a sharp, black insect falling at him. He could see it still and it had the insignia of America on its side. Suddenly from its belly a small, black object dropped. A bomb. He could remember that, in his dream, he had thought this is the end. The black bomb fell slowly, gracefully, to the ground and the whole world exploded in a hot, searing wave of red light. That image had stuck with him so clearly that he could still recall waking up in a sweat, as if a real blast of heat had seared across him in sleep.

-Funny. Queer. Never had a dream like that afore. Maybe I have the second sicht and saw the end of the world, a holocaust, like the Brahan Seer. He must have been a funny mannie, wandering aboot the glens wi a small, round stone wi a hole in the middle, looking through it wi his darting eye, looking richt into the future.

Of course he did not talk to anyone about these things, or about his dream. Well, who was there to talk to? None who would not laugh and scratch their heads and say that he must be off his nut.

The last turnip thudded against the stable wall. He lowered the sneck on the door.

No, he knew what they would say as they drowned their sniggering in a pint: 'He's no wise, that Dougie.'

CHAPTER TWO

'Ye're no wise, Dougie,' said an angry Rob, hitching up his short trousers around his stomach.

'We can, we can,' whispered Dougie in great excitement.

'Nobody'll see us.'

The darkness of the Halloween night swirled about them and they could barely see each other's eyes in the gloom. Psychology was called for. 'Rob's a cowardie calfie,' sang Dougie at the top of his voice. The taunt spurred Rob to action and they grappled, falling in a flailing of arms and legs on the grass.

'Listen,' panted Dougie at a lull in their fighting.

'I've skinned my knee,' lamented Rob.

'Listen,' persisted his companion, adopting a conspiratorial whisper once again. The air was filled with night noises. They could hear the world breathe as it spun through the darkness. 'I ken how to open the shed and the cart's no heavy. I lifted it masel the other day. We can be in and off wi it no bother.'

'Where til?'

'I dinna ken,' said Dougie impatiently. 'Yes, I do. Doon til the hollow where the whins are. We can hide it there and ould Sannag'll never find it.'

'He'll be oot on the road, his bald head like a lichthoose, stopping everybody and saying 'Have ye seen my cart?' ' Rob laughed and rolled on the ground.

'Come on then,' encouraged Dougie.

They set off along the track to Sannag's croft, grinning

and joking, their eyes bright with their imaginings and eager with the thoughts of the night's ploy, their best trick yet for a Halloween. Just wait until the school on Monday, when they would breathlessly tell the others and be the heroes of the week.

The growl of a car came across the fields and two beams of light stabbed into the sky.

'The bobbies!' exclaimed Rob.

'No,' said a confident Dougie, after a moment's reflection. 'So what if it is. They won't come up here.'

'No, they'll no,' agreed Rob. 'Any bangers left?'

'Aye, I've got one. Have ye none?'

'I set off the last one at the corner. Licht yours now.'

'No, let's keep it for Sannag.'

'Right.'

They passed along the road, the one firework for a victory salute, and soon the darker bulk of the crofts appeared before them. Here and there a square of yellow light shone like a navigation beacon. A few stars winked between the clouds.

It was All Hallows Eve, the last day of the old Celtic year. It was the night that the evil spirits, the witches and the warlocks, the bo'men and beasties, came up from their dark, subterranean caverns and roamed the face of the world of men. Rob, in his shorts that were too big for him, and Dougie, brave stealer of carts, hurried towards their tryst with devilment. As they neared Sannag's croft, they slowed. He had a dog which he always kept chained... maybe, seeing it was Halloween, he had let the brute loose. No dog. No sudden thunderburst of barking splitting the night and making them take to the nearest ditch. They were at the end of the croft now, two still, dark figures against the whitewashed harl. They listened. The breeze moved in a soft sussuration over the grass. They could smell the smoke of the peat fire; Sannag would be sitting by that fire, watching the flames or reading the paper, his socks on a length of string along the mantel-piece to dry for the morn.

'Round the back,' whispered Dougie.

'Ssssh,' hissed Rob, turning to follow his friend into the stackyard, where the cornscroos stood like sleeping giants. Their feet rustled in the straw.

'What's that?' said Dougie.

'Just a cat,' whispered Rob. 'I think.'

They circled the back of the house and crept in towards the barn. The object of the assault lay behind the wide, brown door. It would not be an easy task but Dougie had spied out the land several days before, when his mother had sent him over with some milk for Sannag, the old man's cow being ill and dry. Sannag had been locking the barn door when he had arrived; the key to the padlock was to be found between two stones in the wall. Round the corner of the barn they scurried, their hands touching the rough stones in case they lost their direction and the darkness, the witches and the bogles claimed them.

Dougie felt over the stones to find the key. There it was, a cold, rusty finger with a ring at one end. Now for the padlock. As he touched it, it creaked on the hasp. The noise stopped the blood in their veins and they both froze, their hearts pounding, every muscle taut, ears straining and combing the dark air for a clue. Nothing. No dog. No scrape on the stone.

'Hurry up,' hissed Rob.

'It's all richt.' Dougie pushed the key into the lock. It fitted easily enough. Turn to the left. To the right. To the left again, this time more pressure.

'It's stuck,' he whispered.

'Try it the other way.'

'I have done.'

'Gie me a shot.'

'Wait.'

Turn to the right, to the left, the right. Push as hard as he dared.

'Come on.'

'Go til hell.'

The key was making rusty, scratching noises.

Dougie decided that the situation was desperate. He

gave a savage wrench to the key and it turned in the lock with a clatter. The padlock slid open.

'Got it.'

'Dinna lose the key,' whispered Rob. 'We can put it back.'

The final elegant touch to the robbery. Closing the door of the safe. It could be days before Sannag discovered his loss. Dougie hung the lock on a ring in the door and carefully put the key back in its slot in the wall. The next task was to slide back the bolt that held the two halves of the broad barn door together. As like as not it too would be rusty and stiff and would make enough noise to waken every dog in the parish.

He pushed it slowly and firmly. 'The bolt's stuck too.'

'Let me have a try.' Rob pushed him aside and abandoned his caution in a fever of activity. Dougie stepped back and looked around him. He could distinguish the edge of the roof against the sky. A yellow square of curtained light marked the croft kitchen. He gazed at the window, not more than ten yards away, as if he could see through the pattern of roses to where Sannag was sitting under his drying socks.

The squeak of the bolt made him start. 'Ssssh! He's bound to hear us now.'

'I've got it! I've got it!' Rob's voice was wild with excitement.

Far away across the fields someone had set off a rocket and a bright trail of pink and orange sparks fell like rain.

'Be quiet,' said Dougie nervously. 'Open the door slowly.'

The two barn doors swung forward under their pull, rasping a little on the hinges.

'I canna see anything,' whispered Rob, peering into the barn.

'It's just here,' said Dougie.

As their eyes adjusted to the barn's gloom, they were able to make out the drawbar of the cart, a metal tongue with a cold sheen to it. They moved one to either side of it and lifted it from the floor. 'Ready?' asked Dougie.

'One, two, three.... pull.' They grunted with exertion, but nothing happened. The cart did not budge. Rob had a flash of insight. 'There are blocks at the wheels.'

They felt their way back into the dark, tracing the outline of the cart, the sloping sides, the ridge of the floor, the smooth, cold rubber of the tyres, the colder iron of the wheels. Two stones had been placed in front of them as brakes. They lifted the stones aside and breathlessly tiptoed back to the drawbar.

'One, two, three... heave.'

With a slight bump, they found themselves being propelled forwards into the night air. Out from under the eaves, across the flagstones, onto the grass, with a soft swish. A cart, once moving, was easy to pull but not so easy to steer and, whispering instructions to each other, they made an erratic path towards the road.

'The door,' said Dougie suddenly. 'I left it open.'

'Never mind,' said Rob. 'Come on. Pull.'

But Dougie was not going to be deprived of the master stroke. Rob reluctantly lowered the drawbar.

Dougie ran back across the grass. The lit window shone peacefully. One door closed. Squeaking. The other door. More squeaking, piercing the calm like the cry of a wounded soldier. The bolt. As was so often the case with farm doors, the hinges were old and tired and the shank of the bolt drooped below the slot. Dougie pushed it but it would not go in. He was sweating now. He twisted the bolt to try to drive it home. The metal rasped. He leaned against the door and shoogled the bolt frantically. At last it slipped across. Now the padlock. It took only two seconds to push it home. He loped across the grass back to the impatient Rob.

'Sannag's dog must be as deaf as Sannag himsel,' he laughed.

They picked up the drawbar and resumed their trudge to the road, the black mass of the barn receding behind them. At the edge of the road they had to allow the cart to slide down a slight bank. It bounced and clattered on the chassis.

It was then they heard the car. It must have been approaching for some time because the noise of the engine, when it finally penetrated their senses, was already loud and near. The twin beams of the headlights, which would have warned them, were absent; the driver was using his sidelights only, and Rob and Dougie saw the two dull, yellow stars speeding towards them.

'It's the bobbies,' cried Rob.

'Run,' shouted Dougie.

They dropped the drawbar and fled into the darkness, scrambling a twanging trail through a barbed-wire fence, tearing pell-mell across the grass until they collapsed, gasping, hugging the earth.

The car had stopped, its way blocked by the abandoned cart. To see what was what, the driver had turned on the headlamps, and the object of their mischief sat bathed in light. Someone came out of the car. They heard the door echo menacingly across the fields. They pressed themselves into the grass until they were watching through a fringe of withered stalks. Voices came faintly to them. The burst of activity had awakened Sannag's dog. Barking rose from the dark huddle of buildings. The curtain on the window flickered, a shadow crossed it and a few moments later the door of the croft opened. The boys saw the silhouette of Sannag and heard his voice. 'Who's that? What's going on?'

Sannag's silhouette disappeared and soon they saw him hirple into the light of the headlamps. Then came the loud cry that set them laughing so that they had to press their faces into the ground to stop the noise that would betray them. They would remember that cry, in its way ample compensation for the failure of their primary objective.

'That's my damn cart,' yelled Sannag. 'How did it get there?'

CHAPTER THREE

By the time Dougie had finished unloading the turnips, the sky had become an impenetrable grey and the rain was falling steadily. There was nothing more to be done outside. Bess flopped on the mat before the fire and began to lick her sopping paws.

'When are ye going doon to the shop?' asked his mother.

'It closes at half past twelve,' he said.

'I'll get some eggs for Kathie fae the milkhoose and ye can take them doon wi ye.' She stood at the window gazing through the streaming panes. Her face was solemn, grey in the grey light. Dougie wandered what could be going through her mind. Of late she had aged a great deal, he thought. She had never been quick-witted but now she seemed to have abandoned interest in most things. Her ageing annoyed him, and he thought her mind had become a shopping list of trivia.

'I'll go and get the eggs then,' she said and, taking an old waterproof from the back of the kitchen door, shuffled out of the room.

—Maybe she's lonely. But it's five years now since faither died. She canna still be missing him. I suppose it's just old age and she's getting dottled a bit — as if her nerves, like a bundle o elastic cords, are snapping one by one. Ping, ping, ping. Funny thing. Here's Donald's Jamie, three score and ten, still fit, his brain as sharp as it aye was, or maybe sharper, tuned like a well-running engine. And she's five years younger.

He rose and went through to the bedroom. The curtains had been drawn back and a pale light suffused the room. A large print of a sailing ship hung above the bed, and a bottle full of seashells glinted on the mantelpiece above the lifeless fire. He sat on the unmade bed and eyed the untidy pile of books on the sideboard against the back wall.

There were novels, cheap Westerns and detective thrillers, some Scottish works by a mixture of authors — Scott, Gibbon, Tranter, Stevenson — and a volume or two of history and wildlife. Next to the books lay a mishmash of magazines and old newspapers, yellowing at the edges. He had become of late a voracious reader, absorbing everything that came his way, digesting every word as if on a frantic epic of discovery, and never throwing anything away.

For a long time he had not read a thing. His room always had some books but they remained unopened for years, until dust and dead spiders obscured the type and dampness spread tiny maps across the covers.

When he did eventually open them, he found they were prizes awarded to his father and other members of the family by the parish school. For Attendance, For Endeavour, For Geography — each one bore inside a citation in faded ink, long sloping copperplate letters trapped by swirling bunches of gold and blue flowers. The prizes won by his father, Dougie noted, had nearly always been for attendance. Strangely enough, a mouldy New Testament was awarded once for religious knowledge, and this by a man who had never allowed a good word for the kirk to pass his lips.

'I was a good scholar,' Dougie remembered his father saying, 'Hardly missed a day at the school the whole time I was going to it.'

The first book that Dougie read for enjoyment and of his own free will was one of these abandoned heirlooms: *Treasure Island* by R.L. Stevenson.

It had been a black, wet day and he had been in a black mood to match it. Sullen and rebellious, he sneaked ben from the kitchen, carrying his boredom like a burden. In the room he picked up a book from the literary graveyard.

It was the picture of a pirate with one leg that attracted him, a splash of colour on an otherwise grey day. He turned the pages one by one and then started to read. Slowly he became totally absorbed, savouring every word and phrase and imagining the scenes in the Admiral Benbow Inn, the drunken old sailor reminding him of a tinker who had come to the house one day to buy scrap. He had reached the part where Blind Pew appears when his father's voice broke into his imagining.

'What ye doing, boy?'

'Just looking at a book.' He felt a flush of shame at being caught. Books meant school and his wisdom demanded that school be despised.

'Well, ye can put that doon,' his father said. 'Books'll no feed the animals. Come and gie me a hand.'

And out they went into the wind and rain to carry neeps from the stable to the byre. Dougie had hardly been able to wait to finish the work; his mind was back on the cliffs of Cornwall at the Admiral Benbow.

'Mind what ye're doing wi that neeps,' his father growled. 'What's wrong wi ye that ye're pitching the damn neeps like that? Ca canny.'

'Aye,' Dougie growled in return.

When they had finished and the cows were champing contentedly, he asked: 'Is that all for now?'

He wasted no time in returning to his room and the book. He had discovered a great source of secret pleasure, the key to a world at once private and a part of the wider world beyond the croft, the school, the village and all the places he knew. It was a secret to be guarded carefully, sheltered from the mockery of his friends and family.

Rob thought reading was sissy, or so he said — an opinion Dougie shared. The books handed out at school were instruments of torture and they remained safely in the darkness of his bag until the hoodie-crow voice of Miss MacKay forced them into his hands.

'Douglas, you will read from the top of page eleven.'

'Yes, miss.' And he read slowly and without emphasis, his tongue stumbling over the millstones of words, deliberately making a bad job of it. Miss MacKay, perched on her high stool, her glasses perched on her nose, chalk-dust in her hair, would lament and scold and try to drum up some interest in the mind of her recalcitrant pupil.

'All right, Douglas, that's enough. Helen will you please read the next page?'

And at the end of the next page, the teacher would say, 'Very good, Helen.' And Dougie would be listening to the sound of a tractor passing outside or following a bluebottle battering itself on the window pane in a futile attempt to escape to the sun.

It took several days to finish *Treasure Island*; when he reached the last page, he felt lost, as if an old friend had departed never to be seen again. He turned to the local papers and read them hungrily from end to end.

'Boy, there must be gold in that paper,' his father said. 'For God's sake, put it doon and speak til folk. Ye'll burn the een oot o your head.'

'No, I winna,' he muttered.

'Och leave him when he's at peace,' his mother said. 'Your grandfather was a great reader.'

'And muckle good it did him,' said his father.

And Dougie would put the paper down to speak to folk but there rarely had been a conversation that held the same magic as the words on the page.

Apart from the papers and the occasional magazine that found its way into their house, he soon ran out of reading material. The other books in the ben room were tried and found wanting: turgid stories by turn-of-the-century pedants, moralistic preachings and long-winded descriptions, nothing to capture the imagination and hold it like a delighted prisoner in a magic cell. So it was with great anticipation that Dougie waited for the chance to start his

own library. He set aside a half crown from the tin box in
which he saved what money came his way.

The chance came when he accompanied his father one
day to the town to attend a sheep sale. They rode on the
bus. His half crown sat, a hard, polished circle, in his
pocket; normally it might have been exchanged for bat-
teries, a pock of chips, ice-cream — but not today.

It was lonely being a conspirator but he said nothing
during the half-hour it took the bus to sway and rumble
through the countryside. His father conversed with their
fellow passengers and ignored him.

The mart stood on the edge of town near the railway
station, a labyrinth of pens, fences and gates through
which men and animals made their way to the corrugated
iron shed in the centre, where the auctioneer presided
over the smell and the noise. He stood in a box like a
pulpit above the sawdust ring into which bewildered
yowes were driven by dog, stick and shout to be bought
and sold. Each group of sheep changed hands in a matter
of seconds under the auctioneer's bullying voice and was
hustled out through one of the many exits, while an
elderly clerk scratched in a ledger with a fountain pen.

The farmers, the crofters, the buyers and those who
just watched milled around the ring in their tweeds and
dun raincoats, their hats and their flat caps, a frieze of
intent red faces.

Dougie enjoyed the excitement of the mart. His father
moved through the throng, greeting acquaintances, prod-
ding sheep to see how thin or fat they were, noticing who
was buying and the prices they offered. He followed his
father, learning how to judge a good yowe and spot the
bidders. A wink, a flick of the finger, a tug to straighten
the hat — these were the signs the auctioneer's scurrying
eye picked up and acknowledged with an upping of the
price.

Dougie's father was seeking new yowes for his small
flock. Eventually, among the pens, he found what he was
wanting, a group of three who looked fit enough but were
unlikely to command too high a price. The catalogue told

that their owner was a farmer of repute. That was fine, then. 'I think we can go and sit doon now,' said the father, and they went to find a seat on the rows of wooden benches beside the sales ring.

They watched for a while and at last the group of sheep they had had their eye on came in. The auctioneer began his chorus again. 'Three fine yowes now fae Gunn Knockloch. What do I hear now?' The price rose rapidly at first and then levelled off. 'Come on, now,' urged the auctioneer, his eyes sweeping the circle of hats and bonnets. 'A good bit o mutton there.' He changed the price again, raising his hammer, coaxing the canny buyers to bid.

Dougie watched his father who bid with a quick, almost imperceptible nod. The hammer crashed into the desk and the auctioneer pointed with his chin in their direction. The clerk looked and resumed his scratching.

Dougie's father waited until three more groups of yowes had been sold before he rose and made his way down to the pens. They exchanged a few pleasantries with the seller who gave them back ten shillings as a luck penny.

On the way out from the mart, they met an old acquaintance, a broad, burly man with a face like a bowl of apples and a pipe clenched firmly between false teeth. The reunion was raucous and wreathed in fumes of black twist.

'Dan Bayne,' cried the man. 'My God, how are ye doing? There must be little to do at home if ye're here.'

'Geordie, how are ye?'

'Is this your young chiel?'

'Aye, that's him,' said his father proudly.

'Have ye time for a dram?'

'Well, the young chiel is wi me.'

'Och, he can amuse himsel for a whilie, a big loon like him.'

Dougie's father delayed for as long as politeness demanded and then agreed that he did have time for a quick one in the hotel bar. 'Here boy,' he said, tugging at something in the depths of his coat pocket, 'get this for your mither and come back here. Dinna get lost.'

Dougie's heart leapt. It was the chance he had been waiting for; it would take only a few minutes to buy whatever his mother had written on the crumpled piece of paper his father had given him and then he would have time to visit the bookshop. The two men disappeared into the pub and he set off down the street.

His errand for his mother was to buy a reel of thread of the same colour as the length stuck to the piece of paper. This was not to his liking and probably his father had been glad to pass the job to him. He cautiously entered the shop with all the lassies' things in the window, silently cursing the overloud bell which brought every head in the place round to see who he was. Blushing, he asked for the thread and paid for it; then he left quickly, thrusting the reel deep into his pocket.

The bookshop's windows were full of bright covers, like tiles on a roof but each one different from its neighbour. The array of colours, drawings, photographs and words excited and awed him. He scanned them all but found nothing that was familiar; his excitement faded into fear. How do you know what to buy, he thought.

Through the door he could see someone picking up books, looking at them and putting them back. He slipped inside and stood facing the shelves; pretending to scan the goods before him, he peered from the corner of his eyes at what was going on.

The man he had seen from the door left the shop. Dougie felt suddenly alone and helpless. He pulled a book from the shelf and stared at it; the title meant nothing. He put it back. He checked the half crown in his pocket; it was still there, reminding him of his intention.

After a few moments he grew calm and began to look around more boldly. He quickly worked out that the books were grouped according to their subject matter. But what subject was he interested in? The choice seemed bewildering. The shelves stretched for yards. Some of the books faced outwards, some presented only their edges to the world. There were big books, small books, fat books, thin books, plain books, rainbow books — it would take days to look at them all.

The woman who ran the shop was serving another customer. He eavesdropped on the conversation but learned only that somebody's husband was recovering from appendicitis. Then he found a rack with some paperbacks on it. Picking one out, he turned it over in his hand until he found the price. The sum filled him with horror. It was way above what he had to spend. He looked at a few more and eventually found a small volume that cost half a crown; nothing seemed to cost less.

Bloody books, he muttered, a load o rubbish.

'Are you looking for something?'

The voice startled him and he blushed, saying nothing.

'Just looking, are you?' asked the woman who ran the shop.

'Aye,' he said.

It was time to go, he realised. But can I just walk out? She might think I was pinching. Salvation. He saw an array of comics and magazines on the shop counter; here at last was something familiar, names he knew, prices well within his range. He bought one.

'Thanks,' said the woman, giving him his change. 'Cheerio.'

The sunlight was a welcoming balm for his shattered conscious. He looked back at the shop, at the window, as if he had just escaped from a fatal trap. It did not take long, however, for relief to turn to disappointment. He had come to buy a book and he had failed. He thought of going back but was too shy to do so; that would have to wait until another day, another week. Then he would know what he wanted.

CHAPTER FOUR

He picked up the copy of MacDiarmid's *A Drunk Man Looks at the Thistle* that lay beside the bed. For several nights past, he had been reading parts of the poem, finding some lines funny, some impossible to understand and some intriguing. The language was strange although it was supposed to be Scots — certainly nobody he knew spoke like the poet, except for a word here or there — and he had to refer to the glossary. What with the words and the subject matter, it was heavy going but he found enjoyment in persevering with it and glimmerings of understanding were his reward. A lot of what MacDiarmid was saying, he realised with pleasure, was what he vaguely understood to be true but which he never put into words. The same unshaped fears and misty feelings and uneasiness ran in most of the folk he knew; the poet was striking at something common to everybody.

More and more of late he suffered from depression, a state in which he moped about the house or the steading, avoiding others and attempts at conversation, retiring to a book or a newspaper or the TV to escape from himself. The routine, the semi-isolation, the same neighbours with the same gossip — it was one muckle, boring carousel from which it was impossible to flee. His father was dead and in a few more years, as like as not, his mother would be gone too. Then the place would be entirely his, but what of it. Maybe he would sell it and go south, get a job in a factory or driving a van. If he could only find something to live for, he said to himself, it would all be worthwhile, all this trauchling through gutters and shite.

After his father's death, he had in fact initiated some experiments on the croft, trying new ideas gleaned from magazines and elsewhere, and with considerable success an outsider may have said. He had turned an old shed into a deep litter and doubled their income from eggs; three beehives stood near the house and gave some honey to sell. Nobody had been very keen, however, to eat the rabbits he had raised. He had increased the head of sheep and broken more moorland into grass. In five years, he had made the croft a viable concern far and above the subsistence living it had provided for his father.

But when the dark clouds swirled in his head, he could see only an empty future of lonely existence. At times, to cheer himself up, he stayed overlong in the pub and the dark clouds dispersed in the warm, amber fumes. The book of poetry, along with many other volumes in the room, had been a gift from the minister's wife. How he had come to receive such a collection many years ago had been a lucky circumstance.

The Reverend Alastair MacKenzie had been the Auld Kirk minister of their parish; a gangling, grey-haired man, vague and absent minded, he had been well liked by most, whether they attended his Sunday services or not, and most did not. The minister continued to preach and look after his flock long after retirement age, baptising, marrying, burying and comforting.

A genuine murmur of sadness ran through his parish when the news of his death spread. His going was unexpected, he just quietly passed away in his sleep. Folk said he died as he lived — no bother to anybody.

Two weeks after the funeral of the minister, Dougie happened to be passing the manse when the minister's widow called to him.

'You're young Douglas Bayne, aren't you?'

The voice, high pitched and southern, stopped Dougie on his way. Mrs MacKenzie stood at the manse gate between the stone pillars with the lichened balls on top. She was a short, dumpy woman, hardly taller than Dougie himself, sad faced behind her glasses; a cairngorm brooch was the only splash of colour on her black clothes.

'Aye,' said Dougie cautiously. 'Yes.'

'You've grown,' she continued. 'It's a long time since we've seen you.'

Dougie took this as a pointed reference to his non-attendance at the kirk. Although his mother dragged out her bicycle on a fine Sunday to go the two miles to the village, neither he nor his father was very keen to accompany her. He gave another cautious 'Aye'.

'How are your mother and father?'

'Fine.'

'Give my best wishes to them both, will you? Your mother came round last week with some jam. That was very good of her.'

Something of the sadness in the widow's voice affected Dougie, but her next remark startled him.

'Are you fond of reading?'

He did not know what to say and paused. Mrs MacKenzie went on. 'My husband was a great reader. Over the years he collected hundreds of books and parted with not one. He loved books. And now ... well, we don't need them any more. I don't know what to do with them. Would you like some?'

'I don't know,' murmured Dougie.

'Come in and see them,' urged Mrs MacKenzie. 'They're all here, just as the day...' She paused for a moment and her voice faded.

Dougie stood awkwardly at the gate but the woman took his arm and guided him gently up the path. His mind was confused; the sight of Mrs MacKenzie still struggling with her grief made him shy and want to be away but, at the same time, he realised that this was an unexpected opportunity.

They entered the house. He noticed the smell of polish and dark wood and the faded hall carpet; a man's coat and hat hung on the wall. The widow took him into the large front room, which was warm from the fire. Every wall was a bookcase, crammed with volumes; more sat in symmetrical piles on the small tables around the room. He stood and gaped.

'A lot of books,' Mrs MacKenzie was saying. 'He was a great reader and couldn't bear to part with any of his books.'

'Do you like to read yourself?' Dougie ventured to ask.

'Aye, I read myself. But not all the time. Many's an evening, Alastair would read until past twelve. My eyes would get tired if I read that long and I would say to him 'Do your eyes not get tired?' and he would say 'No' and go on reading while I got on with my knitting or went to bed. I don't know what to do now. I'll keep some of them but the rest I'll have to sell or something. It worries me.'

Dougie was not quite sure what to make of that and said nothing. The silence was awkward but he did not have to feel out of place for long. Mrs MacKenzie continued, her soft sad voice sounding like a whisper in the large room.

'I'm afraid now. Afraid of being lonely. It was a great pity we had no bairns but the Most High was kind to us all the same. I'm going to stay with my sister near Glasgow but it will be a small house and I won't be able to take all this with me.

She took Dougie's arm and led him up to the fireplace.

'You choose what books you want,' she said. 'They'll do far more good for you now than they will for me.'

'Thank you very much,' muttered the boy. 'But I dinna know much about books and I don't know where to start.'

The widow smiled. 'My husband read everything. I suppose it's science you'll be interested in or adventure stories. There are plenty of them. I'll show you.'

She moved along the towering, laden shelves, indicating with a quick word and a gesture how the volumes were classified, pulling out one here, another there and thrusting them into his arms. Before they were half way round, he had to set a heavy pile down.

He was overcome now with delight at the prospect of reading all this and also amazed that a minister should have read so much that was not in the least religious. His guide avoided the sermons, concordances and pamphlets, not small in number by any means but still only a fraction of the total.

'That will be enough, I think,' stammered Dougie, his modesty raising a blush on his face.

Mrs MacKenzie did not turn round from her literary pillaging. 'What you can't carry now you can come back for. Have you a bike?'

By the time they had finished there were three piles of books on the table in the centre.

'If I can find a box, you can take some with you now,' she said and she disappeared briefly, returning with a ball of string and a cardboard box.

Dougie still had difficulty accepting what was being offered. 'Are you sure that it's all right?' he asked.

'Yes, yes,' said the old woman, now busy with the box. When it was filled and tied, she said, 'Can you carry that now?'

Dougie lifted the box and cradled it in his arms. 'Aye.'

'Good. You can come back for the rest sometime. I won't be going anywhere now and I'll aye be in. You can have some more if you like. I don't know what to do with them all. Maybe the library will take some. Alastair was such a great reader.'

She looked wistfully around the shelves and Dougie felt awkward again.

'Now, take that box with you. It's not too heavy, is it?'
'No, no, it's fine.'

They made their way to the front door.

'No. It'll not be heavy for you. You're such a strong, handsome boy,' she said, opening the door. 'Now mind and come back anytime. Tell your mother and father I was asking after them.'

'Aye, yes,' said Dougie, much relieved by the cool breeze. 'Thanks very much, I'll come back...'

The door closed behind him before he could finish, leaving him with a mental picture of the old woman in a swither of loneliness.

The box was heavy and after a short distance his arms ached. He set it down in the road, curbing the urge to open it and examine the books there and then.

Two men passed and greeted him with a short series of questions designed to elicit what he was carrying. He gave non-commital answers and moved on as far as he could before the weight grew once more too much for him.

After some time he reached the croft. His mother was almost overcome by the generosity of the minister's wife and unpacked the box as if she were handling crystal. His father looked on, saying little, soberly puffing his pipe.

'She said to come back for more,' Dougie told them.

'Na, na,' grunted his father. 'What are ye going to do wi all that books? Ye're no a minister. She can put them into the library in the toon.'

'I'll read them,' insisted Dougie. 'They'll no take up much room. I didna ask for them.'

'Ye didna say no either. When will ye have time to read all that? There'll no be a hand's turn oot o ye now, no nor a word either. Better put them to a sale o work.'

'No, we'll keep them,' said his mother. 'The minister had plenty o books. It was awful good o her to gie them to ye. Did ye thank her?'

'Aye.'

'Next time ye go back, ye can take some jam and eggs wi ye.'

'Steady on, wumman,' cried his father. 'We're no made o money. And, Dougie, ye'll no tell anybody that ye got them books.'

Over the next few weeks Dougie buried himself in the printed pages that formed a tall pile in his room, to his own delight and to the incomprehending impatience of his father. Dan Bayne was always busy, if not doing a necessary task, inventing a job; to sit with a book was idleness. He knew the world around him, or so he thought, and what he did not know he did not need. The weekly newspaper was the extent of his literary interest, and this sudden surge of reading in his son puzzled him. He was a crofter; he worked with his hands and his son was destined to be a crofter too, except that instead of fixing fences and watching the corn grow his son preferred to slouch by the fire on his backside, his nose invisible in a book.

'Come on, boy,' he would say. 'Put doon that book and come and shift the sheep.'

Slowly and in a manner seemingly calculated to annoy him, he would watch his son raise his head, absently mutter 'Aye, right' and then come out with something like 'D'ye ken that foxes feed mostly on carrion?'

'Carrion enough by the time they're finished wi them, whatever,' old Dan would scowl. 'They took plenty hens off me one winter.'

Then his wife would come out with something daft about his father being a great reader and the fine way he used to take the books, until he felt that there was not a grain of sense in anybody except himself and the dog. And the sheep would be scarcely through the gate into their new pasture before his son would be footing back to the fireside and the book.

Dougie's new library covered nearly every subject he could think of, from chemistry to wildlife, from war stories to travels in exotic countries. They inspired in him a new interest in his own countryside; for the first time he learned facts that brought the fields and moors to life.

What he read implanted ideas in his mind and gave him, he felt, the means to mould the world to his advantage. Yet his father showed little inclination to change, to read a book for himself or even to take what

Dougie knew and consider it. In fact his father grew more cynical, miscalling, decrying what he told him, until he learned to keep his mouth shut, feeling it would be useless to try and change the old man.

One day, father and son were cleaning a ditch in an attempt to drain the flooded pasture on the edge of the moor. They were wearing heavy oilskin coats to keep out the drizzling rain and the digging broke sweat out of them so that they became damp inside the cumbersome garments.

Dan paused to relight his pipe; his face was red with exertion. 'That should do it now,' he panted. 'Maybe a bit more.'

Dougie straightened and stuck his spade hard into the ground. 'Wi a tractor it widna have taken us long to do that. Ye can get a ditching machine to fix on it.'

'We have no money for that sort o thing,' said his father, releasing a mouthful of smoke that hung about his head in the clammy air. 'D'ye ken that your grandfather took in this field, this whole field, wi a spade. He had no tractors in his day.'

Dougie thought that his grandfather would have been the first to have used a tractor if it had been invented. He said nothing.

'Aye, they kent what work was in them days,' his father was saying. 'None o this reading books all the day. No, boy. Up wi the lark and no in your bed til dayset.'

'Aye,' said Dougie glumly.

'Wi a your book learning ye couldna have turned heather to grass like your grandfather.'

'If ye had a ditching machine, we could take in more hill ground.'

Dan sucked on his pipe, spat and picked up the spade. 'Ye should have read all that books when ye were at school, boy. No now. A man has to work and be content wi his lot. That's the way o the world.'

This piece of philosophy seemed false to Dougie. 'We can change things if we ken how. There are a lot o new things in agriculture we could try.'

'What wi?' his father asked angrily. 'It's only them wi money that can do that sort o thing. I've laboured all my life on this land and I've tried new things — fertilisers, take that now. D'ye ken that your granny and your mother too when she was a lassie took seaware fae the tidemark to this land. Now it comes in plastic bags — it costs a fine penny and deil the better job does it do for us. We're no better off wi it all.'

He paused and dug in his spade. 'Damn laziness — that's what wrong wi the world now. Youngsters dinna want to work. And they tell their elders what to do as if they kent it all.'

All through this discourse, Dan's voice had become higher and rougher. Dougie felt anger and frustration wash over him.

— It's no use. The man is too old to change now. Here am I accusing him almost of having wasted his life guttering wi a spade in a ditch. But he's got it all wrong. Look at this place. Rushes — wet pools — sheep huddling fae the rain. I must go, get away somewhere. He must retire soon. Then he can gie off the croft and live in a council hoose. I canna leave him now though. He's grunting and peching on that spade, killing himself. It won't be long. I shouldna be thinking this.

He picked up the spade and plunged it into the soft moss.

'Canny,' said his father. 'Ye micht hit a stone.'

'It's just moss, nothing but moss. Bog!'

'Bog it may be, boy, but it's all we've got. It mayna be muckle reward but I'll be content the day I see ye in my place. Ye micht see it yoursel then, in your time.'

'I dinna want it.' As soon as he had said it, Dougie regretted opening his mouth.

His father laughed and spat. 'There's many a loon has said that to his faither but when the time comes... ye'll see.'

The mockery and the anger brought red blood to Dougie's face and he said not another word all afternoon.

CHAPTER FIVE

Dougie put down the MacDiarmid and left his room. It was nearly time for the midday meal and after that he would have to take eggs down to Donald's Jamie. In the kitchen his mother was fussing with the kettle.

'Still raining,' she said, hearing him come in.

'Aye.'

He sat down at the table, already set with bread and bannocks, butter, jam and sugar. The main meal of the day was taken in the evening about five o'clock, except on Sundays when they ate at one.

When the tea was ready, they ate and drank in silence for a while. Then the old woman spoke again: 'The last day o the year. Your faither would have been seventy.'

He switched on the radio and the voice of the weather-man filled the kitchen: 'A shallow depression now bring-ing showers to the north of Scotland is expected to clear before midnight...'

'They're aye wrong,' said his mother.

'If it clears it'll be fine for going oot to see in the new year,' said Dougie.

'Ye'll no be late,' she said. 'Your faither aye used to come home early.'

Dougie put down his cup and, picking up his woollen cap, rose to leave. Bess leapt up from the mat by the fire and raced to the door.

'I'm off then,' he said.

There was no answer.

Dougie drove down to the village with Bess beside him

in the van. The rain had eased but the sky still hung in dark folds over the fields. The village was a grey, silent cluster; no one was to be seen when he drew up at the council house where Donald's Jamie and his wife, Kathie, lived.

'Here's your eggs,' cried Dougie, opening the front door and going in.

'Ho ho boy,' Donald's Jamie shouted in greeting. 'Coming in?'

'No, I'm no stopping.'

'Hello, Dougie.' Kathie as rotund and red-faced as her husband, appeared. 'Eggs. Oh ye shouldna. Tell your mother thanks very much.'

'There's no a kinder one in the place,' said Donald's Jamie. 'Ye'll be doon for your new year.'

'Aye,' grinned Dougie. 'I'm for off now.'

The hotel, one of the few two-storeyed buildings in the village, stood next to the kirk, a juxtaposition that did not pass unnoticed by those wo staggered out from the public bar late on a Saturday night. It was equally noticable on the Sabbath when two streams of people mingled and then diverged, a motley almost totally male stream swinging into the bar, a dark largely female stream hurrying on through the creaking iron gate to the pews.

Now, in winter, with no tourists and only the occasional travelling salesman, the life of the hotel revolved around the bar. This was a small room on the ground floor with its own door to the outside world so that the locals need not pass through the carpeted lounge to quench their thirst.

It was furnished only with the essentials, a few small tables with ashtrays advertising cigarettes and whisky, half a dozen upright chairs and a long wooden bench running along one wall. A dartboard hung in a circle of small holes. On the shelves behind the counter the light twinkled in variously coloured liquids. The floor was covered with linoleum.

On the middle of this wet day when Dougie arrived there were few customers in the bar. John Campbell was there because it was a holiday and because he had nothing else to do. A round-headed, bald man, with a frieze of ruffled hair like a monk's tonsure, he leaned on the bar and held just beneath his nose the pint of beer he was drinking. He was a garage mechanic: on a day such as this, he usually managed to clean most of the grease from his hands and wore a gaily patterned jersey.

Next to him stood Magnus Gunn, upright and smart in a new blazer with his clan badge gleaming on the breast pocket. The cut of his clothes was matched by the trimmed neatness of the grey moustache; Magnus was an agricultural salesman and thought that a smart appearance helped him persuade tight-fisted crofters buy his baler twine and sheep dip. In fact, most of the crofters thought Magnus an arrogant gowk, overfond of the sound of his own voice and of giving an opinion when not asked. He had come to have a whisky and show off his new blazer, thought Dougie.

One of the crofters to whom Magnus rarely succeeded in selling anything sat on a chair against the wall at the end of the bar. Will Auld was a stocky, short man, wearing as he usually did a jersey out at the elbows and with frayed cuffs. His bonnet showed evidence of an equally enduring existence and, as John Campbell once remarked when out of earshot, he had half the county on his boots.

The fourth man sat on the long bench, his dungaree-clad legs crossed leisurely as he puffed his pipe. With thick glasses and an untidy shock of grey hair, he had the appearance of an owl newly awakened. But anyone who thought they could take advantage of this apparent glaikedness soon found themselves thinking again, because Jim Sinclair the joiner was a first-class craftsman and nobody's fool.

'Aye,' said John Campbell.

'Wet day,' said Will Auld.

'How are ye the day?' asked Jim Sinclair.

'Aye,' said Dougie.

At that moment, Margaret, the wife of the landlord, came through to do her duty as barmaid. She was a large woman, broad and strong, quick to laugh and equally quick to exert authority. More than one customer, too forthcoming and bothersome when in the blues with drink, had felt the lash of her flyting tongue or even the strength of her arm if the occasion demanded. Today, expecting few customers and those likely to be regulars, she was in a cheerful mood.

'A pint, Dougie?' she asked.

'Aye,' he replied, placing coins on the counter.

John Campbell raised himself laboriously to an upright position. 'Nearly the last o the year,' he sighed, 'and damn good luck to it.'

Nobody responded immediately to this remark. Dougie understood it to be a reference to John not having long to wait to have his driving licence restored. He, a garage mechanic, had suffered the consequence of being caught under the influence.

'It wasna a very good year,' said Magnus at length.

'No, no,' agreed Will.

'Well, here's to the next ain,' said Dougie, savouring his beer.

'It'll no be muckle better,' said Will. 'Gie's another rum, Margaret.'

'I hear that inflation's put prices up again,' said Magnus.

'For sure they'll no come doon,' said Margaret.

'The whole damn country is in a mess,' said Will, and he took his rum.

Silence pervaded the bar in the wake of that remark. After a few moments, Dougie spoke. 'No doubt we'll manage through.'

'We'd manage a lot better if we were our own masters,' said Magnus firmly.

'What d'ye mean by that?' This from Jim Sinclair.

Straightening his blazer to draw attention to the small thistle badge on his lapel, Magnus took a sip of whisky before answering. 'This crowd in Westminster that caas itself a government dinna know what goes on up here.'

'I dinna think they ken what goes on anywhere,' said John, but everybody ignored him.

'They've no more idea o how to run things than that dog o yours oot there in the van, Dougie,' continued Magnus. 'In fact they've probably got less. At least the dog belongs to the place.'

'Well, they're there and we're here,' said Will Auld. 'And that's the way o it, boys.'

Dougie was intrigued by the passion in Magnus's remarks, the stiffening in his body and the defiant gleam in his eye. Although he shared the general opinion that Magnus was a big-headed fool and liable to talk rubbish, he still enjoyed listening to him. Fuel the fire, he thought.

'What should we do, Magnus?' he asked.

'Get our own government. Edinburgh is the capital o Scotland, no London. When that day comes, that our own prime minister sits doon in Parliament Hoose in Edinburgh, then we'll have a government that kens what's what.'

'I dinna think we'd be any better off,' said Will. 'Whether it's in Edinburgh or no, it'll be same buggers running the show and we'll still be traipsing at the arse o a coo.'

John and Dougie laughed. Margaret ignored the whole conversation and busied herself washing glasses.

'No, no,' cried Magnus, rounding on the dissenter. 'Aa them that are standing for us now in Westminster have been blinded by the bricht lights o London and chauffeurs and power. Aye, blinded by power. They've forgotten who put them where they are and what we put them there for. They spend aa their time on English affairs and no a word aboot Scotland, their hame.'

'They spend aa their time thinking up taxes for us to pay,' said John Campbell.

'And that's another thing,' said Magnus. 'Taxes. What happens to aa the taxes we pay. De'il a penny or very little o it anyway ever comes back to us.'

'That's no true, Magnus,' said Jim Sinclair. 'We get our share and ye ken that we do. No us, but the country, the nation o Scotland. Take Dougie here — ye get subsidies for your sheep, do ye no?' Dougie admitted that he did.

'And your mother gets her pension?' She did. 'There ye are. And what's more, Magnus, I was reading that for every pound we pay in tax to Westminster we get more back.'

'I find that hard to believe.' Magnus took another drink and reflected for a moment. 'Well, it micht be true on paper but there are other things. What about our natural resources? Minerals, oil, whisky. D'ye think that aa the profits fae that lot come back to us? No chance.'

'There's plenty o tourists come to see our scenery,' said John Campbell.

'Tourists,' cried Magnus. 'Fine, in the summer. Look at the hotel here. It's empty now it's winter. D'ye think we should make our living washing other folks' dirty dishes and showing them how to catch our salmon? That's no living for young folk. And that's the main thing. All the young folk are leaving. There's nothing for them here. They go off to the university, come home long enough to pick up a clean shirt and then off. London — Manchester — Canada. That's where they are.'

'No everybody,' protested John. 'There's still Dougie and me.'

'And d'ye never wish ye had gone too?'

Silence descended once more, to be broken by a fresh ordering of drinks. Jim Sinclair got up and approached the bar.

'How's your mother?' asked Margaret, giving Dougie a refilled glass.

'Fine,' he said.

'Aye.' Will Auld had been almost forgotten and his voice made them all turn towards him. 'There's the big man and the little man and that's the way it's meant to be.'

This resignation angered Magnus. 'It's thocht like that that got us where we are now. Struggling along on hand-oots fae a foreign government. We should have kicked ower the whole lot years ago and gone our own road. We should never have sold ourselves for English

gold — that's what the song says — bocht and sold for
English gold — when we did.'

Everyone looked puzzled.

'In 1707,' explained Magnus. 'The union. D'ye no
mind?'

Will Auld looked into his rum and said with such
sincerity that Dougie could not be sure of the sarcasm,
'That was before my time, Magnus.'

'And 1745 again,' continued Magnus. 'The king was
quaking at the knees and we could have ridden into
Buckingham Palace and had our freedom back.'

'Magnus, you're talking a load o shite,' said John
Campbell. 'We sit here and drink and when we're done
wi that we shift ower the dyke oot there and that's the
end o't. Leave history to the past.'

'This is history now.' Magnus was not to be put off his
blether. 'It's us that makes history and we should make
it for our ain benefit. Ye can learn fae the past.'

John blushed a little. Was this a reference to his court
appearance? The silence hung heavily for a moment. Will
Auld broke it with a call for more rum. When Margaret
had poured it, he said, 'There's no hope for the Hielands
whatever. We'll just have to manage oursels.'

'There's hope richt enough and I'll tell ye what it is,'
said Jim Sinclair.

They all looked at him.

'The hope is oursels. We waste far too muckle breath
complaining and girning about politicians and taxes and
what not, when all we have to do is get our arses off the
chair and do what we want to do. We can make things
happen.'

The beer was slowly filling Dougie with mellow relaxation, loosening his brain and tongue. 'How?' he asked.

'Take yourself, Dougie.' Jim pointed with the shank of
his pipe. 'Think o aa the things you've done to your croft,
man. Hens, sheep, bees. Hill ground into pasture. That's
what we aa have to do. Take what we've got and work fae
that. None o this crying for a saviour in a bowler hat.'

'That's a fine sermon,' said John Campbell. 'But we're no aa like Dougie. He's got his land. Many o us have none.'

'Aye, that's richt,' Magnus pointed out. 'It's money it takes. We need help richt enough. We canna aa be crofters or farmers and even if we were there's no enough land for every chiel. It's industry we need. Sell. That's the key.'

'You're forgetting the oil,' said Will Auld. 'Money's flowing like water there, I hear.'

'It's no helping us though.' Magnus warmed to his theme. 'The government's taking it aa in taxes, or the Americans or whoever. It's no us that owns it.'

Jim Sinclair ordered another pint. 'It'll only last a wee while anyhow. In ten years time we'll aa be back where we started. No more big wages then.'

'It'll last longer than that,' said Dougie. 'Thirty or forty years, I read in the paper.'

'There's a lot o money in it but they work damn hard for it,' said John Campbell. 'How would you like to be stuck on the ocean for weeks on end?'

'Aye, it's gey tough,' acknowledged Jim Sinclair.

'I maun go,' said Will, getting up from his chair. 'This'll no do!'

His heavy boots echoed on the floor as he made his way out. As soon as he had closed the door behind him, he became the subject of the conversation.

'Will's getting on, boy,' said John Campbell.

'He's a tough auld bugger,' grinned Dougie. 'There's a few winters in him yet.'

'When he goes he'll no leave muckle behind him to bother anybody anyway,' continued John.

'Dinna say that,' said Magnus gently, a little shaken by the morbidity of the remark. Thinking perhaps of the number of times he had had to fight to persuade the old crofter to buy anything, he added, 'He's got a good penny or two laid by.'

Dougie laughed. 'He doesna spend it on clothes whatever.'

John Campbell farted. 'Better an empty hoose than a

bad tenant,' he said. 'Have we no music the day? We need something to cheer us up after all that blether.'

Margaret put a tape on the cassette recorder; after a few seconds the voice of a country and western singer enwrapped the bar in its twangy tones. The men drank and said nothing. Dougie was musing over what the joiner had said about working and achieving success, pointing the way for others to follow. Pride and scepticism mingled in his feelings.

'Well, I'm off home,' said John Campbell suddenly. 'Or the wife'll no let me oot the night.'

'I must go too,' said Jim Sinclair.

The crofter and the salesman were alone now, one finishing his beer and the other sipping whisky. Dougie felt moved to ask a question. 'D'ye think we'll ever be independent again, Magnus?' With an audience of one, the salesman abandoned his bombast. He stroked his moustache before answering. 'Aye. I don't know when, mind, but it's bound to come. It micht be when the oil's finished. When the black stuff stops coming in and the green stuff stops passing, they'll aa wake up and start asking 'What noo, lads? Where's aa the wealth?' Gone — in London or New York.'

'Have ye never thocht o working at the oil yourself?' he asked after a pause.

'I have done,' admitted Dougie. 'Och but wi my father dead I couldna leave the ould woman.'

'No, no. But ye're still young. Make the money while ye can. The chance is there and ye have to take it boy.' He looked at the clock. 'Well, I'm for off.'

With that, he placed his glass smartly on the counter and left. Dougie sat for a few minutes, his fist against his cheek, gazing at the bottles behind the bar.

Margaret bustled in. 'I thocht everybody had gone,' she said, surprised by Dougie's silent presence.

'Aye, they've aa gone,' he said softly.

CHAPTER SIX

It was two o'clock when he left the bar and returned to the van. His footsteps on the asphalt woke Bess from her curled-up sleep.

The sun was already getting low in the west, smearing the sky with a thick, yellowish light as the layers of cloud peeled away to the east before a fresh breeze that had a chill smell to it.

He drove up through the village, past the silent houses, some with twinkling Christmas trees in their windows, past the post office, where the blinds were drawn, over the bridge with its attendant clumps of willow and hawthorn and on up the road homewards.

After the beer and the conversation, he felt content, almost cheerful. Perhaps the new year would be a good one, bringing with it a new sense of purpose and the luck that would turn his intentions to a joyful reality. A lot of things I want have passed me by, he thought, just like those fenceposts sliding past. No like you, Bess — ye get your meat and your runs after hens and sheep, and ye're fine.

'I've often thocht ye've more sense than folk,' he said aloud, pausing before adding, 'Ya daft bitch.'

When he reached the croft he found the old woman sitting by the fire.

'I'm going up the hill now it's dry. There's a fence that needs sorting.' Without waiting for his mother's ackowledgement of this information, Dougie left the house and strode past the steading, through the puddles by the midden and out onto the tangled grass, lying flat and wet in its winter languor. Bess ran before him.

The sheep rose to their feet at the sight of the dog, crowded together and moved to let her pass; Dougie followed, shouting to Bess to behave herself. The yowes were heavy after their morning feed and they did not run but stood, watching balefully. They were heavy too with the new life in them; in two or three months they would begin to lamb — singles, twins or triplets coming into the world at all the awkward hours of the day and night. In spring, Dougie rose before dawn to chase some yowe or other, catch her and deliver her of her offspring, his income. At one side of the field there was a low mound, marking the spot where he had buried one of his flock.

He came to the fence he had to repair. Two strands of wire were broken. Bidding the dog lie down, he pulled and twisted the broken ends together with the pliers he always carried in his pocket. The metal was stiff and cold and the pliers slipped but after a few minutes he had effected a satisfactory mend.

It would not be long now until the sun set and the northern winter night closed down once more over the land. The shadows in the whins, where Bess was sniffing for rabbits, were already black. Dougie set off for the moor, for a last look round before the year ended.

The heather was deep and scraped against his legs as he climbed the rising slope. In summer there would be thyme, tormentil and primroses here, speckling the hillside with yellow and red, but now it was a dark, brown sea with lighter streaks where dead bracken lay flattened by the wind.

— This is a piece o ground that could be drained, split open and dried. It could make good grazing in time. Two tile drains running doon to the ditch there. There's a good depth o moss in it. Aye, this could make good grass.

On the crest of the hill, the wind hit him in the face and forced him to turn from it until he found shelter behind one of the great boulders that sprang from the ground. From this vantage point, he could see a great distance and he paused to smoke and look at the country-side.

Down below the grey and white buildings of the croft hugged the ground, an island in the earth, the hub of a radiating pattern of fences and dykes and ditches, cut through by the straight ribbon of the road. As far as he could see in this direction, the pattern repeated, rect-angles of land of differing sizes and colours; black, where it had already been ploughed, grey-green or dun with vegetation.

It was a bare open land, a country with no secrets, where neighbours could see neighbours be they a mile away or more. It was an empty land, for it asked a lot of a person to live here and many, though born and bred to it, gave up the struggle and sought an easier way else-where. It was a land that demanded simplicity, even humility, the ability to make do and be content. It tolerated the enduring stolidity of the obstinate; it pun-ished careless ambition.

— Perhaps my faither was richt. Perhaps his way was the wiser. He took what he could get and asked for nothing more — what he took was not very much. But I'm damned if I'll give up yet. This place can yield a little more. I'll drain this heather and burn it and from the ashes... maybe more sheep... maybe plant trees. Aye. Trees. That's what the land needs. That's what I need. Elated with his intention, he smiled to himself and looked out with confidence across the countryside, seeing for every fence a line of rustling hedge.

He stubbed out the cigarette on the rock and stepped up once more onto the crest of the hill. With his back to the croft, he was scanning a very different landscape, a rolling stretch of moorland that rose in a series of gentle waves until it finally merged with a blue range of hills. Away to his right the moor ended abruptly and beyond that was the grey, shimmering flatness of the sea.

It was to see this vista of infinite emptiness that the tourists came in the summer. They pitched their tents, parked their caravans and spoke for hours about the weather, the price of petrol, where they had been and where they were going next. Many of them stayed at the croft, buying his eggs and his milk and sometimes his mother's bannocks, whenever he could persuade her to look upon baking as a business activity. He enjoyed their company, answering their questions in patient detail and learning from them about city life.

They were often incredibly ignorant, he thought. 'Have you lived here all your life?' they would ask, as if it were a modern miracle that anyone should. 'Not yet,' he would reply and wait for their reaction.

When autumn drove the last of them away, he missed them. That was the main complaint of life here, he thought, hurrying along the moor, it was so damnably lonely at times. Most of his schoolmates had married and many had left the district altogether. Rob had done well at school and had gone to university; now he was a chemist in America and came back rarely. Helen had become a teacher and had married another teacher; both now lived in the town. His cousin Elsie was now a Canadian.

Only those like himself, who had left school early, still lived in their birthplace, finding work where and when they could, or living on social security.

At that moment the sun burst downwards through the thinning western clouds and shot bolts of yellow light across the hills. He felt the scant warmth on his face. The wet rocks and the heather glistened, and the detail of the vegetation stood out clearly.

— Oh God I love this land despite its darkness, its winds and its thrawn ground. It's a sore struggle but it's worth it, just to be my own maister. That's my sheep down there, my fences, my rigs. If I fail, even that will be mine — it will be my failure.

But the sunlight was waning quickly, retreating towards the yellow sky, which was rapidly darkening to gold and red. The fields grew dim and lights came on in distant houses. Gulls made silhouettes against the western brightness, some hovering, some wheeling and diving; their harsh cries came to him on the wind, the voice of lonely places, mocking, laughing, maliciously arrogant. It was over there, from the top of that cliff, that Tom MacDonald had hurled himself, driven to it, folk said, by loneliness and despair after his wife's death. But then, they said, there had always been a weakness in the family.

Dougie had been only five when the suicide had occurred and he could scarcely remember it. It had been suicide, people were sure of that. Old Tom had not fallen accidentally; no treacherous piece of turf had suddenly given way, no unforeseen gust of wind swirled him off the rock edge. The salmon fishers found his body, bringing their coble close in under the cliffs to pick up the broken corpse.

Dougie started back down the hill towards the croft. The heather slope was in dark shadow, a blank plain lacking any detail except for the occasional boulder that glimmered dully in the fading light.

— It wouldna take much imagination or drink to turn one o them into a ghost, squatting there like a puddock watching a fleag. Slurp would go the giant tongue and doon, doon intil the wraith's wizzan wi ye.

He grinned at his fantasy and called on Bess, who rustled past him in the heather, a reassuring presence. It was at times like this, especially at these times, the gloaming, the dulling of perspective into simple, colourless shapes, that the earth seemed to breathe, to move with some essence of its own. The colour was drained from the land, sucked heavenward into the washed, grey cloud, a simplifying, purifying trick of the light.

At these times it was easy for a man to believe himself not alone, to feel that millions of eyes were watching him. Spirits moved in the world at these times; the past, the present and the still to come blended into universality.

— Til think that this great blanket o moss and heather, scratching on my boots, was once a forest. Birch and pine and willow. Deer grazing where my sheep are now, their loogs and their nostrils smelling and twitching in the same way. The peat in my fire must have been a forest giant, green and strong in the sun. Maybe there were beavers in my ditch at one time. Aye, man, ye've changed the face o the land a good bit in your time but here's one chiel who's going to change it a bit more. I'll plant trees this spring. This spring, trees...

On his way through the steading, Dougie checked the hen-houses and closed the small doorways. A clucking and fuffling from inside told him that all the hens had sought their proper shelter for the night. He moved through the gloom to the old stable.

The single, dusty bulb did little to dispel the damp chill inside. He picked up the docker, a curved knife with a spike on the end, and began to pluck turnips from the pile on the floor, one at a time to be chopped into pieces to feed the cows. Years of repetition of this winter chore meant that it took only a few minutes, unthinking minutes, to fill the baskets. He picked them up and trudged through to the byre; the cows looked around at his approach and stamped their feet.

As they munched on the chopped fodder, he picked up a cat from the straw and stroked it until it began to purr loudly in his arms. In the reflective mood that had been on him on the hill and was still with him, the cat's soft dark fur became the soft dark hair of Helen.

Helen. The only lassie born in the place in the same year as himself. That had been remarked on many times during their childhoods — one of the little burdens that communities keep hitching up on their members' backs. They started the school on the same day and sat more or less beside each other for years, until the shift to the secondary in the town placed them in different streams, for Helen had been better at exams and seemed predestined for what folk called getting on. The inevitable drifting apart was countered only slightly by the social current that manifested itself chiefly at such events as dances; and it was at these that Dougie began to look at Helen with new eyes. He sensed too that by then it was probably too late.

Helen had poise and confidence, nurtured by years of prize-winning and compliments, and in comparison he knew he was just a loon. At a dance she would appear usually with a pal or two from the town and, although she lived in a crofthouse with parents the same as his, somehow she seemed to have shed all trace of an identical origin. Somehow the smell of the byre came with him like a shadow, but not with her.

It was a breezy summer day when he had tried to win her back, a day of wind and sun with the light dancing in the spray on the seawaves and in the rippling grass. Just the weather for walking along the cliff edge and down through the heather and marram to the sand curving between the land and the water. Dougie's boots left a meandering trail in the wet beach, as he strode along, hands in pockets, listening to the gulls and the terns.

A jumble of dunes marked the landward boundary of the beach, a stretch of hillocks and hollows where rabbits abounded and beachcombers laid up seadrift to dry.

When he reached the wide, shallow burn that spewed out across the sand, he turned and made his way up into the dunes. It was there that he met Helen on her way down along the burnside. She wore jeans and a patterned jersey.

'Hi,' she said. 'Terrific day for a walk.'

'Aye.'

'Going far?'

'No, I was just thinking o turning back.'

'Same here.'

She climbed up the side of a dune and sat down at the top. He came up behind her and stood looking along the shore. There was no one else in sight; the sea curled and broke in the wind, and the bright gulls called.

'Fine view fae up here,' he said.

'Aye. I might miss this when I go off tomorrow.'

He looked down at her suddenly. 'Are ye for off tomorrow?'

'University starts next week.'

'Oh aye.'

She got up and dusted sand from her bottom. 'If we go doon this side, we'll get some shelter fae the wind,' she said and took a running step down the slope, her feet causing an avalanche of dry sand.

Dougie followed. The air was still in the hollow and the sun shone warmly. Helen sat down once again.

'What are ye going to do at the university?' he asked.

'English and French,' she replied casually, closing her eyes and turning her face up to the sun.

Dougie said nothing for a moment or two as he shredded to tiny ribbons a blade of marram. 'How long will that take ye?' he asked.

'Three years. Four, if I do honours.'

'Aye? That's a gey long time, too. What are ye going to do afterwards?'

'How do I know?'

'Teacher?'

'Maybe. I could do anything wi a good degree.'

'Will ye miss all this?'

'Maybe. It's a chance to do something.'

'I suppose so,' said Dougie slowly. 'There's no muckle here richt enough.'

'There's nothing here.'

'No muckle,' murmured Dougie.

'I want to get away, to see a bit o the world,' continued Helen. 'To meet new people, see new places. Go to France — Paris, Marseilles, Lyons. Aren't they just lovely words?'

She lay back on the slope of the dune and closed her eyes again.

Dougie began to shred more marram. 'Ye're lucky,' he said at length, 'getting a chance to do that.'

Helen did not answer. He looked at her lying in the sun.

— Her hair looks fine, soft and shiny. Cut short across her brow. Had it done before going off, likely. She's got make-up on her eyes. I can see dark lines abeen and ablow. Looks as if she's sleeping but she canna be. God, but she's lovely. I want to touch her, stroke her wi my fingers. Her nose shines a wee bit. Skin is so smooth. There's a row o peedie hairagies on her upper lip. Ye can only see them in this licht when the sun picks oot every one. She must have lipstick on. They're so red and moist. I wonder what it tastes like — roses, scent, almonds? And her lower lip curves so smooth-like to her chin. I feel as if I could squeeze it and shatter it in scow like a piece o thin laim.

Dougie stared at all the details of her body and felt a passion, an urging move in him.

Whether it was the sun, the warmth and shelter of the dune hollow, her closeness and her subtle smell, he could not have said but he leaned across suddenly and kissed her.

She did not struggle or protest but, slightly to his surprise, raised her head to prolong the touching of their lips.

Dougie drew slowly back.

Minutes passed before either spoke again.

'I must go now,' she whispered hoarsely.

'Aye,' he said automatically.

She stood up, brushing the sand from her clothes and shaking her hair back into place. He rose after her and stroked her hair.

'Helen,' he said, 'ye didna mind? I love ye.'

'Dougie!' she laughed. 'Always the same, Dougie. No, it was lovely. I must go. Bye.'

Turning abruptly, she clambered up out of the hollow and disappeared.

For a long time he stood watching the rim of marram, wavering and glinting. And for a longer time he sat at the edge of the dunes, listening to the rumble of the waves and the crying of the gulls, until the lowering of the sun brought with it a chill to pierce the miasma of memory.

As the months and years went by, he saw Helen on numerous occasions, each time she came home on holiday, usually with a new boyfriend in tow. When she had married, he felt envy — but only for a short time.

The cat was still purring loudly when he gently laid it in the straw and left the byre.

CHAPTER SEVEN

As soon as he opened the door of the house, he caught the smell of a cooking fowl: his mother was preparing the new year's dinner — broth, boiled hen, the traditional feast. In the kitchen carpets had been laid over the linoleum, fresh peats stuck up in the fire like black teeth in fiery gums, and, on the back of a chair set close to the heat, his suit hung airing.

'I took your suit oot to warm it,' said his mother. 'Ye'll be wanting it the nicht. Is it your white shirt ye want?'

'Oh yes, aye.'

'Was ye up the hill?'

'Aye. It looks as if it micht be frost.'

'Oh. Ye better watch wi the van. Wi ice on the roads.'

'Aye.'

'Dangerous that ice. Treacherous dirt. Dinna drive fast.'

'No, no, mither. I ken how to drive.'

With the curtains pulled and the fire pouring heat into the room, the croft kitchen assumed a cosy air. He switched on the radio that nestled among the Christmas cards on the sideboard and to the accompaniment of some anonymous music sat down to read a war thriller. Bess stretched out before the fire and closed her eyes. There was a clattering of pots and muttered comments from the scullery where his mother was doing something.

After a few minutes the smell of frying liver and onions sneaked into the room.

'Is that the time?' called his mother. 'The news'll soon be on.'

– What does she want to listen to the news for? As soon as it's done, it's forgotten and when she's listening, she's no hearing half o it.

The music stopped and the news programme began with its usual dramatic headlines; more fighting in the Middle East, an earthquake somewhere, another strike threat. It all seemed very remote from the croft and Dougie devoted most of his attention to the novel. Usually he took a greater interest in world events – he certainly did not subscribe to the maxim with which many of his neighbours summed up international affairs, 'That foreigners are never at peace' – but not today, the last day of the year, the end of the old and the start of the new – today was for personal reflection and relaxation.

More clattering of pots cued the entry once again of his mother.

'Ye'd better put more peats on,' she said.

'Is the dinner nearly ready?'

She had already returned to her cooking and did not answer. Bess opened one eye, as if to concur with her master's feelings on the old woman's vagaries, and yawned. Dougie resumed his reading.

Some minutes later, as they ate, Dougie said, 'I was thinking maybe I'll plant some trees.'

'Trees! Where?'

'Here. On our place. Around the edges o the parks. Hedges would be grand shelter for the sheep.'

'Take a while to grow.'

'Aye, but it would be a fine sicht.'

'Whatever ye want.' She gathered the dirty plates and took them through to the back room for washing.

Dougie lit a fag and sat for a few moments, seeing in his mind's eye a flourishing plantation of fir, pine and hawthorn, hearing the birds in it singing, imagining the warmth in the lee of it. Then he rose and went out. Bess followed. It was dark now but most of the sky was clear and the faint sheen of starlight illumined the land. The frost was imparting a chill nip to the air and the ground was hard underfoot. In the byre the breath of the cattle billowed and condensed on the walls.

It did not take long for him to complete the milking, give a skint to the cats and shut the dog in for the night.

Back in the house, he returned to his reading.

With the noise of the TV and being engrossed in his book, he did not notice the approach of the car until the headlamps sprayed two moons on the curtain. His mother said, 'Who's that?' They heard a door open and close and then the clatter of heavy feet on the flagstone pavement. 'They're coming here,' said Dougie, rising and going to the door just as a heavy knock came to it.

In the light that flooded out behind him, he saw a short, stocky man in a thick donkey jacket, a scarf wound loosely round his neck. The square face with unshaven jowls and high cheekbones, the grey heavy eyebrows and brown eyes marked the visitor as a tinkler. Dougie recognised him to be the one known as Pogo; the man's real name escaped him.

'Aye, aye,' said Pogo in the lilting accent that the tinklers used. 'Sorry for disturbing ye at this time o nicht but we've come tae catch some rabbits on your land.'

'Rabbits?'

'Aye. Ye see, my dug ran aff wi the turkey we had for our new year dinner and the wife was that mad that she threw baith the dug and me oot and tellt us no tae come back til we replaced the damn turkey.'

Dougie started to grin and moved into the gloom to hide his face.

'Noo I ken ye've got rabbits here,' continued Pogo, 'and I thocht ye widna mind if me and the dug took ain or twa aff ye.'

'No, no,' said Dougie. 'Ye're welcome. But how are ye going to catch rabbits at nicht in the dark?'

'That's easy enough. Thank ye.' Pogo grinned. 'Ye can come and watch if ye like.'

'Aye, I widna mind.'

Dougie went into the house to collect his jacket. His

mother was standing in the kitchen where she could hear the conversation outside.

'Who is it?' she whispered.

'Just some tinks for rabbits, I'll go oot wi them.'

'Tinks? Rabbits? Now?'

'Aye.' He tugged on his jacket.

'Where at this time o nicht?'

'I dinna ken.'

Pogo was standing on the crisp grass outside. 'The van's ower here,' he said and made away towards it.

Two other men got out of the van; the larger one was old, possibly Pogo's father, guessed Dougie, and he had a sweeping moustache that gave him the appearance of a walrus. A strong smell of tobacco drifted from the short pipe in his mouth. The other man was much younger, tall and thin, shivering a little, and had lank hair sprouting from under a ski cap.

Pogo did not bother with introductions, 'Richt, lads?' he asked. 'Got the dug?'

The beast emerged from the van. In the dim light it had the substance of a wisp of grey smoke, a thin trembling thing of a whippet, its tail curled forward between its legs to keep its hurdies warm. Is that the beast that took the turkey, Dougie asked himself. The old man bent and clipped a length of rope to the dog's collar. 'Come on, Rover,' he said.

'Ye'll be auld Dan's loon,' said Pogo. 'I mind auld Dan a while ago. Hoo many years is it noo since he died?'

'Five,' said Dougie.

'Aye, aye,' mused Pogo. 'There's a lot o watter geed doon the burn since then.'

There was a moment's pause and after the respectful silence Pogo became the general again.

'Got the battery?'

'Aye.'

'Pock?'

'Aye.'

'Lamp.'

'Here.'

'Where's the best place for rabbits?' This to Dougie.

'There's a stretch o whins doon near the hill. Plenty o rabbits in it.'

'Grand. Grand. Come on then. I dinna want tae be oot aa nicht. It's cauld.'

Their breath hovered in the air and the dog was visibly shaking. Dougie led them, the young man and Pogo carrying sacks, down through the steading and into the parks beyond. Away from the electric glare of the croft window, their eyes adjusted quickly to the starlight and they moved easily through the night.

'Married?' asked Pogo.

'No,' said Dougie.

'Tak my advice — dinna. Wimmen are mair bother than they're worth, them and their damn turkeys. It wisna the dug's fault he took the turkey — the poor brute's only human. She, the daft bitch that she is, left it oot. We's lucky tae escape wi oor heids whole. Everything she threw at us — plates, cups, glasses, coal — when the bread knife came oot I says to mysel 'Time tae go' and tae the auld man here 'Come on, we'll go and get something for oor new year's dinner'. 'And where are ye going tae get a turkey at this time o day?' says she. 'Tae hell wi ye and your turkeys,' says I, 'we'll hae a rabbit.' 'There's nane o thae stinking rabbits coming in this hoose,' says she, and she lets hiff wi anither cup. 'I'll clean it mysel,' says I, 'ye needna put a finger near it. Damn rabbits was good enough for ye once and they'll be good enough for ye yet,' says I. So we got the gear and came here. Och she'll cool doon by the time we get back but she can damn well sleep alane the nicht.'

'Do ye often go after the rabbits?' asked Dougie.

'Och aye. The butchers in the toon tak them. Ye can get a good price for a rabbit noo? As long as there's no myxi in them. D'ye no like them yoursel?'

'I tried raising them once.'

'Did ye noo?' Pogo was momentarily intrigued and

Dougie saw from his manner that an idea had been filed away in the man's head. 'Och but a tame chiel hasna the flavour o a wild chiel.'

By this time they were nearing the whins. Dougie noticed that the whippet was no longer trembling. Pogo dropped his next remark to a whisper. 'Richt, Jock?'

The three men were obviously well practised at whatever it was they were about to do. The old man moved off to the right with the dog, downwind of the whins. Pogo fiddled in the sacks and produced a lamp, which he carried in one hand and which was connected to a car battery in one sack slung over his back. The young man moved off slightly to the left. Pogo motioned to Dougie to stay back a bit.

— Amazing. Funny folk, the tinklers. They look different, speak different and have stayed separate fae the rest o us for as long as anybody can mind. Pogo's grandfather used to live in a tent in the summer and in a seacave in the winter, a brawling, drunken, fechting hushle o shither by all reports. They moved about the countryside as regular as the seasons, selling besoms and pans, poaching, doing odd jobs, working at the harvest, brewing their own forms o poison, living off the land. Now Pogo lives in a council hoose and fleshes oot his broo money and his social security wi buying and selling scrap, poaching, doing odd jobs at the harvest. They are as often in the jile as oot o it. I wouldna be surprised if that ould chiel has a hundred convictions. Who else but Pogo would go after rabbits at half past six at nicht wi a licht, a car battery and a dog as thin as a raindrop?

As Dougie watched and grinned to himself at the absurdity of the scene, the three tinklers edged forward quietly. Suddenly Pogo switched on the light and there in the heart of the harsh glare sat a rabbit, bedazzled. In a brown blur of movement the whippet shot into the pool of light and seized its prey. A bite, a snap and a shake, and the grey bundle of fur lay twitching on the grass.

The young man moved forward silently, patted the dog and put the rabbit into his sack. Pogo switched off the light and the old man softly commanded the dog to heel. After a silent pause, they moved forward again. The pool of light, the kill, the retrieval — the tinklers repeated the series of actions four times.

Dougie was astonished by their efficiency and their quiet sense of purpose: he had the feeling that if the world were to end at that moment somehow these men and their stupid-looking dog would survive.

Pogo turned and spoke. 'That's four, lads. I think that'll do. It's cauld and I could do wi a dram noo.'

The old man and the youth grunted acknowledgement.

'Would ye like one?' said Pogo to Dougie, and he plunged his hand into the sack and pulled out a dead rabbit; there was blood on its nose and blades of grass between its teeth.

'He's no very clear in the een,' said Pogo, 'but he'll be all richt for all that.'

'No thanks,' said Dougie. 'That's kind o ye but we've still got our hen and I can always get one again.'

'Okay, boy,' said Pogo. 'Well, we'd better be awa noo. I'll have tae clean the wee buggers mysel maist likely.'

They returned through the fields to the croft. When their equipment and their harvest had been stored in the van, Pogo climbed in and started the engine. He opened the window. 'Well, good nicht and thanks. And a good new year til ye when it comes.'

'Aye. Good nicht and the same til yourself,' said Dougie.

With a cough and an ominous backfire, the van reversed and turned onto the road, and then roared off into the night, leaving a discordant tootle on the horn hovering in the frosty air.

CHAPTER EIGHT

A little later, he stood in the bathroom, waiting for the hot water to fill the basin. Razor, soap and brush were set on the shelf. Wisps of steam began to curl up and obscure his reflection in the mirror. He washed down to his shoulders and up his arms to the elbows; it was too cold to strip further. Thin slivers of ice were already forming in the water on the window sill and if the frost kept up, as was likely, the face cloth would be as crisp as crumpled paper by morning.

He shaved carefully to avoid nicking himself and mused over growing a beard in the coming year. It could be convenient, save all the bother with shaving, and with a fresh image to present to the world there could come fresh fortune.

He went back into the kitchen to retrieve his white shirt and suit. He did not wear either of these garments very often; only funerals, weddings and new years demanded a suit and for the rest of the time it hung in the wardrobe, hiding in a fog of moth balls.

The first time he had worn this suit had been five years previously — the time his father died.

Old Dan's death had been sudden, or so many people said at the time. Dougie had thought his father had been ailing for months; he coughed more, grew short of breath more quickly, took longer to trudge around the steading and left heavier weights to be lifted by his son. Not that he ever admitted to any of these failings — he kept plodding, like a convict on a treadmill, and the wheel kept turning beneath him until it became too much and he died: and everybody said it was sudden.

It had happened towards the end of June, towards the end of the hay cutting. Most of the crop had been baled — by this time, Dougie had a tractor — and had been driving around the park picking up odd wisps to make an extra bale or two.

Bales of compressed hay are heavy, fifty-six pounds or more if tightly packed, and strong backs are needed to lift them. Old Dan, unable to look at a job to be done and not attempt it, was gathering some bales together and stacking them. The first two or three he managed to place on top of each other but then the extra effort for a fourth proved too much. Dougie saw the old man stagger, slump to the ground and not move.

— He's fallen. Has he tripped? No, he's no getting up. Has he hurt himself?

He clambered from the tractor seat and rushed over, shouting a question, his boots threshing the brittle stubble. By the time he reached his father, Dan had turned over and lay, his head and shoulders against the bales, the rest of his large body sprawled on the ground. The bale he had been lifting lay across his shins.

His face was a purple-grey colour and the grey stubble on his chin stood out like hoar frost. His breath came in short, rasping pants and his hands were clutched across his heaving chest. As Dougie looked in horror, a dribble of saliva ran from the corner of the open mouth.

'What is it?' cried the son.

The grey lips worked and the voice was low and hoarse. 'My chest. It's like a vice.'

Dougie's first reaction was one of anger. Why here? Why now? Couldn't he have left the damn bales alone? Then, panic. Christ, what can I do? A doctor! Anybody! Dinna die here.

'Don't move,' he said. 'I'll get the tractor.'

He rushed across the field and tore the hitching bar and the drive shaft of the baler free. In his panic and haste, the bolts seemed to be welded. Look back. Is he okay? Too far to see. Come on... dammit... that's it... one more... into the seat... clutch... gearshift... dinna stall... throttle...

With a great jerk, the tractor moved forward. He slammed to a halt beside the cart and leapt down. Push off the bales... tears now... gasping... red-faced... panic and anger mingling in him, crushing him with their intensity.

It took several more precious seconds to drag the cart into place and pin it to the tractor. The need to concentrate calmed him a little.

His father's breathing had eased by the time he returned and the livid colour in the face had gone. The eyes were open and moving like trapped animals.

'How ye feeling now?'

'Still pain,' gasped Dan.

'Right. I'm going to lift ye onto the cart.'

Dan must have weighed thirteen stone. Dougie dragged him, holding him under the oxters, across the grass and into the cart. He put the old sack from the tractor seat under the man's head. The cart was short and his father's legs hung over the end.

He drove as quickly as he dared to the house, looking back continually although all he could see of his father's recumbent form was the knees rising and falling as the wheels bumped in the ruts.

At the front door he stopped and shouted "Mither!" but he had to call several times before she appeared.

'What is it?' she asked.

'It's himself. He's collapsed.'

Then she saw the legs and cried out as she rushed to the cart.

Dougie told her to go and prepare the bed and she hurried away. He climbed into the cart and tried to lift his father at the shoulders. But the strength that the initial panic had put in him had gone and he struggled. Dan grunted and moaned.

'I've got to get ye til your bed,' cried the son in desperation.

His father lifted his right arm and felt the side of the cart until his fingers reached the top of the wood. Dougie pushed him up into a sitting position. The man's breathing came in loud gasps and sweat trickled down his face. By moving a little at a time, Dougie got his father's feet to the ground and his arm across his shoulders.

He half-carried him, half-dragged him into the house. When he had laid him on the bed, he collapsed in a chair, drained.

His mother busied about the room, weeping and twisting her hands and punching the pillows and pushing the blankets.

'Gie him a drop o whisky,' said Dougie and he went to the press in the kitchen to fetch the bottle and a glass.

'Are ye sure?' his mother asked.

'It'll no hurt him,' said Dougie angrily. At the front of his mind was a simple desire just to do something. 'It micht help him — revive him a bit.'

He held the glass to his father's lips and gently tipped a drop into the mouth. Immediately the old man coughed violently and turned his head away.

'Canny,' cried his mother.

Dougie set down the glass. 'I'll get the doctor,' he said. 'Put him to his bed.'

And he rushed out into the open air, glad to feel the sun on his face, to escape from the claustrophobic misery of the bedroom. He did not have a van then and had to use his bicycle. He dragged it out and pedalled off on the two-mile journey to the village and the nearest phone.

'Put him to his bed and keep him warm,' said the doctor when he got through. 'I'll come as soon as I can.'

Dougie cycled back home and found that these instructions had been carried out. His mother was sitting by the fire, tense and wiping her eyes with an already wet handkerchief.

'How is he now?' asked Dougie softly.

Her voice was high pitched and quivering. 'I kent it and I said it to him. 'Take it easy. Let your son do the work.

Ye're no fit.' But he wouldna listen. Now he's gone, just like his faither. I told him that. If ye dinna slow doon, ye'll drop like your faither afore ye. But he widna listen. He widna listen. Oh dear God...' And her voice trailed away into a high keening sound and her wet-reddened eyes stared into the fire.

Dougie was momentarily confused. Is he dead? He canna be — he was getting better when I left.

'He's sleeping now,' said his mother suddenly and in something like her normal voice.

'He'll be all richt after a rest.'

'No, no,' she said. 'I've seen this coming. It's too late.'

'The doctor'll no be long,' said Dougie and he went back outside.

He was confused by the speed with which a transformation from the routine to the totally new had taken place. So far he had acted by reacting — and he had acted in anger. Now these feelings passed and faded into nothing but a gnawing fear. What was happening now was totally beyond his control or even his understanding. There was nothing he could do, nothing except wait for somebody, possibly the doctor, to tell him what to do.

Was his father going to die? His mother thought so; indeed she seemed to have made up her mind that the old man was dead already, or maybe it was just her way of speaking. Perhaps he would recover and be forced to keep his hands off any work. If he did die, this place would fall to Dougie. How many times the son had dreamed of being his own boss, of being able to do this or that without reference to his father for approval; but now that the possibility was real it frightened him.

The cluttered yard of the croft was all around him: the jumble of rusting implements, the old tyres, the grind-stone, the old iron pot with water for the hens, the coils of fencing wire and piles of stabs. It was his, or likely to be. Despite the fowls clucking and scratching in the peatstack, it seemed an empty, lonely place, haunted by the past.

— Surely he'll get better. I need him still. He kens so

much about animals and crops. Maybe it's no his hert. An ulcer maybe. Indigestion. Appendix. No it canna be. He would spew. Come on doctor. Where are ye? It's ages since I phoned. It's this waiting. End this waiting... what's it like to die? No see the sun anymore, no hear the hens or smell the hay. Is it like sleeping? D'ye dream for a whilie when ye're dead? Before your brain stops? I can feel my hert thumping inside me. Does it keep going for all these years and never stop? D'ye feel cowld as ye die? Doctor, where are ye? Get here, man. He'll come. He'll come. In his car, black bag, stethoscope, needles and bottles... 'Keep him in his bed for a day or two and give him one of these three times a day after meals. It's just a grumbling appendix. Common at his age.'

Dougie took the tractor and cart back into the yard, walked to the hay park and saw that the baler was okay. He knew it would be: the walk was an excuse to keep himself away from the house for a bit longer. On the way home, he felt guilty about acting this way. It was childish and selfish. These thoughts quickened his step but the nearer he got to the house the more reluctant he became to enter. It was a great relief indeed when the doctor's red car swept up the road.

The doctor was a large man in his early fifties; he wore a tweed jacket but no hat. His voice had a southern burr to it, despite the fact he had been resident in this area for twenty-five years.

'Ah, Dougie,' he said. 'Is he inside?'

'Aye.'

'How is he now?'

'I don't know.'

They went inside. Dougie's mother met them in the kitchen; her face was calmer now — it didn't do to show too much grief to strangers and the doctor was after all a stranger — but her eyes showed the effort of self-control.

'Mrs Bayne,' said the doctor. 'Now where is he?'

'Ben in his bed.'

During Dougie's absence, his mother had removed most of her husband's clothing and he lay with a pyjama jacket over his flannel undershirt. His face was pale and marked with red veins. When they entered the room, his eyes flickered open and he tried to struggle up.

'Is that ye, doctor?' he said in a pathetic kind of voice.

'Aye, Dan. What's this ye've come to? Lie still now til I examine ye.'

The doctor busied himself with his stethoscope. Then he asked Dougie what had happened and dragged out the full story of the collapse. He nodded but said nothing. From the end of the bed, the old woman asked what was the matter.

'Your husband has had a heart attack. He has to rest, stay in his bed for a few days. I'll try to come back tomorrow.'

Dougie wanted to ask how bad his father really was, what his chances were. The doctor's solemn expression gave nothing away or if it did it was not reassuring.

'Doctor.' Dan's word took them by surprise. 'The ould pump's no good.'

'Aye, Dan, it's the pump,' said the doctor.

'Can ye do something for her so that I can gie Dougie a hand here to get the hay in?'

'You'll not be getting any hay in,' said the doctor. 'You'll stop in your bed and do as you're told.'

The old man laughed — a hollow, sniggering sound.

'I'll come back and see you tomorrow, Dan,' grinned the doctor. 'In the meantime stop in your bed and dinna get up to any mischief.'

'Oh no no,' said the old man, and he laughed again. 'What could I do lying here anyway?'

Back in the kitchen, the doctor's face was grave.

'He's no great, is he?' asked Dougie's mother. The doctor did not reply.

'I ken fine,' she went on. 'Your silence speaks like a book. Oh weel, what can we do but put our faith in the Lord. It's in His hands noo.'

'Husht mither,' hissed Dougie angrily. 'Will ye tak a cup or a glass, doctor?'

'No, thank you all the same. I've got some more visits to make. Another time, Dougie, another time.'

Outside, getting into his car, the doctor said, 'Your father's very ill, Dougie. He's had a bad attack and his heart is still very weak. He's got to rest.'

'Aye,' said Dougie thoughtfully. 'I'm sorry my mother was like that.'

The doctor looked up. 'Your mother knew exactly what was in my mind. I didn't have to say a word.' He paused. 'I'll be straight with you, Dougie. Your father may not get over this.'

With that, he started the car and drove away. Dougie looked after the blob of colour for a few moments and then went back into the house.

His mother was filling the kettle to make tea. 'He wants to see ye,' she said.

Dougie hesitated a little before entering the bedroom; cold fingers of fear touched his mind and he opened the door slowly so as not to make any sound. Even the faint noise of his breathing had an eerie foreboding to it. His father lay as he had been lying.

'Come in, boy. Sit doon here a minute. Noo, listen. It may be the last chance I have to tell ye this...'

The speech was hesitant and slow with pauses while he fought for breath.

'Husht, man,' protested his son. 'Dinna speak like that.'

'I'm telling ye. That first shot — that was the scythe being sharpened. He'll be back for me before long so dinna husht me yet. There's a higher hand abeen us, boy, and I ken that although I've never been a man for the kirk. The pain is still in me and it'll no be long. What I wanted to tell ye — are ye listening — what I wanted to say was that everything's been taken care o. I've seen a solicitor and the croft is going til ye. The Commission ken and they said there would be no bother. It's all yours noo. There's a bit for your mother too.'

'Faither, ye'll get better. All ye have to do is no take so muckle oot o yourself.'

'Na, na! Ye micht as weel get used to it now. Promise one thing.'

The old man pulled his hand from below the blankets and gripped his son's wrist.

'Look after your mither, Dougie, and the land. It's a hard trauchle at times but it's good land and it'll be all your own. Promise me that.'

Later that night, Dan Bayne died. Dougie's mother woke him at sunrise, sobbing. 'Your father's gone,' she cried.

What with the woman's cowning and his lack of sleep, he took a long time to come to himself, get his bike out and go once more for the doctor. As he pedalled away, he looked back at the house. His mother was drawing down the blinds to tell the world of the death. Tread quietly all ye who pass by here. Her face was a pale glimmer before the white sheet descended.

The chill morning air woke him and the full import of his father's death came home to him now. And his father had known he was not likely to see another sunrise; all that about the will must have taken quite a bit of thought for the old man. Perhaps he had underestimated him. Anyway it was his croft now, but he did not think on it for long because there were the unfamiliar matters of the kisting and the funeral to arrange. He wondered how he would manage to cope with his mother in her grief. Looking back on it later, he realised that she had coped very well. True, she cried and sobbed and carried a sodden hankie with which she alternately dabbed her eyes and blew her nose, but it was not the display of anguish he had feared.

Donald's Jamie's wife Kathie came round as soon as she heard, and Jean from the shop, Mary Ross — though with her bad leg it would have made more sense to stay at home — and Betty the district nurse. The women continually made tea and comforted the widow.

'Mind him as ye knew him,' said Kathie.

'A fine strong man,' said Mary Ross. 'I warrant he was

fifteen stone. A brave man.'

'He was a good man to me,' said Dougie's mother in the thin voice of sorrow. 'But he had reached his time. There's a higher hand abeen us.'

'He's in a better place now,' said Mary Ross, who was a little pious.

Betty the nurse washed and cleaned the body, shaved the chin and combed the hair, and prepared it for lying-in with a towel and cotton wool. Then the widow brought out a new pair of pyjamas to dress the body and, during this, at a time when such intimate contact could have provoked the most violent remorse, showed such control that Betty was moved to relate it afterwards to her man.

'She was as calm and clear in her voice, the like I've never seen, and ye ken the number o funerals I've been til. She said that she knew this was going to happen, that she'd seen it coming since many a long day. She said that he'd been fading away before her eyes and that in a way it was a blessing that he went so quick when he did, before he lost all his strength. It was God's mercy, she said. I didna ken what to say for a minute or two and then I asked how Dougie was taking it. And she said that she didna ken but as he was a bit soft he micht take it hard, they were aye together, him and his father, and he micht miss him. She said that Dougie had all sorts of ideas but he had been a good son til them and she hoped the croft would be good til him. It's a wife he needs, says she. Then she did a funny thing. She bent and kissed her man on the lips; I thocht she'd broken doon but she said, cool as anything, 'It's many a long day since ye kissed me, Dan Bayne, but I've got ye at last'. And then we went and had some tea. I asked her if she wanted something stronger to steady her nerves like, but no — tea would be fine.'

Dougie's grief exploded to the surface when he was alone, standing in the empty byre. His feelings had been a crazy mixture all morning since the doctor had come and declared a finality with the signing of the death certificate; and there in the diffused sunlight of the byre he could contain his sorrow no longer. 'Faither, why, why, what for?' he cried, slapping his hand on the wall and resting his head against it while the hot anger coursed from his eyes and down his face.

People began to come and go from the late forenoon onwards. Jim Sinclair the joiner measured the body for the coffin and commented on the size. Donald's Jamie dropped in briefly to give his condolences and to say that he would be back in the evening for the kisting. Somewhere, somehow, the gravedigger had got the news and called in on his way to the cemetery to verify his information.

The funeral was set for the following day at noon and Jim Sinclair sent his eldest son off on his bicycle to carry the news to the outlying crofts. Dougie looked out the addresses of relatives in the south and arranged for telegrams to be sent.

Donald's Jamie and Dougie, now composed again but wary and solemn, had a dram together.

'Sudden, boy, sudden,' said the visitor when he heard how Dan had collapsed. 'A big man, your faither. We'll miss him.'

Dougie said nothing.

'It's no a bad croft,' continued his companion. 'Ye'll be keeping it on yourself. Ye'll get a chance to put some o those ideas o yours til practice.'

Donald's Jamie's eyes twinkled at Dougie's sudden look. 'Maybe this is no time to say it but say it I will. Your faither knew his land and his animals, none better, but he widna budge when it came to trying something new.'

Mr Bremner the minister arrived early in the afternoon, clad in black and with his head slightly bowed. He shook hands with everybody and spoke with a great quietness, refusing any tea and staying only for a few minutes and a prayer before leaving. In the evening he returned for the kisting.

It was a well-attended kisting, as people commented afterwards; indeed it was one of the last kisting services in the parish, for after that time remains came usually to be placed in their coffin without ceremony. Many crofters and villagers came, so many that not everyone could find a place to sit and some of the men stood in the lobby of the small house. Outside the sun was still shining in the sky; and it said a lot that so many of the crofters left their fields to attend when it was such grand hay weather. Inside, the light, filtered through the drawn blinds, was thick and yellow.

Mr Bremner went round and shook hands with all present, which took him several minutes. It was noted wryly by some that it was the biggest congregation he had seen for many a day and that as like as not he would try to make the most of it.

Dougie's mother sat by the fire with the nurse and Kathie. All the visitors came to her and shook her hand, murmuring a few words as they did so. Then they moved back and shook hands with Dougie, now in his suit and a black tie that had belonged to his father. Many commented on Dan's sudden death in hushed tones and exchanged quiet remarks on the weather and the hay. Dougie managed a smile or two; he knew that the worst pangs of grief had passed out of him but he worried about how his mother would take this intense, communal expression of sorrow. From where he stood he could not hear her speaking but he was anxious she should bear up; seeing sorrow in others upset him.

Mr Bremner gave a slight cough and silence descended on the room. Everybody looked to the minister, who stood with eyes closed, his head bent, his hands clutching a heavy bible with a spray of coloured bookmarkers hanging from it. He was an old man himself with a bald head and a prominent nose.

'Let us read from the Holy Word of God,' he said suddenly, raising his head and opening his Bible. A rustling of paper sounded as others opened to the correct chapter. 'From the Gospel according to John, Chapter 3, Verse 1.' And the minister began to read. When he reached verse fourteen he read more slowly in the singsong intonation beloved of ministers, the cadence rising during the first part of the sentence and falling quietly towards the end.

'And as Moses lifted up the serpent in the wilderness, even so must the Son of Man be lifted up: That whosoever believeth in Him should not perish but have eternal life. For God so loved the world that He gave his only begotten Son, that whosoever believeth in Him should not perish but have everlasting life.'

When he finished his reading, Mr Bremner closed his Bible and said, 'Let us pray.' There was a general shuffling of feet and some coughing. Dougie felt that the prayer was long and verged on a sermon; several times he opened his eyes to study the linoleum and once he looked up at the minister and was surprised to see him standing with his face upturned to the ceiling, his eyes tightly clenched, all the time praying away.

'Amen.' More coughing and shuffling of feet. Outside somewhere, a sheep bleated.

'Friends,' said the minister, 'we are gathered here this evening to mark the passing away of one of our number. Daniel Bayne, or Dan as we all knew him and will continue to know him, was a man of the soil, the salt of the earth, the tiller in the vineyard of the world. Now he has reaped his final blessed harvest and the Lord God Almighty, the creator of all things in heaven and earth, has gathered him to His bosom. We are gathered here to mourn his passing. Most of you have known Dan longer than I have but we all share the sorrow at his being no longer among us...'

Mr Bremner went on for quite a while and one or two of the men surreptitiously checked their watches.

'...and now, my friends, a new hand is on the plough-handle and a strong, worthy hand...' Dougie suddenly realised that he was being talked about and reddened. '...our heartfelt sympathy goes out to the widow, Mrs Bayne, and to Dougie, and we pray that in their hour of need their faith will remain unshaken and that the Lord's blessings will continue to be made manifest to them.'

At length the minister came to the end of his discourse and bent his head once more for a final, comparatively brief prayer. Then there was a great outbreak of coughing and shuffling of feet, and a fag or two were lit. The men and the women came forward once again to take their farewell of Dougie and his mother.

With the last of them Dougie went out himself and had a smoke. The shadows were falling across the land, the fence posts throwing long, dark pencils on the grass.

After the kisting, the funeral passed off well. Kathie counted thirteen cars as well as the hearse and there was a large crowd on foot and bike too. The sun did not shine but neither did it rain. Dougie, directed in all he had to do by Jim Sinclair, was kept very busy, asking friends of his father to take a cord on the coffin, thanking everybody afterwards and dealing with the minister and other officials. When it was all over and the black-clad figures had mostly departed from among the gravestones, Mr Bremner came over and gripped his hand tightly.

'The Lord will sustain you in your loss,' said the minister. 'I'll be seeing you in the kirk come the Sabbath most likely.'

In the days after the death, he worked long hours, late into the evening as long as the weather was good, to bring in and secure the hay. When that was finished, he took his baler around some of the other crofts, as was the custom. Later in the year, when the barley and the oats ripened and the tatties needed lifting, they would give him a hand. By the end of July, a lull in the year's cycle set in and he turned his mind to what he might do to improve the croft. He read magazines and books, sought advice from the Board and the Commission, and had a few ideas of his own.

It was a period of great excitement; plans and dreams whirled in his head and he read more and more, dipping into ecology and even history and politics. Many of the crofters had jobs to supplement their income: some kept boats and set creels, other had a trade and some provided communal services such as the gravedigger and the man who sold the Sunday newspapers. Dougie discovered the idea of self-sufficiency and decided it was for him; the independence it seemed to guarantee appealed to him and the work kept him busy.

CHAPTER NINE

He knotted his tie carefully and took a look at himself in the mirror. His suit was growing a little baggy after five years but it would do for a while yet. A new suit was an expense he could hardly afford: dungarees and waterproof jackets were more important garments for a person working the land — let the oil boys buy suits and flashy shoes.

Hogmanay. Only four more hours and it would be a new year. But would there be anything really new about it? Probably not: the sun would rise and set three hundred and sixty-five times and spring, summer, the back end and winter would follow each other as always.

Dougie thought suddenly that the world was the same as a puddock pool, filled with weeds and dim light, hotching with craiturs that spent their time fighting and spravelling about, one with another; each puddock puffed up his chest and croaked his anthem, but to what purpose? Maybe he would get married this year; a wife might give some purpose to the whole stramash, someone to work for. A man left nothing if he did not leave his seed.

Tocher, from the Gaelic tochar, a dowry. A bonny word. What tocher would the new year bring? Riches, gold, jewels, like the daughter of a prince. Or fleas, rags, the flu, like a tinkler's hussy. There was nothing to do but wait and live it out. In your own corner of the puddock pool.

— I wonder what Mary Lousie is doing now. She would

have made a good wife. A good worker. She could fairly lift bales and upend yowes. Och but that's in the past, and the past is gone, a corpse.

Dougie put on his jacket and checked his pockets, pulling out lumps of fluff and forgotten raffle tickets and stuffing in cigarettes and matches. It was a cold night, a tant frost. Scarf and muffles weather.

'I'm off,' he shouted in the general direction of the kitchen.

There was a scraping of feet. 'Take care o yoursel,' warned his mother, coming through into the lobby. 'Ye'll no be home late?'

'No.'

'Okay then. Ye're going to the pub I expect.'

'Aye. Tom'll be having a do after closing time.'

'Watch for bobbies. They'll be on the go the nicht. Dinna drink a lot for mercy's sake.'

'No, no. I'll be all right.'

The world lay still and resonant under the frost; the blades of grass cracked under his feet and the sky was shot through with shimmering points of light. Might see the merry dancers, he thought. On such nights, the aurora borealis did paint the sky with ghostly sheets of pink and yellow that moved and disappeared and tempted man to look above him.

The cold made the van cough and splutter before it started properly. His breath quickly silvered the windows and he had to wipe them with a chamois several times on the short journey to the village. Someone had spread sand across the street and it crunched beneath the wheels.

The hotel was lit from ground to rooftree; two spot-lights in the privet bushes bathed the front in a yellow glow and caused the iron letters pinned above the door to throw distorted shadows across the wall. Five or six cars stood in a row at the gate.

Dougie went into the lounge bar. This was a long, low room, carpeted and curtained, with a great peat fire burning at one end and a pinewood bar at the other. The predominant colour was a warm orange. Above the bar, tinsel letters spelled out 'A Merry Xmas and a Happy New Year'. Above the fire hung a framed print of a herd of shaggy Highland cattle standing up to their navels in a loch. A fruit machine glowered at one side and not far from it stood an electric organ and a couple of microphones on stands.

'Ho, ho, it's yourself.' This jovial greeting came from a tall, elderly man, the only person in the room.

'Aye, John, and how are ye?'

Better known as Jonah but never addressed as such, John MacKay was a good-natured buffoon. Now in his late sixties, he had worked on a whaler in the Antarctic for a while after the war; his tales of ice, blubber and derring-do had earned him his nickname. He had a long-jawed face and a nose like a buttress in the Cairngorms, and when he grinned, which was often, his teeth stood like a row of lichened fenceposts. Dougie thought that John was not as daft as people made him out to be; he had an innocent curiosity in all technical things and a runaway, childish tongue — in contrast to the air of sober, silent understanding that most men presented to the world to fool others into thinking they had brains.

'Hard frost,' said Jonah.

'Aye, it's cold.'

'A drappie o John Barleycorn'll soon thaw ye oot.' Jonah laughed and showed his teeth.

The landlord, Tom Manson, appeared behind the pinewood counter. He was a large, florid man with wavy hair going grey at the temples. As it was Hogmanay he wore a kilt; the great silver buckle on his belt flashed before him like a headlamp.

'Aye, Tom, I'll have a nip and a pint.' said Dougie. 'What are ye drinking, John?'

'Och never heed me.'

'Yes, yes.'

'Weel, thank ye very much. A rum and pep, if ye will.'

'Music the nicht?' Dougie nodded towards the organ and the microphones.

'Aye,' confirmed the landlord.

'Oh ye canna see in the new year without a hooch and a skirl,' grinned Jonah.

'I mind one new year's nicht I spent in South Georgia. We had a richt fill and music — music I'm telling ye, ye never heard such music in your life. There was one Norwegian chiel wi a fiddle and we danced roond the deck, all men like, though nobody kent the steps or whatever they were dancing. It's a wonder we didna go overboard.'

Dougie and Tom exchanged glances. Jonah's memories were common property in the parish and whenever he began his recall men's minds drifted away on their private courses, leaving the old gowk to relive his day.

Dougie was halfway through his pint when the door opened behind him and some people came in. Jonah looked at them and Dougie watched the old man's face but it betrayed no signs of recognition of the newcomers.

'Is that Dougie Bayne?'

The voice was confident, obviously local but with a hint of something else. Dougie swung round to see a tall man of his own age, bearded, dressed in a checked jacket and a polo-necked shirt. The newcomer's face was smiling broadly and there was a joyful light in his eyes. I know him, thought Dougie.

'D'ye no ken me, boy?' said the stranger. 'Hello, John. How are ye?'

'Hello,' said Jonah slowly, hiding his curiosity with a grin.

'Rob,' cried Dougie suddenly. 'Good God, I didna ken ye wi that beard.'

They shook hands heartily, both laughing. It had been several years since the boyhood companions had met. Jonah recognised the visitor now and also shook hands, flashing his teeth in delight.

'How are ye, Rob?' he burbled. 'It's been a lang while.'

'Aye, John, it has,' said Rob, and the American edge to his accent was now apparent. 'But ye're looking well.'

Rob's companion, a tall girl with auburn hair and the whitest teeth Dougie had ever seen, said, 'Hi.'

'Oh sorry,' laughéd Rob. 'This is Tammy, my wife. Tammy, this is Dougie. I told you about him. And John.'

'Hi,' said Tammy again, and shook hands with the men.

'Pleased til meet ye,' said Jonah.

There was a moment's silence.

'Well, can I get you a drink?' laughed Rob, suddenly full of energy. 'The usual?' He glanced at the beer and rum just to remind himself what the usual might be.

'Just a small one for me,' said Jonah.

'Thanks very much,' said Dougie. 'I didna recognise ye wi that beard.'

'That's what everybody says. Tom, how are you? Fine, fine, it's great to be back. What was it now? A rum, a nip, two nips. Honey?'

'Have you got Martini?' asked Tammy.

'Surely,' said Tom. 'Ice and lemon?'

'Terrific,' laughed the girl.

'When did you get home?' asked Jonah.

'Just today,' said Rob. 'This afternoon. We drove up from Inverness.'

'Boy, what a drive,' cried Tammy. Her voice seemed unusually loud. 'Those hills and the snow.'

'Aye, aye,' nodded Jonah. 'They've had a puckle snow doon there.'

'A puckle?' queried the girl.

'A little bit,' said her husband, handing her a Martini.

'I'm gonna find it a little hard to understand you guys.'

She's beautiful, thought Dougie, especially when she laughs. You lucky bastard, Rob, with a wife like that.

'Och, no,' Jonah reassured her. 'Twa or three days here and yc'll be spouting like us.'

Tammy looked at him quizzically.

'Ah look, there's a fire,' said Rob. 'Let's get warmed up,

Dougie, and gie us your crack, man.'

The three of them moved to a table and sat down. Dougie offered his cigarettes but neither of the newcomers smoked — not tobacco anyway, added Rob cryptically.

'You arrived the day?' asked Dougie.

'Yup,' said Rob. 'We flew into Prestwick yesterday morning and took the train to Inverness. I hired a car there.'

'Boy, were we bushed,' laughed Tammy. 'Jet lag really knocks you out.'

Silence, while they sipped their drinks.

'This'll be your first time in Scotland,' said Dougie.

'Yeah, it sure is.' Tammy's open-hearted enthusiasm was becoming a thing of wonder to the crofter; her voice filled the room. 'It's great. I've been reading about Scotland for months and months, and Rob has told me all about it. But gee, it's... it's far better than I expected. It's so beautiful, even in the rain.'

Dougie grinned and admired the girl's eyes over the rim of his beer mug.

'On the way up,' said Rob, 'we rehashed all the stuff Tammy had read, all the corny rubbish that you read in tourist literature. All that crap detracts from the real thing and we had a great time tearing it to shreds.'

'Oh yeah, that was fun,' said Tammy. 'What was it about the locks brooding in the mist-clad glens?'

'She means lochs,' added Rob unnecessarily. 'Let me see now.' He looked to the ceiling for inspiration. 'We drove out of Inverness, the capital of the Highlands and the home of the best English according to the novelist Defoe, into an ancient country where the past rubs shoulders harmoniously with the present...' he put on his best American accent and Tammy glowed with delight, '...into an enchanted land of heather, purple adjectives and lone pipers, competing with the distant cry of the curlew as they finger their pibrochs on the bonny banks and braes, into a land where Grannie's Hieland hame squats peacefully in the shadow of an oilrig repair yard or

a nuclear reactor, where the turbulent northern seas crash
on silver sands and the scent of peat, bog myrtle, haggis
and chips comes on the gentle breeze out of the incom-
parable calm of the gloaming. Set a stout heart tae a stey
brae, as the locals say, and keep right on to the end of
the road where ceud mile failte, a hundred thousand
welcomes in the ancient tongue of the Gael, awaits on the
lips of the friendly people. Hospitality is a by-word in the
Highlands, the home of salmon, grouse and whisky, and
nothing compares with a dinner in an old castle, in
modern comfort amid stone walls built centuries ago,
where the lilt of foot-tapping strathspeys has long since
replaced the clash of claymore on targe. Time has no
meaning among these hills and lochs. Forget the office
and the supermarket as you cast your fly on the gleaming
troutpool, while high above you a golden eagle wheels,
watchful, and the monarch of the glen sniffs the breeze.'

Rob drained his whisky, pleased with his monologue,
and Tammy laughed loudly. Dougie watched them both
with admiration. Rob has done well for himself, he
thought, he must have plenty money now.

'There are plenty o good books, too,' said Dougie. 'I
hope ye read them.'

'Oh sure,' said Rob. 'I saw to it that Tammy got a fair
picture and now she can see for herself. But tourists like
that kinda thing. It adds to the excitement of the holiday,
I suppose. If the trip doesn't match up to the brochure,
they blame themselves or the weather for missing something. But Dougie you've got a way with words yourself...'
he resorted to a stronger Scots accent, '...I mind ye writing
poetry once.'

'You write poetry?' said Tammy, far too loud for comfort.

'Na, na,' blushed Dougie. 'I'm nae poet.'

'False modesty, pal,' said Rob. 'He wrote verses,
Tammy, he really did. We've a Burns, a Hogg in our midst.'

'I wrote some poems once,' admitted Dougie, 'but it
was nothing... just a few lines... anyway, how long are you
home for?'

'Three weeks,' said Rob. 'Your glass is dry.'

'This is my round,' stated Dougie. 'Is it the same again?'

As Dougie was at the bar, Rob's father and mother came in, which was an unusual event for a start. Although Davie Sutherland did come to the hotel of an evening, no one could remember the last time he had brought his wife with him, and her wearing the same green coat she wore to the kirk. This was for Tammy's benefit; likely Davie had had to indulge in a good deal of preeging to get her out.

Davie was bluff and serious and spoke without removing the cigarette from his mouth. 'Aye, aye, Dougie. Rob said ye would be here.'

Isobel Sutherland walked as if the floor was covered in ice. 'Aye, Dougie,' she whispered.

'Hello. They're ower by the fire. What d'ye want?'

'A rum. Whit aboot ye?'

Isobel was confused by the array of bottles. 'Oh I dinna ken. Have they orange juice?'

Davie took matters into his own hands. 'Gie her a glass o sherry.'

'Aye. All richt, then,' she agreed.

'Cold nicht, David,' said Jonah, still perched on his stool at the bar and who had observed everything with a gleeful twinkle.

'Cold, boy,' agreed Davie.

'John,' said Isobel softly, acknowledging the man's presence.

'Aye, Isobel,' said Jonah, louder than necessary and throwing a wink at Dougie.

— Just the same old carry-on. Nobody in this place has anything better to do than miscall their neighbours. We all know why Isobel is here but she's probably been dying to come for years, scared to come on her own or suggest that she might be taken, and she had to wait until Davie and his pride saw fit to bring her. Well, I hope the old biddy makes the most o it because it'll be a damn long while afore she's here again.

'I was just saying,' said Davie, taking his rum from the

tray of drinks Dougie brought back to the table, 'that Rob'll see a difference here noo.'

'Oh no,' said his son. 'A bit maybe but overall it's still the same place. I don't want it to change. I always like to think that I can come back to what I knew.'

'The prices o things are awful now,' Isobel ventured to say.

'Och, that doesna bother Rob,' her husband said. 'He's got a good wage. How much did ye spend on that hoose ye bocht, boy?'

'I couldna have got a place like it here,' said Rob, slightly embarrassed.

'Anyway, how's the old croft?'

'Fine,' said Dougie. 'Why don't ye both come up some time?'

'That would be great,' cried Tammy. 'Sure, we'll come along, won't we, honey?'

'Crofting's a lot easier than it used to be,' said Davie. 'Plenty o grants and subsidies compared wi what we had in our day. The government gies money away like sand fae the beach.'

More people had come in and the chairs and tables were filling up. Nods and words of greeting flew across the room and eyes quickly sought out the strangers. Isobel blushed and fidgeted, sipped her sherry and smiled.

'Rob Sutherland,' cried John Campbell, advancing through the crowd, the light making his fringe of hair into a halo. 'Good God, boy, is that a dead rat on your face?'

'I thought it safer to come home in disguise,' laughed Rob, shaking hands heartily. 'How are ye doing?'

'Fine, canna complain. Boy, it's good to see ye back.'

Davie grunted and drank his rum. John Campbell added loudly, 'How are ye, Isobel?'

About this time, the musicians arrived, bearing accordion and fiddle.

'We're ready for a tune now,' shouted Jonah. 'Right ye are,' said Alistair the teacher and the player of the organ.

'We'll soon swacken your ankles.'

The trio took their places and began to prepare their equipment. Booms and piercing shrieks roared and fell away from the amplifiers.

'Do they play traditional music?' asked Tammy.

'Aye,' said Davie, although he did not quite know what she meant.

Bright sparkling notes spilled from the electric organ. The fiddler made some minute adjustment to the head of his instrument and his brother, the accordion player, carefully laid a cigarette at his feet. Alistair nodded one, two, three and they were off with a reel.

'Noisy,' said Isobel. 'It's hard to speak.'

'Never heed speaking,' said Davie, 'listen.'

Rob was smiling. 'No muckle has changed in the music field,' he said. 'Still the old boxie and the fiddle. Kate Dalrymple is still lowping.'

Dougie laughed when Tammy said 'Kate who?' and explained that it was the name of a tune. Rob went to the bar for another round. The music stopped and the players responded to the scattered applause by raising their pints.

The silence at the table was awkward. Davie said nothing and Isobel sipped her sherry, apparently scared to tip the glass too much. Dougie lit another cigarette.

'Do you play an instrument?' asked Tammy.

'Me?' said Dougie. 'I'm no musician, but I like listening to it like.'

Another silence. Then Rob came back with a laden tray and an excuse for talk.

'There's a fair crowd in now,' said Dougie.

'What does everybody do here entertainment-wise?' asked Tammy.

'No much,' said her father-in-law. 'Och, everybody has cars nowadays and they run aboot the countryside at nicht. And there's the TV, though there's a lot a rubbish on it aa the time.'

The schoolteacher began to sing in a plaintive, mid-Atlantic drawl, backing himself with throbbing chords on the organ.

Dougie savoured his beer and allowed the warmth of the alcohol to suffuse his being.

— I wish Rob hadna mentioned my poetry. Nobody kens about it, nobody, no a soul kens but him. I just dabbled. And it was years ago. She walks like a cat through a jungle o men. That was my opening line and I canna mind the rest, even though I wrote it myself. It was for Helen, it was aboot Helen. She was a tiger, striped orange and black, stepping regally fae man til man and leaving behind her empty souls like bones behind a cat, the flesh all consumed. Why did I ever write it in the first place? I suppose I must have loved her, jealous.

— Why has Rob come back now? In winter. He's done well for himself though, but we aa knew he would. Crofter's son makes it big. Fae peatbank til palace. He's had the chances and he's got the brains to make the most o them. And his faither didna drag him oot the school. Mind ye, I wasna sorry to leave. If only I'd started earlier wi the books. I missed my chance and he didna. I could have been a chemist in America and married to that woman. She's lovely, like an advertisement. There's nobody wi skin or eyes like that in this place. If she would only speak a little softer.

Jonah had also been admiring Tammy and he came over, weaving his way between the tables to be included in the group so that he could talk to her. Davie Sutherland was not too pleased at his coming and Jonah, aware of it, played on it for devilment.

'Aye, Rob, and how are ye?' said Jonah. 'It's good to see ye back, looking so hale and hearty, as fit as forty cats. And wi a wife, too. Man, man.' And he shook his head in mock disbelief.

Rob laughed. The returning exile is always tolerant of the foibles of his countrymen.

'Aye, John, ye're still here,' said Davie.

'And what think ye o Scotland?' asked Jonah.

'I think it's terrific,' said Tammy.

'No too cold for ye?'

'Well, maybe a little bit,' she laughed.

'Are ye fae California?' Jonah was obviously determined to show off his knowledge of the world.

'No. I'm from Vermont. Do you know it?'

'No, no,' admitted Jonah. 'I ken — know where it is like, but I've never been there. I was in Florida once.'

'Really? It's warm down there. When were you in Florida?'

Jonah shook his head to signify the passage of time. 'A good few years now. I was on a whaler coming back fae South Georgia. In the Antarctic, ye ken.'

'It'll have changed a bit since your day,' said Davie with a solemn firmness, at once statement and rebuke.

Jonah was not to be put off. 'Aye, aye, as like as no it has, Davie. It aa changes if ye live long enough.'

'Some things never change,' laughed Rob. 'And ye're one o them, John. Ye'll never die, they'll have to shoot ye.'

This sally swelled Jonah's smile to wide proportions and his eyes twinkled. Davie's laugh was unnecessarily loud and long; Isobel simpered.

Dougie admired the tiny creases that formed at the corners of Tammy's eyes as she frowned, trying to follow Jonah's spiel. There was something about the girl that was familiar and it took a few moments' brain-searching for him to realise that she resembled Sandra, the lassie who had come home with Rob once from university and who had brought Mary Louise into his life. The band launched into another song that began, 'Don't condemn me for being human.'

The first thing about Mary Louise that impressed Dougie was her size. At least six feet if she were an inch, she had huge hips and bosom; he had never seen a woman of such proportions. Were all American females this size? Beside her Rob and Sandra looked very small and weak. Sandra came from somewhere near Ullapool and had a pleasant west-coast accent. She was a classmate of Rob's and his current sweetheart. All three had come home for a week during the Easter vacation and had spent most of the time gallivanting about the countryside in a small car. Davie Sutherland was reported to be going mad with their carry-on and he spent as much time as he could in the hotel to get some peace and quiet. But he could not say much because he had agreed to the visit in the first place; Isobel hirpled about the house, grinning and saying that she enjoyed mixing with 'young folks'.

On the last Friday before they were due to return to the university, the trio invited Dougie to join them to a dance in the village hall.

Rob had obtained a half-bottle and they passed it one to the other as they swigged their way through the dark. The amplified guitar music and the stabbing lights of vehicles marked their destination. Village dances were raucous affairs. Mary Louise overflowed with enthusiasm for what she termed an ethnic experience and the other three reminisced vigorously about previous social gatherings.

When they arrived, a young lad with stringy hair and a patent leather jacket was vomiting against the wall.

'Oh gee, he's real bad,' cried Mary Louise.

In the hall lobby, there was a powerful smell of cigarette smoke, alcohol and cheap aftershave. Two girls, shivering in the fug, dragged each other past; 'so I says til him, if ye touch me again I'll thump your face,' said one, to which the other replied, 'He's an animal so he is...'

The newcomers paid the admission fee to the hall-keeper, a tall, angular man with skin like stained sandpaper and a sour expression. He looked totally out of place as he took coins and stamped a letter B in indelible ink on hands to show that admission had been paid. As soon as they were stamped, some went outside and tried with saliva and much pressure to transfer the magic symbol to the hands of their friends. No one ever succeeded in conning the hallkeeper in this way but they tried again and again.

The man's eyes flickered when Mary Louise cried, 'Gee, a stamp. I've never seen this before. Wait until they hear about this in Kansas.'

The hall was a cavern of noise and gloom. At one end the band was playing, making conversation impossible. Along one wall, the males phalanxed, dark and solemn; along the opposite wall was a bright whirl of girls, some of whom were dancing with each other. There was a steady to-ing and fro-ing between the dance floor and the toilets, the doors of which were continually opening and shutting, sending beams of light and a pungent smell of disinfectant across the floor. The whole hall was lit by half a dozen red bulbs in the ceiling.

'Well, this is it.' Rob had to shout above the music.

'Terrific,' cried Mary Louise. 'Get that beat.'

She grabbed Dougie and dragged him onto the dance floor to his intense embarrassment and the delight of Rob and Sandra. Others started to dance and the floor filled quickly with a mass of moving bodies.

The American girl danced with such voluptuous vigour that she intimidated those around her and cleared a space. Dougie's footwork was not of the best; he shuffled and waved his arms and tried to emulate the enthusiasm of his partner. By the time the dance finished he was pouring with sweat. The lull in the music was too short by far; as the bass chords rumbled, he shouted to Mary Louise that he had to go outside. 'Okay, see you later,' she yelled and turned immediately to seize another unsuspecting lad from the onlookers. Dougie found Rob standing near the door.

'Where's Sandra?'

'Lavatory.'

'Come ootside.'

Round the back of the hall, Rob uncorked his half-bottle and they both took a large mouthful. They were among a fairly large crowd; glass glinted in the pale light and the red eyes of cigarettes glowed.

'She's a real goer, that one,' said Dougie.

'Ye can say that again. Even when she's sober.'

'God.'

'Another one?'

'Aye, ta. Slainte.'

'Want a fag?'

'Have one o mine.'

'Ta.'

The match flared and burned out before they could use it. Rob struck another. They drew deeply on the smoke and leaned against the wall.

'Sandra's a fine lassie,' said Dougie.

'Aye, no bad,' agreed Rob.

Silence, except for the distant crash of the music and the whispered drinking going on around them.

'Going back in?'

'Aye.'

They joined the men grouped near the toilets. Sandra squeezed her way towards them and slipped her arm around Rob's waist. Dougie felt a twinge of envy. As like as not they would be flattening somebody's grass before the night was out. A great lad for the girls was Rob, or so it seemed, because he never had any trouble attracting them.

Mary Louise swept up to them, the bystanders recoiling on the bow wave of her approach.

'Hi guys. Isn't this terrific? Can you get a drink in this place?'

The hallkeeper's brother sold bottles of orange squash from one dim corner; it was either that or what you took outside behind the wall. Mary Louise had an orange squash.

The next hour passed in dancing and standing near toilets, smoking and shouting to each other above the din of the music. Normal conversation was impossible unless you retreated out of doors and it was getting a bit cold to be doing that too often.

The fight started at about eleven thirty and none of them could tell who was responsible. The epicentre of the ruckus was over near the band platform and the shockwaves rippled out from it. A scream, an exodus of girls, their eyes bright with fear and excitement, a converging of loons, just for a look. The hallkeeper sent three henchmen to sort it all out and the singer made a plea for calm over his microphone that only added to the racket.

'Oh come on,' groaned Rob. 'Let's go. The coppers'll be here any minute.' They stumbled outside.

'Now what?' asked Sandra.

'I don't know,' said Rob. 'Let's go for a walk. We can finish off the whisky.'

'It's cold.'

'I've a great idea.' Mary Louise's enthusiasm was growing tiresome but they listened. 'There must be a hayrick somewhere where we can shelter.'

'Hayrick?' queried Dougie. 'Ye mean a gilt?'

'Aye, she does,' said Rob. 'And I know where there's one. In Sannag's muckle park.'

'Where?' asked Mary Louise. 'It doesn't matter. I just don't understand you guys half the time. Is it far from here, this place?'

Sannag had been dead for years but the largest field on his croft was still called his muckle park. A stretch of rough pasture, it ran from the road down to a small loch, and towards one corner stood the haygilt, a square structure with a broad, sheltering end where the bales would be broken and loose and comfortable.

Much joking and laughing saw them over the gate and through the coarse tussocks; they were all beaming with exhileration when they flopped in the hay. It was not too damp and the clamminess in the legs went away after a few seconds. They passed the bottle back and fore and smoked. Beyond their outstretched feet the distant surface of the loch glimmered.

'It's empty,' said Dougie disconsolately, holding the bottle up to the sky and peering at the stars through it. 'She's dry.'

'So be it,' rejoined Rob. 'To him that hath it shall be given and to him that hath not even that which he hath will be taken away. All good things must come to an end. Thus saith the Lord and the distillers. Why? Why should they, come to think of it.'

'Eh?'

'I think — pardon — I think it is time we started our own still. D'ye ken that eighty percent o the price o a bottle o whisky is tax? Jink the gaugers, Dougie my lad, and mak our ain. Like in the olden days.'

'All we need is a copper coil, barley and a fire. Any old pot would do.'

'And lots of bottles,' added Sandra.

'Tae hell wi bottles. Cut oot the middleman. We could take turns lying below the tap wi our mooths open.'

'Moonshine forever,' cried Mary Louise.

It was cosy in the lee of the hay and very conducive to togetherness. The odd stalks of grass and thistle purrs that penetrated their clothing heightened their senses, and after a while Rob and Sandra betook themselves to a corner.

Dougie suddenly became very aware of Mary Louise's presence.

'Have you lived here all your life?' she asked.

'Aye.'

'Never been abroad?'

'No. No even England.'

'I think that's great.'

'What's it like in America?'

'It's big, like really big. Huge. Vast. I've hitched over a good area but there's still a lot to do. But it's boring in places. Just the same for miles and miles. Nothing higher than a roadsign. Everything here is so neat and cute and small.'

Dougie was not sure whether that was a compliment.

'Mind you, your weather is nothing to rave about.'

'We rave about it all the time,' said Dougie. 'Never stop complaining.'

They lapsed into silence and studied the metallic glitter of the loch. A rustling and stifled giggle came from Rob and Sandra's corner. Silence again.

'That whisky was good,' breathed the American girl. 'Boy, was that great? I feel fine, real fine. All cosy inside, like a little fire burning in my stomach. Do you ever feel that way? Tiny, tiny flames flickering and dancing, yellow and red and orange, little arrows of heat running through your veins, up your arms and down your thighs, your shins, skipping around your toes. And the whole world is outasight...'

Dougie stopped listening because as she spoke she had put her hand on his thigh and had snuggled closely to him, stretching her legs along the length of his. She ended with a gentle sigh and her head on his shoulder.

Had this woman taken a fancy to him? He was alarmed and also intrigued. Or was she just drunk? Anyway, the warmth of her lying against him was pleasing but she was too heavy and he could feel himself sinking a little in the hay. Her next words took him like a trout on a cleverly cast fly.

'You're so strong,' she whispered, running her hand along his thigh.

He didn't know what to do and, in the hay, could not move quickly.

'Rob told me all about you. I like country people. I made it once with a Mexican peasant. He was big and strong and nearly twice my age. Nearly old enough to be my father. Imagine that. He never said a word. We just did it. Wow, I'm telling you, he was terrif! He didn't have none of these books or anything like that, just a joint and the biggest organ south of the Rio Grande.'

All Dougie could manage was a weak 'Aye?'

Then her hands were behind his neck and her lips crushed against his. The world became a whirlpool of tongues and whisky breath, and she pulled him down on top of her. Caught and landed, he was helpless.

'Come on, come on,' she urged. 'Don't stop now.'

Then she pushed him off, sat up and peeled off her sweater over her head. Her flesh was grey-white in the darkness and it loomed and glimmered. 'You'll catch cold,' hissed Dougie. 'Never. I made it once with a trucker in Oregon when it was ten below.' She unhooked her bra and unzipped her jeans. 'Come on, what's the matter with you?' And she grabbed his belt, opened it and plunged her hand into his trousers. 'Ouch!'

'That's better. You're great!' And she pulled him back on top of her.

Dougie remembered afterwards how comfortable she was. Her breasts were fat and milky coloured, plump as two Christmas geese, and her hips were snow-covered hillocks.

'Canny,' he gasped. 'I'm no a horse.' This made her laugh and she threw her head back and shouted, 'Be my stallion!'

'For God's sake, they'll hear us.'

'Who cares?'

When the first frantic session came to its glorious end, she clutched Dougie to her as if afraid to let him go. He also remembered that for a moment she averted her eyes and stared into the darkness, and a tiny droplet glistened on her cheek.

'Mary Louise,' he whispered.

She looked up at him and smiled. He kissed the tear and destroyed it.

'Thanks,' she said softly.

They lay that way for a long time until the cold made them shiver and Mary Louise retrieved her sweater. The world became a dark pool of haunted silence.

'You can add me to your list,' said Dougie after they had lain together, his hand on her breast under the wool.

'Ehhm?' she queried dreamily.

'You can add me to your list after the Mexican chuchter and that trucker in wherever it was. And ye can tell the next one that ye made it wi a Scottish peasant.'

'No, Dougie,' she protested. 'It's not like that.' She kissed him. 'C'mon, let's do it again.' And her hands began their magic roving.

The next day the trio departed and that was the last Dougie ever saw of either Sandra or Mary Louise. To his surprise, however, she did write to him, without enclosing her own address, just once and soon after. Basically it was a wordy thank-you but there was, he thought, an undercurrent of sadness running through it, as if the writer had been genuinely grateful for something, as if she had been desperately seeking the answer to a question she did not know how to ask.

CHAPTER TEN

Fada siar air aghaidh cuain
'Se mo dhuansa Cruit-mo-chridh
Guth mo luaidh anns gach stuaidh
'Ga ma nuallan gu tir.

Alistair the teacher, who was from Stornoway and had the Gaelic, was singing the Eriskay Love Lilt.

'There's a grand swing to the Gaelic music,' said Davie knowingly.

'Is there anyone here who speaks it?' asked Tammy.

'No, no. Just broad Scotch we speak.'

The crowd in the bar was beginning to thin out. There was a great deal of drinking still to be done before the next sunrise and it was best to take it easy until midnight. There was a feeling, too, in most people that the fireside was the proper place to be at this time, in the last hours of the dying year.

Davie Sutherland looked studiously at the big pocket watch he always carried and, giving Isobel a tap on the knee, said, 'C'mon, wumman, it's time we was oot o here.'

'Oh mercy,' said his wife in her pathetic little voice. 'Time fairly flies when ye're enjoying yourself.'

She would be happy to stay here all night knocking back the sherry, thought Dougie, but she'll go home now and make Davie his tea.

'We'll be along later,' said Rob.

The musicians launched into a selection of wild jigs and a chorus of hoochs and handclapping kept time.

Dougie began to give himself over to John Barleycorn.

Every mouthful slid down his throat with a silken smooth-
ness and in his brain all the dragons, kelpies, slithering
beasties, bogles, warlocks, dinosaurs and brownies stirred
and awakened, flashed their red eyes and girned, plotting
mischief. Behind the mask of jollity, the facade of good
humour and comradeship — oh he's a richt fine chiel,
Dougie, a good case, fine sort — there was the realisation
that the drink-induced gaiety was part of the charade of
machismo that the Scottish character required. Och, it's
the new year. A man can take a fill at new year and be
forgiven, not a blemish on his character, neither mote nor
plank in his eye. It's the time o year for it — we aa expect
it.

Margaret made her way among the tables, collecting
dirty glasses. 'Ye'll be coming up for a whilie after ten,'
she said to selected customers.

At ten o'clock when the last of those Jonah called the
Gentiles had left, Tom Manson closed the bar, dimmed
the lights and summoned everyone to continue the party
upstairs. Dougie, Rob and Tammy, Jonah and several
others were invited. Margaret decided that some of her
guests needed coffee and went to the kitchen to make
some. Tammy offered to help and was put to work slicing
a large black bun.

'Do you have a party like this every year?' she asked.

'Just about,' said Margaret. 'Just for our regulars, you
know. Tom says that they put a good few pennies through
our hands in the year and this is a way o saying thanks.'

'I'm really enjoying myself. Everybody has been so
friendly. Especially that old man with his stories about
hunting whales.'

'Jonah's an old blether.'

'It's funny but the younger people are more quiet.
Dougie seems a nice guy but he doesn't say much.'

'Dougie's a fine loon but he's no aye so quiet. I feel
sorry for him sometimes. We shouldna be speaking aboot
folk like this, but he has this croft all to himself and

nobody on it wi him but his mother. I think that at times he wants to sell the whole lot off and take a steady job.'

'Trees, Rob,' Dougie was saying. 'I'm going to plant shelter belts and copses on all the odd corners o land I've got. It'll break the wind and gie the sheep some shelter.'

And he saw the deep green needles rustling in the wind, smelt the resin and traced the rough bark with his fingers.

'Sounds like a good idea to me,' said Rob.

'That's what we should have done years ago,' continued Dougie. 'D'ye ken, of course ye do, that the land was all forest once — after the Ice Ages. Christ, there were bloody wolves then. Diversification o the environment, they call it. It's aa to do wi succession and climax vegetation and aa that. Och but ye'll ken what I mean. The problem seems to be finding the richt kind o trees to stand up to the wind, to start the succession. Noo, I fancy pines myself, or fir — Douglas fir, no named after me I doubt — and the sitka spruce has a bonny branch.'

'It'll take a while to get them started,' cautioned Rob, who was more sober.

'Aye, maybe, but ye canna let that stop ye. It micht take years but nothing worth doing was ever done quick. Aye, pines and spruce it'll be and maybe a sprinkling o deciduous — birch, there's a bonny tree, flickering and dancing in the licht — and sycamore'll grow anywhere. I'll get in touch wi the Forestry Commission. They've been planting for years and should ken what grows best where, and there's been lots o bitties in magazines aboot it.'

Jonah leaned across.

'I'm no thinking ye'll get trees to grow here,' he said.

'Och, ye've never tried man,' cried Dougie. 'What d'ye ken?'

'The wind, boy, the wind. It leaves nothing alone. No even a kail plant'll grow strecht if ye dinna put a wall aroond it.'

'Ye've nae faith, John,' laughed Rob. 'Nae faith and nae pioneering instinct. I bet ye the next time I come home there'll be a forest roond Dougie's hoose.'

'Then ye'd be a fool to part wi your money so easy,' argued Jonah. 'Trees micht grow but it'll no be quick. Mind ye though, Dougie, I'll say this, that if any chiel can do it ye'll be the one.'

He looked at the carpet before continuing. 'For there's nobody else. They all up tail and fly off after money. There's damn few like ye, boy, and good luck to ye.'

Coffee and plates of black bun appeared; the conversation lapsed into appreciative noises. Jonah began to recount to Tammy how good the coffee made by the Norwegians in South Georgia had been and how the cup would freeze solid if you let it stand at all.

The musicians were prevailed upon to play another tune. Alistair sang again and Tom opened a new bottle of whisky. There was a tension in the room, a mixture of mourning and high spring-wedding excitement, the death of the old year and good luck to it, the expectant birth of the new, good health to the bairn. The last twelvemonth had brought its usual melee of fortune and ill-luck, wisdom and foolishness, change and decay. The next would bring more of the same but it was in the people's nature to wish that somehow this time round the wheel would miss the ruts and the glaur and turn smoothly.

The clock on the mantelpiece struck eleven. 'Only an hour to go,' said someone. The door opened and the tousled, sleep-heavy head of Margaret and Tom's daughter shyly appeared. She wore a long nightgown and clutched a teddy bear.

'What are ye doing up?' cried her mother.

'I couldna sleep,' came the almost inaudible reply.

'Is Tommie sleeping?'

'Aye.'

'All richt then. Ye can stay for a whilie just till the new year comes in and then it's off to your bed wi ye.'

The little girl came and sat near the fire, sharing the couch with Jonah and Alistair's wife, who began to make much of her, asking her questions about this and that.

'D'ye want a dram?' asked Jonah.

Her mother thrust a tumbler of fruit juice into her hand and she sipped it slowly, gazing wide-eyed at the assembled crowd, knowing she was a privileged witness of a strange adult ritual. She knew almost everyone in the room except the man in the polo-necked sweater and the lady with the high-pitched voice. Later she would ask who they were.

Dougie was staring into the dregs of his coffee as if he could see through the cup into some private world. His mind was grappling with whiffs of thought, chasing through his head like a pack of dogs pounding over hard snow, their paws leaving faint depressions, barely detectable traces of their furious passing.

'Rob,' he said, 'd'ye think Scotland's changed much?'

'Eh?' Rob was obviously taken aback by the serious tone but he went on. 'Changed much? No, I don't think so. Why?'

'I don't think it's changed one damn whit. That's the problem. Nobody wants it to change.'

'No, maybe not. It's no a bad place for aa that.'

'Weel can ye say it now. Ye dinna live here now.'

Rob flushed slightly.

— Dougie is drunk, full as an egg, and he's going to make a fool o himself, saying what he would never say, never think, when he's sober. There's always one, one like this at new year, full o barming shite, drowning in pity. When drink's in, wit is oot.

'What I mean, Rob auld friend,' continued Dougie, 'is... is... and ye'll understand this, because ye're an educated chap, and in America and everything. Ye ken what I mean? What I mean is that Scotland is still a developing country, just like them places in Africa and Asia and... ye ken what I mean...'

'Aye, I ken, boy, I ken.'

— Best to humour him. Never argue with a drunk.

'We're just the same, the very same as one o them Third World countries. Naething going for us but the land and most o that no in our hands and undeveloped. Folk canna get work and emigrate. A factory here or there and whole toons depending on it, and as like as no the factory is owned by a foreigner. Worst o all, though, is that we seem to have no spirit ... no wish to do things for oursels. What's gone wrong, Rob?'

'I'm no sure.'

— Shut up, Dougie, for God's sake. Although there's a grain o sense in what ye say, the trouble is that as soon as ye've sobered up ye'll have forgotten the whole subject.

'This country was great once. Fine music and poetry.'

— What's worse than an educated Scotsman? A drunk, educated Scotsman. And this obsession with the past and place. A drunk American complains about his divorce, a drunk Englishman curses his wife and tries to chat up the barmaid. Us? A drunk Scotsman cowns for his granny and the mist on the brae. Robert the Bruce rides again, and Bonnie Prince Charlie wins the replay of Culloden.

'We did,' Dougie insisted. 'Ye're no listening to me, are ye? I'm no drunk, just had a droppie. Look man, d'ye no feel nothing for this place that made ye at all? We used to make things. We invented steam engines, ships, all kind o things. We built a bloody empire for this country. What happened to us?'

'I dinna ken.' Rob was becoming annoyed.

'No, neither do I.' Dougie gave a sudden laugh, raised his arms like a preacher and recited:

'This is my country,
The land that begat me.
These windy spaces are surely my own.
And those who toil here
In the sweat of their faces
Are flesh of my flesh and bone of my bone.'

Everybody stopped to listen to the poetry and when Dougie finished a silence filled the room.

Perhaps because he still had some of the Celtic love of words in him, Alistair cried, 'Well done, Dougie!' and to his wife, 'Come on Mairi, give us some puirt a'beul.'

The others called for the dark-haired woman to sing

and after some protestation she nodded and grew quiet, gathering the words of the song within herself. Then she sang and enwrapped the company in the pure rapid rhythms of the old mouth music. When she finished, breathless, the crowd applauded and shouted their appreciation.

'Grand, grand,' laughed Jonah, flashing his teeth. 'That's better than the TV any day.'

'Come on, folks, recharge your glasses,' cried Tom. 'It's nearly the midnicht hour.'

He switched on the television but left the volume control at zero. We'll be seeing what the new year programme is like,' he said.

Dougie rose unsteadily and made his way to the bathroom. When he came back the musicians were playing a tune on the accordion and the fiddle.

'It's cold oot there,' said Dougie, collapsing into a chair. No one answered him, intent on the music as they all were.

After a few moments, Tammy's voice broke into his thoughts. 'Tell me about your farm.'

'Och,' he said with a smile, 'it's no a farm, it's a croft.'

'What's the difference?'

That was a question he had never had to answer before. Everybody knew the difference but putting it into words was no easy task. He thought for a moment.

'Size, I suppose. Aye, size. A farm's bigger.'

'Have you got cattle and sheep?'

'Aye.'

'Sounds terrific. It must be fun with the cuddly lambs.'

— Poor lassie. She doesna ken much but how could she. Cuddly lambs. I suppose they are at times but she's never chased a pelly ould yowe in the rain, slipping and sliding in the gutters, or risen at five to the lambing when the sleet's like to break your face.

'Aye,' he said. 'If only they were like that all the time.'

'I would love to live in the country,' Tammy went on.

'Are your folk Scottish?' Dougie asked, offering her a

cigarette which she refused.

'No. My father's family were Swedish and my mother's family came from Germany. Quite a mixture.'

'Aye. Mixture richt enough.'

The conversation lapsed for a moment, as it often did when talking to a stranger; you never knew what might offend them.

'I'm a teacher,' she said, 'though I'm not working at the moment. I've been fixing up a new house we've bought. So when Rob goes off to the office I get busy with the paint brush.'

She laughed and another silence descended between them. Dougie felt the need to continue the exchange and make the girl feel welcome among them but whisky, the brown man with the silken voice and the big club, was starting to bewitch his brain. Silently he began to concentrate on staying sober.

'No long now, boys,' cried Jonah.

Chimes sounded. A hush lay over the folk. This was a sacred moment. Throughout the length and breadth of Alba, men and women were at that minute silent and listening — waiting for the single sound that would release... DONG!

'That's it, boys,' shouted Jonah. 'A happy new year til ye all.'

They all turned to each other and a chorus of greetings echoed from the corners. The men shook hands solemnly, wishing each other 'a good new year', 'many o them', 'all the best', and broke open their bottles. The women shook hands likewise with all present and kissed the men they knew best. The little girl stared open-mouthed and delighted at this swirl of activity and Tammy, the stranger, did her best to imitate her hosts.

It was as if a charge of electricity had passed through the company. Whisky was poured into glass after glass until they overflowed and slopped on the carpet. It flowed like sunlight on a bright summer day — warm, corner-seeking, heart-lightening, step-thumping. Even those who did not like the stuff and never touched it to their lips at

other times did their duty by it and threw down their
measure. And on top of it all came the sound of the pipes
from the television.

'Who's going to be our first foot?' cried Tom.

'Oh I never meint,' laughed Margaret. 'Dougie, Rob, ye
should've gone oot afore the clock struck and come in
again. Both o ye are tall, dark and handsome.'

'There'll be somebody here before long,' said Jonah.

After twenty minutes and numerous glasses, Dougie
said to Jonah that he was going to firstfoot Donald's Jamie,
and was he coming. 'I'll come up wi ye for a whilie,' said
the old sailor.

They made their farewells and staggered out into the
night. The cold hit them like a wave and they bundled
their hands into their pockets, weaving a trail over the
silvered, slippery ground.

'Hard frost,' said Jonah.

'Aye,' grunted Dougie. He slipped and collided with his
companion.

'Canny. Watch my bottle.'

'She's all richt, boy.'

There were lights shining in most of the houses and
smoke rose from the chimneys, dark pillars against the
star-brightness.

'I must go behind the dyke,' announced Dougie.

Jonah stayed on the road, gazing around him, while the
other went to relieve himself at the convenient wall.

'That's better.'

People were out and firstfooting; the drumming of
water on stone mingled with echoing, distant shouts and
footsteps.

'I think I'll go too,' said Jonah. 'Ye've given me the
thocht.'

'What a fine, clear nicht.'

'Look at all the stars.'

'I wonder if it's new year up there too.'

'Likely it is.'

'Just think. Somewhere up there, there micht be two

mannies pishing and looking up and thinking if we are having a spree like they are.'

'Ye're a great boy for the imagination,' laughed Jonah. 'Weel, if they're there, I hope they're enjoying themselves as much as I am.'

'D'ye think they micht have invented whisky yet?'

'No shooting stars to be seen?'

'There micht be a satellite or two if ye watch for a whilie. Just like a star but slow moving.'

'Boy, it's great when ye think on it.'

'Aye. Come on, we'd better get a move on. Done?'

CHAPTER ELEVEN

Donald's Jamie welcomed them effusively, his red face perspiring slightly. Kathie had a good fire on and the newcomers soon began to sweat.

'Ye're no our first foot, but ye're welcome aa the same. Get some clean glasses, woman. It's a hard frost but most likely ye're no feeling it.'

'Magnus Gunn was in earlier,' said Kathie.

Donald's Jamie poured two generous libations.

'Canny,' cried Jonah. 'I'll go aground if I take all that.'

'Husht wi ye. It's new year. Your health, boys.'

Dougie sank back into the couch and eyed his brimming glass. The golden eye played with the light and winked at him. He concentrated on the mantelpiece and wondered why the clock moved when he looked at it.

— Steady. Steady on. A little too much o this stuff... it's warm in here.

Kathie's china dogs, one guarding each end of the mantelpiece, were much admired.

'A good new year, Jamie,' said Jonah.

'Good new year.'

'Good new year,' cried Dougie.

'Same to yourself, boy.'

'Your mither'll be in her bed?'

'Eh? Aye. She's in her bed.'

'That's a drop o good whisky,' said Jonah, smacking his lips.

'It should be. Paid enough for it.'

— Here I am. Nobody but old shither for company. I

shouldna be thinking this. Damn Jonah and his wind, saying my trees wouldna grow. I'll show him.

'Have a piece o cake, Dougie,' said Kathie.

'Thanks.'

'No saying very much the nicht, boy?'

'Never heed him. Leave the boy alone, Jamie.'

'Saying plenty when he wants to,' said Jonah.

Dougie laughed and spilled some of his drink. 'I'm sorry, Kathie.'

'Magnus said he was expecting a crowd in,' said Donald's Jamie.

'Hear that?' Jonah poked Dougie in the ribs. 'We'll go to Magnus's in a whilie. I micht get a young ain for myself.'

'A young what?' cried Dougie. The waves of the amber tide had receded. Visibility good.

'A young ain like one o Magnus's twa daughters.'

The tide raced in again, rushing and roaring in black pools. Visibility poor. The clock and the guarding china dogs multiplied.

'D'ye want some tea?' asked Kathie.

'No, no, no for me,' cried Jonah. 'I'm as full as a sponge.'

'I havena given Jamie a dram.' Dougie's statement was grave and brooked no dissent.

'Aye ye have. I've got her here.'

'Did I?' He could not remember pouring it and doubted the old man.

'John, have ye given him one?'

'Yes. I did too. We've all got our drams.'

'Jamie, ye havena had one fae me at all. Gie's your glass, Jamie. Come on. This is ... is ... Hogmanay ... no, it's new year now and I must gie ye your new year.'

'Oh Dougie man, I dinna want anither one. Save your whisky, boy.'

'No, no. There's plenty more where that came fae. Kathie ...'

'Yes, Dougie?'

'Kathie ... gie your man's glass. That's an order.'

— They don't want me to do this but I'm going to do

it. Jamie's been a good friend to me. 'Jamie, ye've been a good friend to me. Where's that glass?'

Kathie put it in his hand and he made to get up to pour the toast.

'I'll pour it for him, Dougie,' said the woman.

He surrendered the glass and the bottle, and the couch engulfed his defeated body. The ceiling was a pale green colour.

'Well, here's tae ye, Dougie, and all that's yours, boy,' said Jamie.

'Same to yourself. A good new year. Kathie, ye've got to take one, too.'

'Oh no, Dougie, no for me. I dinna like the taste o it.'

'Ye can take one. It's new year.'

'Take one,' said Donald's Jamie, giving his wife a commanding glance.

'Just a small one,' she said.

'Small or big, doesna matter,' said Dougie. 'Ye can pour it yourself.'

She filled a small glass and held it up. 'Your health, Dougie, and your mother, too.'

'Thanks, Kathie. Same to yourself.'

She touched the whisky to her lips and shuddered. Then she moved quietly to the table where Dougie's bottle had been placed for safe keeping and tipped the bulk of her portion back in. Only her husband noticed her do this.

— Poor loon, he's had too much. He canna take it and now he's making a fool o himself. Och, men and drink. And Jamie, sitting there with a face like glowing coals, bald head like the moon, will not stop him. They go on handing drink one to another like the old fools they are. It's a wife the boy needs, something, oh I dinna ken what ... that would keep him oot o trouble. A fine loon, a credit to any mither, going the way he is. He'll have a sore head the morn, curse himself for being a gowk and be off to the pub before he's changed his breath. Somebody should put him home to his bed, but will they? No, they'll gie him more drink and watch him droon in it and then say what a grand chiel he is. Can men no take a dram and enjoy it? No, they must pour it into themselves as if life depended on it.

'I think I'm for home,' Jonah was saying.

'Ye said ye were going to Magnus's hoose,' protested Dougie.

'Are ye going there?' Kathie asked, looking at the three men, all slouched around her fireside, the old and the young. The old cock crows, the young cock learns.

'I micht pop in for a whilie,' said Jonah.

'Ye and your whilies,' argued Kathie. 'Your whilies stretch out for a good long time. Dougie, ye needna bother going. Stop here, take a nap on the couch and then ye can see Magnus tomorrow when ye're feeling better.'

'Eh?'

'Ye havena got the van?'

'At the hotel. I left it,' murmured Dougie.

'Stop here the nicht. Ye canna go home all that way.'

'Kathie, leave the boy alone,' said her husband. 'He'll be all richt.'

Five minutes later, the two were making unsteadily for Magnus Gunn's front door. The sound of laughter, talking and bagpipe music grew as they approached and swelled to a crescendo when they opened the door and stottered in.

Magnus's living room was filled with people. John Campbell was there, rotund and beaming, and the musicians from the hotel, and Magnus himself of course, now in his kilt to mark the occasion, and Betty the district nurse, and Peggy, Magnus's wife, and his two daughters, Jean and Catriona, and many more. The light glittered and danced on the rows of bottles, cans and glasses; sherry, whisky, rum, brown ale, pale ale, lager, advocaat and vodka, an army of delights waiting to invade and capture the soul. Over it all floated a diaphanous cloud of tobacco smoke. Peggy bustled from end to end of the room with plates of shortbread and cake.

Jonah grabbed her, stifled her skirl with a kiss and shouted, 'A good new year til y'all.'

'Come in, boys,' cried Magnus, proud as a cock robin on a fencepost, a muckle sporran with grouse claw decorations bouncing on his belly.

They produced their bottles, the old sailor and the young crofter, both now shaky on the legs, one brimming over with words, the other slowly sinking into moroseness. Drams were exchanged and swallowed and more whisky soaked into Peggy's carpet.

A huge picture of Eilean Donan Castle hung above the mantelpiece, on which stood upright a polished, brass shellcase, a souvenir of Magnus's wartime adventures. Dougie held his glass so that both the shellcase and the flames of the fire were seen through the amber; distorted sources of light, the brass a steady, dull gleam and the flames, red and moving below it.

His mind was away on a drink-fuelled course of its own.

— Licht. All licht comes fae the sun. Licht can be a wave or a particle at the same time. Barley traps the licht and photosynthesis produces sugars. Does the plant ken whether the licht that feeds it is a wave or a particle? Och I suppose not, as long as the green shoots get the sun they dinna care how it comes, in bucketfuls or greipfuls or poured oot fae a thimble. Photosynthesis makes sugars and sugars makes starch and we make bread fae the starch, and whisky. All plants use licht. Plants die but dinna rot and all the dead stuff piles up through the centuries, a great midden o rottenness that doesna rot, and in the end we cut it wi our tuskars for peat. And we burn the peat for warmth and licht. The sun gangs doon but we still have it here on earth, lowing in a million grates. It all comes fae the sun. All is licht. Whisky, peat, barley, ourselves.

'Consider the peat,' he said aloud.

'Aye,' said someone. 'That's the peats richt enough.'

Magnus bent and threw a piece onto the flames; a

fountain of red sparks shot up the chimney.

'D'ye ken what peat is?' asked Dougie.

Magnus had seen many a drunk man in his time.

— During the war, boy, it was terrible. I swear that alcohol killed more men than bullets. No just the men, the officers too. I swear that the officers were worse than the men. I had some roch times myself. Many a fill I had.

'Aye,' said Magnus with an empty grin. 'I ken.'

'But d'ye know what it is?' persisted Dougie. He paused to claw the next part of his argument from the crazy patchwork of thought in his head. 'Peats and coal are the same thing, only coal's older. And it was all plants once. Consider the peat. It's all there. If ye can understand that, ye have it all.'

'Are ye on aboot peats, Dougie?' asked John Campbell, his face that of a monk in his cups. 'Ye're a bit early. It's no summer yet.'

Dougie waved his hand in the air.

— They've all got the wrong meaning. Why does everybody take the wrong meaning from what I say? But I've still got my wits...

'No, no, no,' he protested. 'I ken aboot the summer. What I mean is... consider the peat. It's burning there and it'll be nothing but ashes in the morning. Dust to dust.'

— Ashes to ashes. Dust to dust. Daniel Bayne, we commit thy body to the earth. The dark wood, the rough face of the ground shining where the spade had cut down through it. The gentle clattering of the eight cords as they formed eight curling snakes on top of the coffin, his the last to fall. The stepping back of the black coats. Rook-caw. The wind curling and whipping around them. And the rows of stones, their lettered faces to the sunrise. Marble angels. Granite books. Books. 'A lot of books. He was a great reader and couldn't bear to part with his books.' 'Douglas, will you read from the top of page eleven?' Gold-rimmed glasses perched on a thin nose and hair strangled in a bun.

Dougie closed his eyes and tried to calm the swooping and diving of history in his brain.

'No,' he said suddenly to no one in particular. 'I'm talking aboot evolution. D'ye ken that funny things have been dug oot o peat? It preserves bodies for hundreds o years. In Edinburgh, I think — in a museum somewhere — there's the body o a man that was found in a peatbank. Clothes and all. Just as it was the day he died.'

'Husht, Dougie,' cried Peggy. 'Ye're putting ears on me wi aa that yarns.'

'It's no yarns. It's God's honest truth.'

'Fancy that now,' said Jonah. 'Ye better watch when ye're at the peats this summer, Magnus.' He paused to light a cigarette. 'It was the same in the Antarctic. The ice keeps a body. I heard stories o chiels that fell into holes turning up miles away years after it.'

'It's treasure I'd be wanting,' laughed Peggy.

'I've read aboot the ice, too,' said Dougie. 'Ice and peat. This whole place was under ice once, long before there was peat. Ye can see the scratches the ice made on the rock.'

'Aye,' said Magnus absently.

'Ye needna say aye. I can show ye. Ye dinna believe me because ye think I'm drunk and barming my head off. But it's true. Ye ken what I'm speaking aboot?'

Jean and Catriona, sitting with glasses of sherry in their hands, both giggled.

'I dinna ken,' said one softly.

'I ken ye dinna ken but I'm telling ye,' cried Dougie. He paused. 'What d'ye mean ye dinna ken? D'ye no read aboot that things at the school?'

'I've left the school,' said Catriona the elder.

'Oh aye. That's richt. No long, though. Ye should mind if ye learned it or no.'

'I canna mind.' She looked at her father.

— Ye needna look at your faither. He doesna ken either though he sits there, solemn as a judge, wi a look though as to say I ken it all. Silence becometh the idiot.

'D'ye read a lot?' Jean's question drew dagger looks from her sister and her father.

'Aye, a lot,' replied Dougie.

'We never got that at the school,' said Magnus.

'Neither did I,' cried Dougie.

— A desk rough on the elbows, the wood almost black with the ink and dirt of decades, engrained in long lines joining the initials to the carved sailing ships. An inkwell, deathtrap for bluebottles. You sit there, the end of your pencil chewed to sawdust, listening to the tractor in the field outside. Dad will be sharpening the blades for the mower. 'Douglas, will you pay attention? Douglas Bayne, do you hear me talking to you? Say the six times table.' 'Six times one is six. Six times two is twelve six times three is eighteen six times four is twentyfour six times five is thirtysix ...' 'What did you say, Douglas Bayne? Come out here. Do you want to be a crofter all your life?' The tawse, the long leather snake with the forked tongue. Hand up, eyes closed. The whistling of it through the air with all her pith behind it. The stinging bite of it across the fingers. A hero for a day. If I had my schooldays back I would have been a scientist like Rob.

'Dinna waste your chances,' said Dougie urgently to Jean. 'Stick in at your books.'

'Aye.' The girl giggled and took a sip of her sherry.

— Ye're a bonny, young thing. Fine legs. Keeping your sherry warm in your hand. Ye're thin. It would take four or five o ye to make Mary Louise. Her with a lover on every continent and me one o them. There must be a book somewhere wi a list o us all. Mexican peasants, Eskimoes, black boys fae San Francisco or Nairobi, Chinese crofters and Scottish crofters. Are there Chinese crofters? Aye, ye're a bonny thing, all dolled up in your fine clothes, your body as firm as a grape. And ye're only fourteen.

'Darwin,' he said, spitting the name like an oath. 'That was a great man. And what's-his-name? What d'ye call him?' This in a pleading voice as if the others could read his mind easier than he could himself. 'Newton. Isaac Newton. And Oppenheimer. Do you get them in the school?'

Jean did not answer. Others were coming and going but the crowd in the room was gradually diminishing. Magnus rose to see some of his guests away.

'How's your mother, Dougie?' asked Peggy.

'Fine.'

'I havena seen her for a while. Ye must tell her I was asking for her.'

'I'll tell her.'

— Dinna spin so fast, world. I've only got my feet to keep me on. I'm only a human being, no a piece o wood nailed to the ground. Ye keep birling on. Slow doon, world, slow doon. Time's passing fast enough. Another roon o the clock, another roon o the sun, another new year. I'm in no hurry for another year if it's the same as the last. Slow doon, world.

'Slow doon.'

Everybody looked at him from the silence that suddenly filled the room.

'What was that, boy,' asked Jonah.

'Eh? I'm drunk. I've had too much but it's new year and I'm going to have another one.'

'No, Dougie,' said Jonah. 'Give it the go-by this time.'

'Haud your tongue and go back to the Arctic where ye belong.'

'Antarctic.'

'Ye can go there too. I've going to gie my old friend Magnus Gunn here a dram. Magnus, gie ower your glass.'

'Oh never heed, Dougie. I got one fae ye already.'

'Deil take ye and your ones already. Take another.'

Rocking in his seat, Dougie began to unscrew the top from the whisky bottle. Magnus passed over a glass and tried to ignore the frown from his wife.

— Keep him humoured. I can tip the whisky into the flowerpot when he's no looking. I wish he would go home.

'Magnus,' said Dougie, trying to steady the bottle over the glass. 'Ye've got twa bonny dochters, my old friend.'

'Aye,' agreed Magnus cautiously.

Peggy took the bottle and glass from the crofter and poured a measure for her husband. 'Here's your bottle back. Make sure ye put it in your pocket and dinna fa and break it.'

Jonah was highly amused. He was laughing at Magnus, the ultimate Scotsman, afraid to throw Dougie out lest he have one less customer for his binder twine as much as through unwillingness to commit an unneighbourly act.

'D'ye want some tea, Dougie?' asked Peggy.

'Dinna gie him tea,' said Jonah. 'There's nothing faster to make ye sick.'

'It's a wife ye need, boy,' said Magnus, raising the glass. 'Here's tae ye. A good new year.' He took a sip and grimaced.

'A wife! Where will I get a wife here?'

'Ye can never tell. A young strapping chiel like yourself. I hear that Rob Sutherland's back home and a fine young ain in tail.'

'Aye, she is that,' said Jonah. 'We saw her in the pub. A bonny lassie she is.'

— Faither, why did ye no keep me at the school? 'What are ye going to do wi all that books. A man has to work and be content wi his lot, the way o the world.' Why do they no leave a man to live his own life? Freedom is ane noble thing. John Barbour. He lives at ease that freely lives. Scotland and me, we are both thirled aboot wi gowks and thochtless fools. Here's tae us, they're shouting. Here's tae us, wha's like us? Damn few and they're aa deid. Deid. Dust to dust. Ashes to ashes. Flesh to peat. Maybe we're burning some chiel in the fire richt now. Who was he? A great hero wi a claymore and a sgian dubh? A witch that had just set a boat on the rocks and drowned the crew? Or some poor crofter who was born, lived and died on the same bit o ground, never bothered anybody, never left home, never touched a sword, never had an evil thocht in his head? Born a nobody, died a nobody. If he had a dream at all, he died and it died wi him, or maybe it died before he did. That's what I am — a nobody who'll die and gie a lowe to somebody's fire.

'Hey, Dougie, wake up man.' Jonah's voice was urgent.

'I wasna sleeping.'

'No.'

'What's the matter anyway?'

'It's nearly three o'clock in the morning. Time we was off home.'

'We've aa got to rise the morn,' said Magnus.

'I'm no going yet,' cried Dougie. 'It's time we had another dram to see the new year in.'

'Oh no, Dougie.' Magnus shook his head. 'No more for me. And I think ye shouldna have one either.'

'I've never paid attention to what ye thocht, Magnus, and I don't intend to start now. Where's my glass?'

Magnus blushed and tightened his knuckles. Then he laughed a forced laugh.

'Where's that glass?' The dinosaurs had a grim sense of prurpose. Dougie's hand shook but he filled the tumbler. He collapsed backwards but held the glass high. It skinted and fell on him; dark spots appeared on his suit.

'In vino veritas,' he announced triumphantly. 'That's Greek. No, it's Latin. D'ye ken Latin?'

Silence.

Jonah put his hand on the crofter's knee. 'Come on, boy. Get that doon ye and then we're off.'

'John,' said the other. 'I'm a failure, a bloody failure. A disgrace to my faither and mither.'

'Husht, man.'

'See that fire there. Ashes. That's all I'm coming to. Nothing but a heap o bloody ashes in some chiel's fireplace. Ye can throw me oot wi the aise in the morning.'

'Haud your tongue. It's your bed you're wanting. Ye've got trees to plant, mind.'

'I'm no going to plant trees. They're richt. They'll never grow here.'

'Who are they?' cried Jonah. 'They've never tried. Oh they'll tell ye what'll happen but they've no more idea than fly to the moon.'

Magnus did not follow this part of the conversation but

felt he should remain in control of the situation and reminded the others of his presence by saying, 'That's the way o it, boys.'

Peggy, hovering behind the couch, agreed that that was the way of it.

'I lost my chance at the school,' said Dougie.

'Aye,' said Magnus softly.

'Here!' Dougie grabbed Jean's knee. 'Here!' She laughed nervously and moved away. 'Listen, I'm no going to touch ye. Here's some advice. Dinna waste your time at the school. Dinna laugh. It's the truth, the God's honest truth. I wish I had my schooldays again.'

'I left the school when I was ten,' grinned Jonah, 'and I was never so glad.'

Dougie glared at the old fool, the sagging, grizzled chin and the grinning mouth with a glistening dollop of spittle on the lower lip. Christ, this is myself twenty years from now.

'And what did ye get?' he cried. 'Ye've wasted your bloody life...'

'Steady on!' Customer or no customer, Magnus was thinking that Dougie had gone too far.

Jonah was taken aback and stared at the carpet for a moment. 'I dinna think my life's been wasted,' he murmured, adding more loudly and more defiantly, 'I've done a bit o sailing in my time.'

'Aye,' said Magnus. 'ye have that, John. Take me now. I left the school early. Youngsters nowadays have it easy. Dammit, I had a war to fecht. I went off like many another loon. I know that war's no a thing I would like to see again but it was the best school I ever went to. If ye'd been there, Dougie, ye'd be content wi a peaceful life.'

'The war, the war,' repeated Dougie, shaking his head. 'Fools sending bigger fools to be shot. For what?'

Magnus began to frown and the heat in his face glowed red. 'Dinna say that now. I lost a lot o good pals in the war. We saw sichts and happenings that ye couldna dream o, that ye wouldna want to dream o.'

Dougie started to laugh, a drunken, mocking laughter.

'Ye can go now,' cried Magnus. 'Ye're in the blues wi drink. But, drink or no, I'll tell ye this. I've been on ground that ye've never seen...'

Dougie rose to a half-crouch, interrupting his host. 'And ye wouldna have been there if ye hadna been taken by the scruff o the neck.'

'Shut your mouth,' shouted Magnus. 'Get oot o my hoose. Ye're nothing but a drunken waster.'

'Magnus!' cried Peggy.

The girls screamed and Jonah took his companion by the arm. 'I'll see him oot,' he said.

Dougie drew himself up and glared at the kilted figure. All his pent-up frustrations seemed to boil out from that angry, red face and, shaking himself free from Jonah, he aimed a blow at it.

The clumsy punch glanced off Magnus's shoulder and did not harm him. But it unbalanced him and he fell heavily back into his chair. A great screaming and yelling rose from the women. Almost immediately Dougie regretted what he had done but before he could say anything Jonah had dragged him away.

CHAPTER TWELVE

Outside, the two men staggered down the path; Dougie almost collapsed on Magnus's hedge but Jonah caught him and guided him through the gate. On the icy road they slipped and fell together.

For several moments they both lay there, an entwined bundle of arms and legs and clothing.

'My bottle,' cried Dougie. 'I've broken my bottle.'

'No,' said Jonah. 'Ye havena broken it at all. I heard no crash.'

'Ye wouldna hear it anyway, ya deaf auld bugger.'

Jonah burst into wheezing laughter. 'Oh Dougie, Dougie, ye're a great lad. Ye're nothing but a bloody professor. That's what ye are. A professor.'

They got to their feet, clambering up each other for support, both laughing now, their voices echoing down the village street and out across the frosty fields.

'Ye fairly sorted Magnus whatever,' chortled Jonah.

'I shouldna. I hope I didna hurt him. Maybe I should go back and apologise.'

Jonah restrained the crofter. 'Stop where ye are. Ye're going nowhere but your bed. Anyway ye didna hit him. Ye missed but he still fell doon.'

'I didna hurt him?'

'Ye should've seen his face.'

'I didna ken what came ower me.' Dougie's voice had a frantic edge.

'Never heed.'

They set off down the road, taking both sides before

them in their meandering. Most of the lights in the houses had been switched off but still here and there a yellow shape winked at them. Their breath hung in long, wisping trails.

'I'm for home,' said Jonah.

'Me too.'

'Good nicht, professor, and a happy new year t'ye.'

'Want one for the road?'

'No! Awa home wi ye.'

'Good nicht and a happy new year t'ye and all.'

Dougie struck out on the two-mile walk to the croft.

— What a nicht. I shouldna have struck Magnus. Damn ye, John Barleycorn, damn ye black and blue and black again. I'm going to gie ye up. Never again. Where are ye anyway? Oh, ye're in my pocket, still whole, still safe, though there's no muckle left in ye. Hech, what a nicht! What a way to start the new year. I must get home now. The road looks bonny stretching strecht before me. Watch your step. There's a lot o ice. Ouch! Damn! I've fallen. I thocht I bounced on that bit. Must get up... canny... take your time... concentrate... there's some chiel in them saughs. No, it's just a trick o the licht. I need a pumpship. Better get off the road. I'll never get ower this barbed wire. Ah, there's a dyke here. This'll do. It's cold. That's better. The stars are all oot. There's the ploo and the pole star and Orion. I've had a hell o a lot to drink. This is never going to stop. Dinna fall now or ye'll wet yourself. If I shouted they'd hear me for miles...

'Anybody there? Can ye hear me? Can ye hear me up there? I'll show ye. I'm a professor. The world is sitting in my hand. Can ye hear me, faither? Can ye see me? This is your son doon here and he's drunk, as full as the sea.'

— Folk'll think I'm mad, clean gone. Ach, tae hell wi them. What have they ever cared aboot me, anyway? I'm my own maister. I don't need them and I'll show them. I'll have more lambs than any o them this spring and I'll have trees growing green around the place after I'm gone. That'll be my monument after I'm gone. No marble angels or granite books but trees growing strong, waving in the

wind. Folk'll come by to see them and they'll say Dougie
planted that trees. Everybody thocht they would die but
Dougie was richt. Are they no fine? A richt clever chiel was
Dougie. All the women in the parish were after him; he
was a professor.

'D'ye hear that, faither? I'm a professor.'

— I feel as if I'm going to be sick. Why did I drink so
muckle? Stomach's churning just... oh no...

And he fell across the dyke at the road side and vomited
loudly and violently in the night.

— That's better. I canna hang here all nicht. Must keep
going. I canna mind what happened the nicht... at the
hotel, Rob and Tammy were there... hit Magnus. I'll have
to say sorry to him and Peggy and Jean and Catriona.
Jean's a bonny craitur... bricht amorous een where love
in ambush lies. Who wrote that? I must have read it
somewhere... canna mind. It's quiet, quiet... I can hear
my footsteps echoing afore me.

He continued on his way until he crested the final rise
in the road and came home. The house was in darkness
and its black bulk sat solid against the sky. His feet
clattered on the pavement and he rested against the wall
as he searched for his key. His fingers were clumsy and
when he drew out the contents of his pocket he dropped
the lot. A tinkling metallic chorus sounded.

He fell on his knees and began to scrabble for his
possessions but in the dark all he came across were a few
coins. The key. Where was it?

He spent a considerable length of time after it, moving
and probing and cursing his own folly. Then the cold
began to work on him and he began to shiver.

— I canna spend the whole nicht oot here. I ken. I can
go and warm up in the byre for a whilie and come for
anither look.

He hauled himself to his feet, using the corner of the
gable, and stottered off to the steading. The byre door
was not locked but it took him a few moments to fumble
for the sneck and lift it. A gush of warm, stinking air met

him full in the face as the door swung back. There was a light switch on the wall and he found it.

The cows were lying in their stalls and two cats slept curled around each other on a heap of straw. One of the cows raised her head and made to get up.

'Lie doon,' he growled. 'It's no morning yet.'

He pushed the cats from their bed and sat down. A sudden wave of tiredness swept over him as he looked at the four low walls, dripping with condensation, and the rafters, silent in their dust. Then he fell asleep.

When he awoke he did not know where he was at first. His mouth could not have been drier if it had been stuffed with blotting paper; there was a great thirst on him. And a pain in his head such that when he sat up the byre swooped and reeled. One of the cats had been sleeping in the crook of his arm and it sat up and mewed. The dim amber bulb still burned in the ceiling and the skylight was a black square. It was not yet sunrise.

He staggered to his feet, tripped and dropped onto his knees. His suit was a mess with bits of straw and scuff-marks. He got up again, slowly this time, the blood threatening to burst the skin of his temples, and crossed to the door. Opening it, he saw that the frost had been severe. Ice was thick on the puddles and the chill pained his nostrils.

But the sky was lightening a little in the east. He remembered the key; maybe he could find it now and let himself in. The pavement at the door of the house was speckled with coins and there was the key, as plain as day on one of the flags. The stooping to pick it up sent more painful tides of blood surging through his head and he held unto the window sill to steady himself.

Once inside he went straight to the kitchen and swallowed a glass of water. Then he lit a cigarette and smoked it slowly as he put together bit by bit what he could recall of the night. Then, to bed.

The electric kettle and a pan were boiling merrily when he came through in the morning. His mother had spread the breakfast things on the table and the radio was on.

'Here ye are,' said his mother. 'A boiled egg for ye.'

'Ta.'

'Had ye a good nicht?'

'Eh? Aye.'

'Och, I nearly forgot. A happy new year t'ye.'

PART TWO

DOUGIE'S LAND

CHAPTER ONE

It was one of the long, hot Saturdays of June with just enough of a breeze to keep the midges away from your blood. A good day for handling sheep, as their fleeces were dry and you could catch them without soaking yourself. Dougie had penned his flock in one corner of the Hill Park, where he had set up a complicated arrangement of gates and planks, tied with binder cord and twine to keep the animals the way he wanted them.

He had worked out the plan for the new pen beforehand and had sketched it on a sheet of writing pad. It was a cunning design and he was very proud of it, for it enabled him to work with his sixty yowes with the minimum of physical effort. This was its first test in action and so far all was going well.

'Haud up, ya bissom,' he muttered to one recalcitrant yowe, a large, old one, a leader of the flock, who was afraid of neither man nor dog and regarded him with a glittering, yellow eye. He stood with one leg on either side of her, gripping her between his thighs and cupping her jaw in his left hand while he tried to poke the nozzle of the worm drench through her clenched jaws.

'Open your mooth,' he growled.

Bluebottles settled on his forehead. Bess lay panting in the shade of a tuft of rushes. Overhead somewhere, a lark was singing.

At last the yowe permitted the nozzle to enter her mouth and he squirted what he hoped was an adequate dose of the medicine down her throat. Released, the animal bolted forward, coughing and shaking her head.

Dougie put down the drenching gun and straightened his back.

— Boy but it's warm. Still, that's half o them done.

Bess looked up at him and thumped the grass twice with her tail. He eased his bonnet up and wiped his brow with the back of his hand. His fingers were raxed and stiff with gripping the sheep, and the smell of lanolin and sharn was powerful.

Next was a thin, nervous yowe, a poor craitur with a short jaw. He dragged her forward, straddled her and reached for the gun. Bess suddenly rose and trotted off up the hill.

— Where are ye going, dowg? Oh there's somebody coming doon the brae. A lassie.

Bess skirted around the newcomer, who was wearing a pair of jeans and a bright yellow sweater. Dougie saw her bend to greet the dog who, muckle soft brute that she was, sat and received the attention with shameless sycophancy.

'Hello,' said the girl as she came up to the pen.

— English. Brown hair. Cheery-like face.

'Hello,' he replied. 'It's a grand day.'

— Must be a tourist. Been walking the hill most likely. Nice looking.

'It's hot down here,' said the girl, 'but it was cool up on the hilltop.'

'Aye,' agreed Dougie.

'I hope you don't mind me crossing your land,' she said.

'I don't know the paths.'

'That's alricht,' he said. 'There are no paths anyway.'

'I didn't want to trespass.'

'Och.'

She looked at his pen and the sheep crowded inside it, standing nose to tail, their flanks heaving. The air above them wavered with the aime of their heat.

'What are you doing?' she asked.

'I'm dosing them for worms,' he explained.

'Oh.' She paused. 'It must be hot work.' She laughed in an embarrassed way.

'Gae warm.'

Bess was playing around the girl, seeking her hand and more attention. 'Sit doon, dowg,' he commanded.

'Never mind,' said the girl. 'I like dogs. What's his name?'

'Bess.'

'Sorry, you're a girl,' she laughed and patted the grateful collie, who sank onto the grass and loved every second of it.

'She's a petted lump,' stated Dougie. 'Are ye on holiday?'

'No,' said the girl. 'I've come to live here.'

'I'm sorry. I didna ken.'

At that point, there was a rattling, creaking noise and down the road appeared a man on a bike.

'Oh ho!' cried the rider as he came to a halt and laboriously swung his leg over the crossbar.

— Donald's Jamie. It must be a good day.

'Aye, Jamie,' said Dougie.

'I heard ye was dosing the sheep and I came to see if I could gie ye a hand,' cried the old man. 'But I've see ye've got a helper already. Hello, Alison. Is it warm enough for ye?'

— He kens her. God, there's no muckle goes off him.

'Hello, Jamie,' said the girl. 'It's hot.'

'Aye,' agreed Jamie with a wink. 'We get a good day now and again.'

He propped his bike against a fencepost and bent to stroke Bess, who had run to meet him. Then he straightened and said 'Och ye're more than half done' in mock surprise.

'Trust ye to turn up when work's half done,' said Dougie maliciously.

'He's an awful chiel, this Dougie,' said Donald's Jamie to the girl. 'It's a wife he's needing to keep him under control.'

— The old goat. What does it matter to him? What can I do now? Standing here like a glaiked chiel.

'Have ye enjoyed your walk?' asked the old man. His face was red with the sun and the exertion of cycling, and he mopped it with a grimy handkerchief.

— It's a wonder he's no ashamed to take that oot in front o the lassie.

'Marvellous,' enthused Alison. 'I must have gone miles. I've been out for hours anyway.'

'Where did ye go?'

'I don't know. Everywhere, according to my feet.'

'Ye'd better rest. Dougie here can gie ye a lift home.'

Dougie blushed and glared at Donald's Jamie.

'Thank you, but I think I'll manage the last two miles. I can't give up now or I'll be ashamed for the rest of my life.'

Alison turned away from the pen and went to cross the fence. 'Goodbye,' she said gaily. 'It was nice meeting you, Dougie.'

— My name sounds funny in an English accent. Nice backside she's got.

The two men watched her go up the road, the yellow sweater standing out against the tall, green grass along the ditches.

'Who is she?' asked Dougie.

'An English lassie. She's moved into Shore Cottage and is here to stop for a while. She's a potter. She got some grant or something fae the Highland Board to set up a workshop for herself.'

'I thocht she was a tourist.'

'No. She's a fine ain. I've been speaking to her at the post office twa or three times.'

Dougie grinned. 'Taken a thocht o her?'

Donald's Jamie cackled and began to cough. 'Oh Dougie, Dougie. Is your mither in?'

'Aye.'

'Ye wouldna have some eggs to spare, would ye? I'll tell ye why. Donnie's coming home and Kathie wants to make sure there's plenty o meit in the hoose for him. The shop's shut.'

'We could likely spare ye one or two,' said Dougie lightly. 'When's Donnie coming? Is he coming by himself?'

'Monday. Aye, he's coming by himself on the train. I'll have to go into the toon to meet him. Och he'll be alricht. He's twelve now, a big loon. Ye wouldna be going in a run, would ye?'

'No. I wasna planning it.'

'Never heed.'

Donnie was Donald's Jamie's grandson, from near Glasgow.

'I'd better get a move on or I'll be here the whole day,' said Dougie. He grabbed another yowe and thrust the drenching gun into her mouth.

Donald's Jamie shook his head. 'Great stuff that, boy. What is it? Is this it in this drum here?' He squinted at the plastic container leaning against the fence. 'Worm drench for sheep and cattle for the control of roundworms, lungworms and tapeworms. Boy, boy, what will they think o next? It'll be dear, that stuff?'

Dougie did not answer but got on with his work. The old man followed the plastic pipe leading from the container to the gun in the crofter's hand. 'Ye'll have to be canny putting that in a sheep's mooth. That could break their teeth.'

'No, no,' grunted Dougie. 'D'ye want a dose?'

The man eased his bonnet and grinned. 'I'd rather worms. They'd be less bother.'

The yowe ran out from the pen, bleating in her indignity, and Dougie seized another.

'Och ye'll soon get through them at this rate,' said Donald's Jamie.

— That means ye're for off.

'What's this, though?'

Alerted by the urgent tone in the question, Dougie looked up. A car, white in colour, was coming down the road towards them. Neither recognised it. Bess sat up and cocked her ears. The windows of the car were open and when it drew to a halt beside them the driver stuck out his head and asked, 'Is it okay to park here?'

— Dark hair, glasses, English I think.

'Well, no really,' said Dougie. 'This road is used all the time. Ye'd better go on a bit and turn up the side o the byre there. Ye'll be alricht there. The ground's hard wi this dry weather.'

'Thanks.' The driver passed on to where Dougie pointed.

'Who's that now?' asked Donald's Jamie.

'No idea.'

The sheep were forgotten as the crofter and the old man stood gazing at the visitors as they parked by Dougie's byre. Clumps of nettles and thistles interrupted their view and Dougie reminded himself to cut them down, but they saw the men clearly when they got out of the car and stood up. They shouldered haversacks and walked off towards the hill.

'Towrists,' said Donald's Jamie, as if the word explained everything. 'Birdwatchers or something. Or that crowd, what d'ye call them, geologists.'

'Maybe,' mused Dougie. 'They've gae big packs, whatever.'

'Aye.'

They watched the men until the distance made it unlikely they would discover anything new about them. Dougie returned to his work.

'Well, I'll away in and see your mither,' said Donald's Jamie.

'She'll be in the hoose, I expect,' said Dougie without looking up from the yowe he was doctoring.

Donald's Jamie picked up his bike and pushed it down the road to the house. Dougie did not see him pause and have a good look inside the strangers' car as he passed it.

— That yowe's walking crooked. Feet rot.

He upended the creature and set her on her backside so that he could reach and pare with his knife the infected foot. Though not a delicate operation, it required some care. Too deep a cut and the hoof would bleed. The rotten material was soft and he had to saw rather than cut it. Then he dosed the yowe and let her go.

— Ochanee it's warm. Blinded wi sweat. Still, if this keeps up, the hill road will be bone-dry and I'll get the peats home next week. Where's that two mannies now? Oh, there they are, going oot ower the top o the hill. Birdwatchers. It must be grand to have holidays — do what ye like, get clean away fae the daily round. I canna leave the animals. I let the tourists, the towrists, come to me. I could have given Donald's Jamie a red face in front o that lassie, saying that I needed a wife. For evermore in her eyes I'll be the chiel that needs a wife. She was nice-looking, though. Maybe I'll see her again. Ach, but she mayna stop here long. Another one o them shither that think living in the country is great, escape fae the toon and come here wi their dreams and their bit money, doing their grand ecological thing, wi no a clue as to what it's really like. Come the first winter, when the nor-easters rattle the hoose about their lugs, and they're off. Potter she is, Donald's Jamie said. Can ye make a living at that? Selling milk jugs to tourists. They're oot o sicht now. Maybe they're archaeologists, looking for mounds to dig up.

CHAPTER TWO

Half an hour later, Dougie dosed the last of the yowes and suddenly felt very thirsty. He went into the house, pausing on the way to look at his plantation, as he liked to think of it. The two rows of pines had been growing now for more than four years and they had come on well — well, some of them had. Lopsided, made so by the westerly gales, they stretched upward like spindly, hesitating hands. They reached to his waist.

Visions of a rustling, solid, green shelter belt still filled his mind on occasion. On calm nights, a fine resiny scent hung around them. The three beehives had been more successful, though the wee, buzzing devils had taken a bit of getting used to at first, and produced dripping falls of honey.

Donald's Jamie was still in the house when he went in. His mother had made tea and the old couple were sitting one at either end of the table.

'Are ye done noo?'

'Aye.'

His mother poured him a cup. The tea had been a long time in the pot and he could smell the tannin.

'I'd better be making tracks,' said Donald's Jamie. 'Thank ye for the eggs, Jessie.'

'Och,' replied his mother.

He watched her struggle to her feet, to see the visitor out. She was growing frail now, but no more dottled than she had been for years. Her skin was almost the colour of peat-moss and had a brittle texture.

'I hope this weather keeps up,' she said.

'Aye,' said Donald's Jamie. 'The cold is no kind to auld craiturs like us.' He looked through the window. 'There's another car coming doon.'

'It's getting like a sale day here,' commented Dougie. 'I'll start charging for parking soon.'

'That's a local car,' went on the old man. 'But I dinna ken who's driving.'

All three stood where they could see through the net curtains. The car, blue and a little battered, turned into the road at the end of the house and glided to a halt. The driver, the lone occupant, got out.

'He's coming to the door,' said Jessie.

Bess released a little warning bark and was told to shut up.

'If it's visitors ye're having, I'd better go,' said Donald's Jamie.

'I dinna ken him,' said Jessie.

The newcomer passed the window and they heard the sound of his fist on the door.

Dougie opened it and Bess scooted out, wagging her tail.

'Hello,' said the man. 'I was looking for the men in that white car there. D'ye ken where they are?'

'No where they are now,' answered Dougie. 'They went oot ower the hill a good whilie ago.'

'That way?'

— Local by his tongue.

'Aye.'

'Thanks, I micht catch them yet.' And the man turned quickly and strode off round the corner of the house.

Donald's Jamie and Jessie appeared at the door behind Dougie, their expressions bright with curiosity, but they were too late to catch a good look.

'It's all go the day,' said Donald's Jamie.

He retrieved his bicycle, and he and Dougie stood on the road and watched the face of the hill. Bess sniffed around the blue car.

'That's him going up the brae,' said Dougie. 'He's shifting.'

'He is that,' agreed Donald's Jamie, who was loth to leave when so much was happening. His big face was screwed up and red with concentration, forcing his eyes to focus on the distant figure.

'We'll no see him again for a whilie,' said Dougie.

Donald's Jamie reluctantly and laboriously mounted his bike. 'Cheerio then.' He pedalled slowly up the road, staring at the hill and steering in a series of arcs, taking the whole road before him.

— Nosey bugger. Still, I wonder who that chiel is. I've seen him before somewhere. He seemed awful excited. A thin, half-chewed craitur. The car's no awful new, whatever. Cushions in the back seat, a book, sweetie papers. There's a map in the front, and newspapers. That's who he is, now I ken — a reporter. Excited he was. Why should he be after two birdwatchers for a story? Odd.

Dougie thought over the sequence of events, as he went about his work. He cleaned and stored the drenching gun, tidied the pen, and changed the oil in the tractor. It wore on towards tea-time and there was still no sign of the three men. The news came and went on the TV, and they did not return. Dougie took in one of the cows for milking, and his scanning of the brae-face revealed nothing. He fed the cats and listened for any sound of the strangers.

The reporter was the first to return, alone. He was hurrying and his thin face glistened, his glasses threatening to slide from his nose. He almost collided with Dougie at the corner of the house and his voice crackled with excitement.   'I found them, I found them.'

'Did ye?'

'I did. Dinna let on. Wait for the paper on Friday. Oh boy, boy.'

'What's happening?'

'I canna tell ye now.' And he rushed to the car and rived the door open.

'Come on oot o there, Bess, or that chiel'll run ye doon.'

The car started and belched black exhaust fumes. Gravel leapt like bullets from the back wheels and it sped away.

— Reckless gowk. Like to shite himself. But there's something going on here. I'll have a look in the other car. No muckle to be seen. Maps, a rucksack, shoes, a thermos.

Dougie's speculative powers were greatly exercised for the rest of the evening. His mother annoyed him, too, by making inane suggestions as to what might be going on. The mystery tantalised him, but she seemed just to accept the existence of mysteries and her suggestions were mere verbal playthings, spoken for the sake of speaking and not directed at solving the problem at all.

It was the gloaming before the two men returned to the white car. They did not come to the house but got into their car and drove off in a quiet, dignified manner, leaving their mystery behind them. It would be a whole week before the paper appeared with the promised explanation.

On Monday, Dougie drove to the hill to take home a load of peats. The road was a long and rough one, with rocks, mossy pools, clumps of rushes, shingle, troughs of fine black dust, muckle bools, and crumbling clay; and the tractor creaked and roared. Bess ran in the heather, an altogether more comfortable journey. But the day was good and the breeze fresh and scented.

— Well, Mr Bayne, let me begin this interview by saying that you have achieved a lot with this croft of yours. Aye, no bad, for a chiel like me. Could you describe for us some of the improvements you have made in the last few years? Well, I dinna ken where to start, but let me see. I've taken more hill into grass and I've more sheep. They've been doing well. And there's the beehives, and my trees, though they've had a tough time o it, wi the awful bad gales we get in the winter.

— But, Mr Bayne, many of your experiments have failed. That wind machine for electric power was no good. It nearly worked but it blew away one nicht. Bits o it turned up ower half the parish.

The tractor lurched over a large boulder and left the driver suspended in the air, interrupting his daydream.

— I need a thicker pock here for a cushion. Mr Bayne, I understand that you've acquired more land for grazing? Aye, I was lucky to get twa or three more acres. It's considerably more than that. When I say twa or three, that's just a manner o speaking, aye it's a fair amount. I've heard it said, Mr Bayne — can I call you Dougie? — aye, if ye want — you've been highly praised for your work in trying to make your land the basis of a good livelihood. Have I? Well, och, I havena done muckle, I just had a few ideas, ye ken, and, well, the land, when it comes to the land, that's all we've got, is it no? Withoot land there's nothing.

A hare rose from the heather and sped, hulluping, across the ground. Bess paused, one paw raised, and watched it go.

— Dowg's got sense whatever. Mr Bayne — I mean, Dougie — it has been said that you lead a very lonely life. What would you say to that? I suppose it is, in a way. Aye, I do feel lonely at times, but I keep myself busy. I'm my own master. And you've never been tempted to sell up and live in town? Never! Never?

'Bess,' he shouted, as the dog began to sniff at a sheep carcass. The clutter of bones and grey wool had been lying for months.

— It micht be fine in the toon, too. But I think I would feel hemmed in. Nae view fae your window but your neighbour's heid keeking at ye fae across the street. I go in often. I'm a member o the library and I've been to the pictures on occasion, but I canna stop fae home for long.

— I wonder can ye make something o that cotton grass. There's acres o it, just a sea o wee, white flags.

Far away across the moor, he saw another tractor, slowly rocking its way towards him. Behind it tossed a stacked trailer of peats. The noise of the engine was an indistinct throb in the breeze.

— Who'll that be? It's a wonder there's no more folk in the hill on such a fine day. It's early yet, though. They'll all be coming at nicht, when they get home fae their work.

— Mr Bayne, what do you think will become of you during the rest of your life? That's a bonny question to put to a chiel. Come back in thirty years and ask me again. Likely I'll still be here, taking home peats, sharing this ground wi maas and puddocks. But things are aye changing, we canna predict. 'An' forward, tho' I canna see, I guess an' fear.' It would be fine to share it all wi somebody, though. Yes, Dougie, is it not about time you took a wife? You've forsaken the joys of wedlock for too long, some say. Aye, there micht be something in that, I'm thinking aboot it.

'Aye, Dougie.'

In the midst of the waste of heather, rock and cotton grass, two tractors meet and their hardy pilots exchange news. John Campbell's round face is black with peat stoor and the blackness extends in a fine dusky shade over the expanse of bald head, fringed with curly brown hair. On the ramparts of the peat on his trailer, his children cling like mountaineers. Their faces, too, are black.

'Aye, John.'

'Grand day for the hill.'

'Topping.'

Brakes are applied, gears disengaged and throttles eased back.

'I was off early,' says John, his teeth a white wall in a field of black. 'Got the day off. Must try and get as many loads home as I can.'

'It'll no take long wi the bairns to help ye.'

'They should be at the school but the exams are done.'

'Aye, aye. Did ye see any chiel else on the way?'

'Not a soul. I doubt we're too early for them.'

'No sign o a fox?'

'I found a nether's skin,' pipes up a young Campbell.

Pause.

'We'd better be off. The breakfast'll be on.'

'Cheerio.'

He reached the bank where his peats were waiting. This part of the moor formed a long trough, a U-shaped valley he had surmised, after reading a book on the Ice Ages, though it was hardly a valley, more a long crease. On the west side, the brae rose steeply to an edge marked by protruding white walls of stone. Frost and rain had carved slices from this cliff and boulders studded the slope, rising like white islands in a sea of bracken. In the trough, the moss was thick and black; viscous, oily stuff, the death-distilled essence of millions of heather and sphagnum leaves. A month or so before, he had flayed the turf from the ground, howking it out with the tuskar and letting it fall in mossy dollops into the bank, the ditch left where he had dug the previous year's fuel. Beneath the top few inches of roots, flowers and stems, the moss was clean and smooth, like chocolate custard, only blacker, and his tuskar had sliced it cleanly into slab after slab.

The air was hot and calm in the trough. Dougie took off his jersey and threw it on the heather. A warm diesel fug rose from the tractor, now still and whimpering, its engine off. He sat down on a tuft of grass and gazed up at the rocks.

— I wonder if yon two mannies came this far the other day. If they were geologists, there's some grand rocks for them here. That's a grand life, climbing aboot wi peedie hammers, knocking junks off and looking at them. Sandstone, granite, whinstone, freestone, marble. There's gold at Kildonan but nobody ever found the mither vein.

A crow flew past the face of the small cliff.

The peats were as dry as bones. And hard, like biscuits. He began to throw them into the cart, picking them up from the serried rows in which they had been set to dry. The cart filled until a cairn of slabs rose in its centre. Then, he climbed onto the drawbar and began to arrange the load to make it stable for the homeward journey.

— Not a sign o a soul. A lonely kind o place, this, even during the day. Ye'd think some of the rocks had een and were watching me. No wonder our ancestors believed in fairies and elves and little craiturs. There could be a great elf city below that edge up there, wi kings and queens and palaces. Maybe they make the gold.

Bess sorned about, sniffing all the hillocks and tufts, going mad in a world of new smells.

At last the cart was full, its tyres bulging and sinking a little in the heathery mattress, but before the homeward trip Dougie decided on a dander up the brae. Man and dog leapt the bank, where the water shimmered beneath the legs of the pond-skaters. On the brae side the bracken was waist high, woven together with webs, silver tendrils safe from the seeking wind. The heads of the unopened bracken curled, beckoning, like fiddle necks.

It was warm in the face of the rocks. The stones were comfortable to the touch, curved and gritty. Below, among the straight, black slashes of the peat banks, the tractor and the loaded cart looked small and desolate. The waves of the moor rolled away from him like the waves of the sea. And then he noticed the bright orange splash of peel, strident among the greens and fawns.

— There's been somebody up here lately. I wonder if there's still a chiel here. It's quiet, quiet. No wind here. This place is putting ears on me.

He spoke to Bess, just to break the silent spell that the rocks and the sun were putting on him. At the foot of the rock shelf he found a splattering of chips, flakes from the mother stone. A clean face gleamed above them.

— Ah, they must be geologists richt enough.

He tried to persuade Bess to sniff the area in the hope that she might pick up a trail but she was no bloodhound and was more interested in gallivanting back and fore after rabbits. He sat and smoked.

Then, on the rising ground beyond the tractor his eye picked on something odd: red, white, more colours that did not belong in this place. He had not noticed them before but now they leapt from the heather like a beacon. Curiosity took him down through the bracken and up the opposing brae. Somebody had been tampering with his hill, though it was not his hill but common ground and free to everybody. But when admitted to a place a visitor was expected to behave; and he was annoyed that someone had been taking liberties with the moor.

The red and white object turned out to be a short post, like a barber's pole but with broader stripes, sunk into the ground and rising some three feet from it. He had seen poles of this sort before, at roadworks and building sites.

— What are they marking this place for? Were they surveyors? I'd better not touch it but if I pulled it up and threw it in the bank they'd be lost. They must be coming back. Maybe they're archaeologists. But the reporter would never have got so excited over archaeologists. They're common enough.

CHAPTER THREE

He took home four loads of peats that day and by evening felt done out. A thin skein of cloud had crept across the sky and the breeze had a damp smell to it. Even if it rained during the night, the sprinkling of water would not harm the road and he planned to bring home the remainder of the peats on the morn. And that would be that for another summer.

But now a drouth was on him and a longing for company, and he drove to the village.

John Campbell was in the public bar, blethering to Jim Sinclair the joiner and Tom Manson the landlord.

'Are ye done wi the peats, boy?' asked John as Dougie entered.

'Done? Dead done.'

'It's been a warm day,' observed Tom, beginning to pour a pint of heavy for the newcomer.

'I got twa load home,' went on John. 'I swear wi the stoor sticking in the sweat on my face I could have cut another load off my cheeks.'

Dougie thought that the size of John's face made such a possibility interesting. His full-moon head was scrubbed pink.

Jim Sinclair, tall, thin, with a full head of curls bestrewn with sawdust, the badge of his trade, leaned on the bar and explained that he planned to go to the hill at the end of the week. He was building a house roof and that had to be finished first.

'Did ye see anybody in the hill the day?' asked Dougie.

'None except yourself.'

'I've been dreaming o this all day,' and Dougie took his beer.

'Where's your bank?' asked Jim Sinclair.

'I've been cutting at the Whitestanes this three year past,' explained Dougie.

'Good, black peats there,' said Tom Manson. 'A good depth o moss.'

'Did ye see any poles, painted red and white, in your bit o the hill?'

The joiner and the mechanic said they had seen nothing like that.

'I found one on the brae above my bank,' said Dougie. 'I was wondering what it was there for.'

'Funny place for a pole,' said Tom Manson.

'Maybe they're putting in a new road for us,' laughed John Campbell.

The door opened and the face of Donald's Jamie appeared.

'My God,' cried John Campbell. 'It's no pension day, is it?'

'Aye, men,' said Donald's Jamie, coming in. He fidgeted in his pocket and brought out a handful of silver. 'I'm no stopping, Tom. Have ye got lemonade or stuff like that? Donnie's wi me and he's wanting something to drink.'

When the old man had bought a tin of Coke, he spoke to Dougie. 'We're for the cuddanes. D'ye want to come wi us?'

'I ken nothing aboot fishing.'

'Och, ye can come oot a run. We've a loan o Alistair's boat. It's a fine nicht for a trip on the water.'

Dougie hesitated. 'I'll gie ye a run doon to the pier,' he said. 'By the time we get there, I'll have made up my mind.'

It took only a few minutes to drive the mile from the hotel to the pier, a simple rectangle of concrete with a slipway on one side where boat-owners could haul their craft. Two yawls bobbed in the water and beyond was

moored Alistair the teacher's boat, a sleek, white hull with
blue gunwales and an outboard motor. The name Aegir,
the Norse god of the sea Alistair had explained, was
painted on the bow.

Dougie sat in the van and watched the name bob up
and down. Donald's Jamie was beside him and over his
shoulder peered Donnie, his eyes bright like the waves
before them.

'I'm no clad for the sea,' said Dougie.

'It's no cold,' argued Donald's Jamie. 'Ye've a gansey
there that'll do ye fine.'

Donnie was a slightly built boy, tall for his age and not
unlike his grandfather in the face. He spoke with a soft,
Lowland accent. 'Will we get a lot of fish?' he asked.

'We'll get none sitting here on the land,' stated Donald's
Jamie.

A caravan was parked near the head of the pier and
some holidaymakers were fishing. Beyond the marram-
fringed braes, the roof of a cottage stuck up like a grey
reef. Maas paraded. Dougie was in two minds.

'Hello.'

'Well, well, it's Alison,' cried Donald's Jamie.

She came up to the van, smiling broadly and wearing
a yellow anorak.

'We're for the sea,' said the old man. 'D'ye want to come
oot wi us?'

'Now?'

'Certainly. Come on. I'll show ye how to catch cuddanes.'

'Are you going out for long? What are cuddanes,
anyway?'

'I dinna ken the English for them,' said Donald's Jamie.
'We'll no be oot long.'

Dougie thought the English for them was coalfish but
he said nothing.

'I'm game,' said Alison.

'Och, I'll come too,' said Dougie quietly.

Donald's Jamie turned a codseye on him and grinned.

They got into the boat and, while the old man footered
wth the outboard, Dougie and Donnie untied the mooring
ropes. The holidaymakers watched them; Donnie was
scornful of their plastic rods and floats — he was a real
fisherman. Alison sat in the middle of the boat, obviously
enjoying herself.

The motor responded to Donald's Jamie's rive on the
starting cord and the good ship Aegir was soon butting
seaward. The old man was familiar with the sea and he
made creels in the winter that Alistair the teacher set for
lobsters in the rocks below the cliffs. Now, Jamie son of
Donald faced the sea breeze and nestled the tiller in his
horny liv.

'This is the life for ye,' he cried.

'Yes,' shouted Alison.

'Will we see a basking shark?' asked Donnie.

— There's a fair turn o speed in this boatie. Jamie the
viking. The waves are no that big. Good job it's calm.
Funny how it's suddenly cooler out here.

'How are the sheep, Dougie?'

— Sheep?

'Oh, they're fine,' he said. 'Have ye been off in the hill
again?'

'No,' said Alison. 'I've been working in the house,
unpacking my stuff. It was such a lovely day that I spent
most of the time sitting at the window looking at the sea.'
She laughed. 'The cottage looks very small from here. It
all looks very different.'

— What took her to live here?

'Is there no sea where ye come fae?'

'I lived in London. There was the Thames but I never
really looked at it. Have you been to London?'

'No.'

'Look, there are some ducks,' cried Donnie, pointing.

'Ye can be making ready your line,' instructed his
grandfather. 'We've nae need to go further oot. The tide
can take us for a bittie.'

He shut off the motor and a great silence fell on the

surface of the sea. They spoke quietly because it seemed a sacrilege to make loud noises. They uncoiled the lines which Donald's Jamie brought out from a biscuit tin stowed under the stern seat. On the ends were small balls of lead and, at intervals, hooks decorated with white and coloured feathers.

'Let the line doon until ye can feel her touch the bottom,' explained grandfather to grandson. 'Then lift her a bittie and jig her up and doon.'

'I can see the bottom,' said Donnie. A vague, shifting whiteness below showed that they were above a sand-bank.

They fished for a while. Dougie offered a cigarette to Alison but she said she did not smoke. The Aegir drifted with the tide, rising and falling, and they watched the coast and worked their lines.

Donnie was the first to feel a bite and he almost went overboard with excitement before he managed to haul the flapping cuddane into the boat.

'There's nothing like that in West Kilbride,' said his grandfather.

'Did my dad fish a lot?'

'Aye.'

'I bet he wishes he was here now.'

'No doubt.'

Then Alison caught one, bigger than Donnie's, and several seconds later Dougie hauled aboard a small, red cod.

'Ye've got none, Grandad,' observed Donnie.

'Just ye wait. We're no among the big chiels yet.'

— I'm enjoying this. Glad I came. It's a fine way to pass the nicht, better than polishing Tom Manson's bar stools. What brocht Alison fae London to live here? Did she rob a bank? Crash through the swing doors, arms raxed wi the weicht o money in pocks wi loot written on them, like in the comics. Bells ringing — stash the cash doon some cundy and off north on the train, wi sunglasses for a disguise. She has a car, Donald's Jamie said. Must have some money. Maybe she inherited it and was looking for a place to buy and fell in love wi Shore Cottage. It looks like a dot fae here. Can hardly make it oot at all. There are some big waves coming in now. The tide must have turned. Moon up there, sooking all the water back and fore. Mind asking in the school where the tide gaed when it went oot. In somewhere else, I suppose — one chiel's flood, anither chiel's ebb. She's a bonny face, the way the wind pulls her hair back fae her cheeks. Is she looking for a man? Brave northern chuchters, fed on brose and kail and tatties and herring. What's that?

He hauled up his line and a large cuddane tumbled over the gunwale, the hook sticking through its jaw in a smudge of blood.

'That's a big one,' cried Donnie.

'It looks like we're in them now,' said Donald's Jamie and he brought up his line with another fish.

After fifteen minutes or so, a pile of flapping white bodies lay in the bilge.

'How do you cook them?' asked Alison.

'Och, cuddanes are no great,' said Donald's Jamie. 'I like one myself but there's a lot winna touch them. I'll split them and dry them in the sun.'

— It's a good job I had only one pint before coming oot. How could ye pish here wi a woman in the boat? Keep it til ye get back, or else she'll just have to turn her head. All this water roond ye puts the thocht in your heid. The sun's low now. Yellowy sky. Maybe she's just come here to get away fae the toon for a while. Six months o this life and she'll be hankering for back again. A lot o southerners have taken crofts and tried to work them, some have stuck it well but a lot havena. She's a potter though. Interesting kind o work, it must be. Maybe she's come looking for inspiration. Or too much competition doon sooth, too many potters, dozens o them sitting churning oot jugs and bowls and cups.

'I doubt we should be going in,' said Donald's Jamie. 'Your grandmither'll be wondering where we are.'

He started the motor again and turned the boat in a wide arc. Donnie was not too pleased and pleaded to stay longer. His grandfather hummed and hawed and relented, saying that they could try a bank he knew a little to the south of them that was good for haddies.

— It's getting colder now. Strange motion, up and doon, up and doon, like as if there was a tickling in my stomach. Better concentrate on something. It would be it, if I were sick here. They would all laugh at me. What kind o viking am I? Dinna think aboot it. Up and doon, up and doon. It's steady. No roch, just a steady up and doon. It would be better if...there are scales on my trousers. Little grey eyes. I can see the rings on them, like little furrows in ploughed land. How old was that cuddane before I plucked it fae the sea? The harvest o the deep — rich cuddanes, cod, haddies, flukes, all kind o craiturs. How do whales never catch cold? Blubber. Up and doon, up and doon and up and...Can I see the croft fae here? My mither will be looking for me. Haddies'll surprise her when I take a fry home. It's been a while since we had fresh fish. Row them in oatmeal and fry them. Delicious, wi a boil o new tatties. Rich food. Brain food. Does it really feed the brain? An old wife's story that. Maybe it's the oil that lubricates the cogs in the brain. Fine clear oil, like the oil for the wheels and gears in a clock. Oil, codliver oil, oh God — up and doon and up and doon. Up. We used to have to take codliver oil in the school. Sticky horrible muck. A spoon happed in a piece o newspaper til the oil made the ink come off on your fingers. 'Open your mouth, Douglas. See. John has taken his. You do want to grow up big and strong, don't you?' 'Yes, miss.' Ooaauugh! Bolt a sweetie to take away the...Christ, I'm going to spew. Up doon up doon updoonupdoonup-doon...damn this sea. In front o them all!

'I'm going to be sick,' he cried and he boked over the gunwale.

'I thocht your face was getting green this last whilie,' grinned Donald's Jamie.

'I dinnae feel sick,' chirruped Donnie, as he watched

Dougie hanging over the gunwale and languidly considered the stain floating away from them on the grey sea.

'Hush, you're a sailor,' said Alison. 'We aren't all sailors.'

Dougie sat up, his eyes rolling like the dead fisheyes in the bottom of the boat.

'It's time we went in,' said Donald's Jamie and he proceeded to start the motor.

Through his glazed vision, Dougie saw him grinning and hated him. 'I feel better now,' he moaned and then to Alison he apologised.

She smiled and he felt better. 'Nelson used to be seasick every time he went out with the fleet,' she said.

CHAPTER FOUR

Next morning, his stomach was still a bit dwannie but two duck eggs at breakfast, hard boiled, soon set it to rights. It was a dry morning without sun and he went to the hill, back to the Whitestanes, for another load of peats. He had another look at the pole but it yielded no clue as to its purpose.

After noon, he and his mother drove to town on her weekly shopping trip. Jessie had put on her best coat and headscarf and sat noticing everything in the passing countryside. She noticed and commented, the shuttling eye capturing the last etchal of detail and the tongue remarking on it and filing it. The litany was familiar to her son.

'The grass is growing tall in the cemetery. Your father's stone'll be disappearing in it, it's time it was cut. Need cutting often wi this warm weather. Has Johnnie Allan no been at the mower? No him. He's aye in the blues wi drink they say. I see Jean has new painted the windows in the post office. Dinna like that blue myself. Duck egg blue, is it? Or it's a bittie darker than that. Jean was saying to Donald's Jamie that she has a bad back. And her a young woman too. But that's no it. Look at that bairns playing on the top o the road. Watch, Dougie. Slow doon til they're past. Lot o towrists aboot. I see two — no — three, fower, five caravans at the Sandend. That's a big ain. It canna be warm in that water, but they're lowping naked like tadpoles. They're for whitewashing the kirk, I heard. Did ye hear that? It's black looking richt enough, ablow the eisewaas. Betty's man's going to do it, they say. There's somebody in Shore Cottage, a lassie fae the sooth. D'ye ken her? Is she English? Oh, she is. What's she here for? She makes pots. Fancy! Oooh. Cooper's Quarry has still got water in it. That hole never dries up, must be a spring. Even in the driest summer that never dries up. When we were bairns we were telt on no account to go near it. Och, but the men were working there then. There was a lot o men at it. A dozen, maybe more. Your faither thocht o going there once, before he got the croft. Then they closed it doon. But ye'll no mind that, ye were just a bairn. Concrete, they said, no need for stone. Tanster's a fine herd o beise there, fine black stirkies. I havena seen Jinnad for ages. I should write, we were grand pals at the school. She's twa month older than me, she was May and I was July. I can never pass that park withoot minding on poor Jockie Sinclair. A fine loon he was, and a grand whistler. I can see him yet, thinning neeps and whistling away, and then he gaed off to the War. Is that Davie and Isobel? They're for the toon too surely. Ye've had no word o Rob lately? No. Building their peat stack at the Ha. Who has it now? I havena been there since auld Cormack lost his life in the blind drift one nicht. That was a while ago. Oh, it must have been near th end o the second War. It was selt off after that because he had no heirs, poor man. Five bairns and they all died afore him. He was drunk the nicht he died. If only he'd had a droppie more, he would've withstood the cold, they said. But the way I see it, if he'd had none at all, he wouldna have lost his road and been oot in the first place. Mossigill's a fine tidy looking place. But they say he doesna own it, it belongs to the solicitors and he's working his fingers to the bone to pay them. That's no like his grandfather. Who's that wifie on the road? Red coat. Must be making for the shop surely. That's Jacob's sheep that Cuddiegeo's got there, funny looking craiturs. Like they had in the Bible. Mind me to buy baking powder, I forgot to put it on my line. Quoydale, that's where we used to go for horses. The auld mannie who had it then was a great breeder o horses and my faither used to get his fae him. Mony's a time we gaed there when we were bairns...'

— And that's a stab, and that's a strainer, and that's a flag dyke, and that's a bull, and that's his doadles hinging doon. Och I shouldna be annoyed wi her, but it's the same damn spiel every time we go to the toon. Like a tape recording. It's like reading a diary o her life for her, a rehearsal o her history. I wonder what it was like then. No muckle different — same hooses, gie or take a bungalow — same parks, same corn, same maas. Horses, no tractors. What'll it be sixty years fae now? That's the teaser. More hooses? No hooses? Forests? Parks? A desert?

At length they reached the outskirts of the town and drove through the white council estate to the older, greyer kernel. Dougie dropped his mother off to let her get on with the messages and steered the van in the direction of the public library.

The polished linoleum and the spacious bookshelves formed a cavern of reflection and faint echo. He handed in three books. An old woman was poking and squinting under a sign proclaiming 'Romantic Fiction'. He headed for the science shelves and, the image of the pole sticking from the heather still in his mind, pulled out a book on rocks and minerals, flicked through the pages and decided on it.

After fifteen minutes, he had chosen another two volumes and left the library. Just as he was unlocking the door of the van, he heard someone call his name. It was Alison, coming along the pavement.

'Hello,' he said.

'How are you?' She was smiling broadly and was wearing jeans and a thick, patterned sweater.

'Fine,' he muttered. 'How are ye yourself?'

'Great,' she said. 'Have you eaten your fish yet?'

'I...I gave them to the cats,' he admitted. 'I dinna think I could have eaten them after all yon.'

'You weren't bad. Anybody can be seasick.'

'Aye,' he grinned. 'Are ye in town for the day?'

'I came to pick up two bags of clay from the station,' she declared. 'Now I can start throwing again.'

'Good.'

— What does she mean?

'Ye'll be at the potmaking again then?'

'Yes. I've got some great ideas. The colours and shapes of the rocks here are so different, so unusual...and the flowers and the shades of brown...oh it's all so much to tackle. I must try to come up with some new glazes.'

Dougie smiled and felt drawn by her enthusiasm. On the almost-deserted, grey street she was a bright butterfly.

'I ken nothing aboot pottery,' he said.

'Why don't you drop in sometime?'

'Aye, I micht do that,'he said.

'Well, I must buy some things and be off home,' she said. 'Bye.'

'Cheerio.'

Dougie went off along the street. At the traffic lights, where he halted, an old man dismounted from his bicycle, propped it against the wall and disappeared into a shop. There were two cars with local number plates, but he could not distinguish the faces behind the light-smeared windscreens. From the back of a large lorry, two chiels in brown shopcoats were unloading boxes of bananas onto a little trolley. The amber winked on.

— I ken that car though. Coming the opposite road. It's the white car that was at the hoose. Is it the same chiel driving? Two men in it. So, they're still in the vicinity.

The white car flashed past him and he had to force himself not to turn around and follow it. But it set him to thinking of the hill again and the red and white pole, and he glanced at the books on the seat bside him. Maybe the answer would be given by something in the minerals book. As his mind raged with suspicion, he recognised that there might be nothing in all the fuss at all. Many a crow had flown over the face of that brae and never landed. Yet there was this nagging doubt...

His mother he spotted on the pavement outside Wool-
worths, bulging plastic bags of plunder in either hand.
She got in, with much shoogling and peching.

'Did ye get it all?'

'Pineapple chunks are up fourpence on what they were
last week. I need some ither things yet. It's warm. We'll
have our coffee now. I got some cold ham for your tea.'

While they took their half-yoking, coffee and a mutton
pie each, in a cafe, Dougie looked at his mineral book.

'What are ye reading now?' she asked in a whisper.

'Hhhm?'

'Ye shouldna be doing that here. Some chiel micht
come in.'

'I'm thinking aboot something,' he protested.

'Ye're aye thinking aboot something.'

But he did not bother to answer and left her to sip her
coffee and gowk at whoever passed on the street outside.
Wolframite, scheelite, beryl — minerals had strange
names. He skimmed from page to page and admired the
beautiful forms and colours of the crystals. He had never
thought before of the array of types which a few chemical
elements — he knew already about elements from a basic
chemistry book — put together in differing proportions
could produce. Like a few simple ingredients in a kitchen
larder becoming under the expertise of a chef dozens of
individual dishes. It was hardly canny. Who could think
that diamond and graphite were composed of the same
atoms? Or that amethyst, citrine, cairngorm, jasper, chry-
soprase, onyx, chert and opal were all forms of quartz?
He was fascinated and dipped into a paragraph here and
a caption there. And as he absorbed all this new knowledge, little pictures of Alison flickered into and out of his
mind, hardly noticed but recurring like water dripping
from the edge of a roof during a shower of rain.

As he had grown older, Dougie seemed to have become
shyer. His teenage years had seen a modest amount of
debauchery, drink mostly, enough to establish him as 'a

bit o a lad but a fine loon really', but of late he had grown more old-fashioned in his morals. He was hardly aware of this change and, although he was definitely interested in Alison and attracted to her, he had no thoughts of 'what micht happen' when he arrived at Shore Cottage one day later in the week in response to her invitation.

It was a wet, cold day, the north wind driving gouts of rain down over the land. The barley and the tattie bleems rustled and groaned in protest at the unseasonable intrusion, and folk hurried from door to car and from bus to fireside, their coats buttoned.

The front room of Shore Cottage caught what little extra light came off the sea and was bright in a pale, cold way. Alison had answered his knock with hands plastered in clay.

'I'm sorry,' he said, blushing a little. 'Are ye busy?'

'No. Come in.'

'I can come back anither time.'

'Come in. You're wet?'

'No.'

She had a fire on. A stack of driftwood stood on end beside the grate and what had been consigned to the flames crackled and sparked as fire met salt. There was little furniture in the room, just a table and three upright chairs. On the window sill, a clutter of books and letters crouched under the broad leaves of plants. The room was dominated by a large potter's wheel and on and under a bench beside it were an array of buckets, basins and plastic bags.

'Would you like some coffee?' she asked.

'I dinna want to put ye to any bother.'

'I feel like one anyway.' She wiped her hands and switched on an electric kettle. She held out her arms in an expression of apology and dismissal. 'Welcome to the tip. A lot of my stuff hasn't come yet. I've hardly any furniture.'

'I've collected all this wood from the beach,' she went on. 'This is the first time I've had the fire on. It seems to burn okay.'

The kettle began to sing. She took two mugs from a wall press.

'Sugar?'

'Aye, please.'

He looked at the wheel. The round plate on top was wet and muddy.

'It was kind o ye to ask me doon,' he said. 'It's a wet day and I canna do much ootside, so I thought I would drop in.'

'You're very welcome. Are you interested in potting?'

'Well... to tell ye the truth, I've never thocht much aboot it before.'

She handed him a mug of coffee.

'That's good on such a cold day,' he said.

'I love my fire. It makes it so cosy here. In winter, I'll hibernate. Stay in bed all day. The pace of life is so slow up here. Everybody speaks, nobody hurries. Such freedom.'

He thought a faint trace of sadness tinged her voice.

'How long have ye been here now?' he asked.

'Three weeks,' she cried, and her face was once again bright. 'It seems much longer. Is the coffee all right?'

'Fine.'

He noticed on the floor behind the wheel a file of wet potshapes, standing like brown soldiers in a line. The clay glistened, like leather left in the rain, like newly exposed peat, like the skin on Bess's nose. There were tall, thin pots — vases, he guessed — dumpy, round pots, medium-sized pots — was amphora the word for them? — pots with curving, graceful handles, pots with no handles, all sorts of pots. As he looked at them, the realisation that he could think of nothing to say crept into his mind, that he was embarrassed by the silence, that he might by some magic trick curl and writhe and disappear into one of the pots. And riding on the back of one realisation came another. He and this girl had almost nothing in common. Not even speech. He was not accustomed to talking in anything but the dialect and it took an effort to remember grammar, and he always blundered. It was like climbing a rickety ladder, when a shaky verb or a false pronoun could suddenly plunge you in shame to the bottom rung. And he had taken the first mouthful of coffee too quickly; a little heat blister formed behind his front teeth.

'I've made a few pots today,' she said.

'So I'm seeing,' he said, grateful for her opening. 'Does it take you a whilie to make one?'

'Pardon?'

He blushed a little. 'Eh — how long does it take to make one?'

'Only a few minutes. I'll show you.'

'Och, I dinna want to bother ye.'

She went to the wheel and sat astride the seat attached to it. With her left foot, she pumped a paddle and the wheel began to spin. Dougie thought of sewing machines. Then she took a lump of clay and slammed it with a force that surprised him onto the spinning disc. Drops of wet mud appeared on her apron. He watched her bend over the machine, her hands wrapping the clay. Her face puckered in concentration and he noticed that her tongue keeked out between her lips; the muscles in her wrists were taut and she grunted now and again. Then the daud became a rounded dome, changed into a flat-topped wheel, melted upwards into a cylinder, growing taller and taller, until she stopped pumping and sat up.

'There you are,' she said. 'It's not very good.'

The transfigurations that had taken place under her hands seemed to him miraculous, some kind of magic, and he looked anew at the conjuror, his shyness lost and replaced by an echo of childhood wonder. 'That's fantastic,' he cried. 'And that's all that's to it?'

'Well...' Alison still had to preserve the aura of the professional.

'What's that ye've made now?'

'Just a basic kind of pot.'

'That's marvellous, that. Just to think a daud o gutter — clay — like that...howked oot the ground, turned while ye wait...ye make it look easy.'

'Do you want to try?'

'No. No me. I dinna ken a thing aboot it.'

The mug was empty.

'I'd better be going,' he said. 'I'll let ye get on wi your work.'

'That's okay. It's nice to have a visit. Come again any time. I hope to have my kiln working soon.'

'Thank ye for the coffee.' He paused as he set the mug carefully on the mantelpiece. He would never look at a mug again without thinking of a woman's hands pulling it into being.

He turned and looked at her and blushed a little. 'If there's anything ye need...'

'Thanks,' she replied crisply. 'I'm all right just now.'

'Still raining,' he said, looking at the running window-pane. 'That's Scottish weather for ye. It's summer, I believe.'

The sound of her laughter went with him like a catchy tune on the way home.

Chapter Five

When he got the newspaper on Friday, at the top of the day, from Jean in the shop, he went at once to the van and eagerly scanned it. What he was searching for was not immediately obvious among the mixture of pictures and headlines that graced the front page. 'He drank and drove', 'Folk star heads south', 'Moderator to pay visit', 'Thurso man's Far East adventures', 'Prizes for flower arranging'. Then he found it. 'American company raises job hopes.'

> 'Geologists from the American mining giant Redriver Inc and the Institute of Geologists have spent the last weeks prospecting in Caithness and Sutherland and are optimistic about the possibility of finding commercial mineral deposits in the north. A spokesman for the firm said that they were about to complete their study of the data but some of the results were very positive.
>
> A number of minerals have been found in deposits with commercial potential, he said, including galena, barite, zincblende and uranium. The uranium deposits are particularly interesting, he added.
>
> The Council has expressed a great interest in the findings, saying that if the company wishes to exploit the deposits they can be assured of every cooperation. Redriver Inc, which has its headquarters in Nevada, has mining interests worldwide. The spokesman said that should they decide to mine in Scotland they would make every effort to employ local labour. The company has a very high opinion of the skill and

hardworking integrity of the people of the Highlands,
said the spokesman. Redriver hope to reach a decision soon and the public and the press will be kept
fully informed, he went on. One of the directors of
Redriver Inc is Charles Edward Bruce Mackay Jr,
whose great grandfather emigrated to the States from
Bettyhill last century. Mr Mackay was looking forward
very much to working in his ancestral home, said the
spokesman, who admitted himself to having a Scottish grandmother on his wife's side.

— That must be it. They were prospectors. And the
pole, they wouldna leave a pole if...commercial deposits...fly buggers. They wouldna say. Suppose if they
gave too much away and then found nothing, micht feel
foolish. Minerals in our hill. I wonder...galena, barite,
zincblende must be for zinc, uranium. Well, we all ken
what that is, they use it at Dounreay all the time. Very
valuable stuff — power, energy. What kind o mining will
it be? Towers rising in the sky, wi wheels and cages like
a coalmine, or great holes like a quarry. It's dangerous
stuff, uranium. Still, it canna be that bad if we've been
walking ower it all these years. Maybe safer to leave it in
the ground oot o sicht. I must look at the book again.

The book offered little help. It told him galena was a
source of lead and barite was sulphate of barium, a silvery
metal used in making glass and glossy paper. The section
on uranium was brief and filled with formulae and odd
names and said little to enlighten him. Curiosity, fuelled
by the uncomfortable suspicion that he was being over-
taken by events, burned in him and he determined to seek
more information as soon as he could.

He did not have to wait long. The next day was Saturday,
normally a quiet, lazy time in the week, a day for chores
and routine work. Dougie was in the kitchen, reading,
when his mother announced the approach of a car. He
glanced casually through the window.

'Looks like Magnus Gunn,' he said.

'What can he be wanting?' muttered Jessie rhetorically.

The car stopped and the occupants got out. Three men.

Jessie began to whisper. 'There's Magnus, and Jocky Shearer and I dinna ken the third chiel.'

Girning, Dougie put away the book and went to the door. Bess, who had been lying her length on the mat, followed him.

Magnus Gunn and Dougie had a kind of uneasy understanding. Ever since the crofter had taken a swing at him four Hogmanays previously they had taken care to be respectful of each other. Magnus had forgiven Dougie for the attack but he had not forgotten it; Dougie had apologised and had bought from Magnus binder twine that he did not really need to make up for his behaviour that night.

The year before, Magnus had stood for election to the council and had been returned unopposed. Jocky Shearer was also a councillor, a slight, short man with very bandy legs, a kind soul with a soft voice who lived alone but for his old mother; he bore the by-name Sprowg, which means sparrow, but it was only used by those who disliked him, and they were few.

Seeing Magnus and Jocky together made Dougie suspicious. And who was the third man?

'Aye, aye, men,' he said as he met them in the close. Two hens clucked their way round the corner. Bess wagged a greeting to all.

'Hello, Dougie,' said Magnus.

'Fine day,' said Jocky.

The third man smiled.

'No bad.' Dougie agreed about the weather.

'How's your mother?' asked Jocky.

Dougie noticed that the two councillors wore ties and jackets, Magnus being particularly well attired in a new checked affair. The third man wore a jersey but no tie.

'She's fine.'

'Hello, Jocky.' Jessie's voice sounded from inside the house.

'Aye, aye,' called back the Sprowg.

Still suspicious, Dougie thought that Jocky did indeed resemble a sparrow. When excited or anxious, he hopped from foot to foot and cocked his head to one side. Pleasantries over, the councillor got down to business.

'This is Mr Nicholl. He's wi the Redriver company, in the mining line.'

'Oh yes, I saw a bit aboot ye in the paper.'

'Pardon?' said Mr Nicholl.

'This is Dougie Bayne, Mr Nicholl.' Jocky completed the introduction.

'Pleased to meet you, Mr Bayne,' said the third man. They shook hands.

'Ye saw the bit in the paper then,' said Magnus. 'Well, ye micht guess why we're here.'

Dougie thought of the pole in the hill. 'I'm no sure,' he said.

'I represent Redriver Incorporated,' began Mr Nicholl. 'It's an American multinational, one of the biggest mining concerns in the world, although we've also interests in shipping, electronics, air freight, you name it. I reckon you know of us...'

Although the man was obviously English, Dougie recognised the American touch in his speech.

'...For weeks now, we've been carrying out a survey in the Highlands, looking for mineral deposits. There have been surveys before but none as big as this one, and throughout we've enjoyed the full cooperation of your local authorities. Mr Shearer here has been very helpful, and Mr Gunn.'

The two councillors smiled and shook their heads, as if to say they had only done what was expected of them.

'I havena heard muckle aboot all this,' said Dougie.

'No, no likely,' said Jocky. 'There wasna an awful lot o publicity. We didna think at first that they'd find muckle and there was no need to raise folks' hopes, ye ken.'

'So far,' went on Mr Nicholl, slightly nonplussed by the exchange in dialect, 'our work has been of a broad, general nature but we have located several deposits which we would like to investigate more thoroughly, with test drillings, etc, etc.' And he made a little wave with his hand as if they all knew what etc, etc stood for.

'What kind o minerals have ye found?'

'A range. I expect you saw those named in the paper, those and a few others...with technical names, eh, you probably wouldn't know...'

'Carnotite?'

Mr Nicholl's mouth dropped open a little at the sound of the word, the name of a somewhat obscure compound of uranium that Dougie had picked up in his reading. But the man's mouth remained open for only a second and turned into a gentle smile.

'No, not that,' he muttered, 'though I dare say it may be there.'

Magnus and Jocky did not know whether to smile or remain solemn, and they decided to speak, almost together, but Jocky was quicker off the mark and Magnus shut up.

'The thing is, Dougie, that they found in the hill here a good place for uranium and they think that the deposit, ye ken, runs below your land.'

Dougie started and and his eyes registered alarm. 'I saw the pole in the hill,' he began, 'but I didna ken...'

'They dinna ken yet themselves,' went on Jocky in his gentle, soft voice. 'That's why they want to drill a bittie to make sure. They can drill in the hill and they want to try a few holes on your land, too.'

'Just mine?'

'No. Will Auld's, too. Just the twa o ye, ye and Will.'

'We've just come fae him,' explained Magnus. 'He signed the permission.'

'What permission?'

'There are papers ye have to sign,' Jocky took over again, 'just to make it all legal, like.'

'Just think on it, Dougie,' cried Magnus excitedly. 'Ye could be living on a gold mine here. If the tests are richt, this could be the biggest thing since Dounreay. This is a great opportunity.'

'Redriver is very conscious of its public duty in bringing employment and other oportunities to marginal communities,' said Mr Nicholl. 'We've learned a lot in the developing world, and the company is proud of its record in this respect.' And he smiled his public relations man's smile.

'Heavens, I dinna ken,' murmured Dougie. 'This is a surprise.'

'We appreciate that you might require time to think, Mr Bayne,' said Mr Nicholl. 'We can leave the papers with you and come back for them tomorrow, if you wish, although it is a little inconvenient. None of us likes working on a Sunday...' and he laughed a dry laugh '...Mr Auld was very understanding and signed his for us.'

The laughter cut through Dougie's confusion like a sword through the Gordian knot.

'I want to think about it,' he said. 'Can ye tell me about the test drilling?'

'Sure.'

'Well?'

Mr Nicholl gave a little sigh. 'We need perhaps to drill two, three, four boreholes to a depth of some hundred feet, maybe, though probably less will suffice. The holes are a few inches in diameter...'

— That doesna sound too bad, but what happens if...uranium on my land...

'There canna be muckle uranium here?' said Dougie.

Mr Nicholl's ear for the dialect was improving. 'You're right,' he replied. 'I must say, Mr Bayne, you seem to know more about this than I anticipated. Frankly, Redriver has set aside considerable sums for the testing of non-viable ore sites, that is, non-viable up to now. There is no shortage of uranium but we believe that a far-sighted, responsible international company should spend some of its revenues checking non-viable sites before they become...' again the little laugh '...the only viable ones left. The veins of granite in the sedimentary rocks here — you with me? — have concentrations of uranium ores just at the limits of commercial viability, at the present state of the art. But who knows? New techniques, an increase in prices, and they could become prime sites tomorrow. As a leading company, naturally we don't want to be caught with our pants down, eh gentlemen?'

Magnus and Jocky grinned.

Dougie scratched his head. 'Have ye got the papers?'

'Right here.' Mr Nicholl thrust forward an envelope.

Dougie took the brown rectangle gingerly and held it lightly between his fingertips. He looked at it, and his face was serious. 'I'll need a wee whilie to think aboot this.'

Magnus frowned. 'Will Auld signed his richt away,' he said. 'Ye canna take too long.'

Dougie and the councillor exchanged looks, two cliffs on opposite sides of a grey sea.

Jocky the diplomat hopped from foot to foot. 'Of course ye need a day or two to think it ower. Will Auld's an old man, and he didna work his land anyway. Dougie's young, this place is still his livelihood. We can gie him two days. Eh, Mr Nicholl?'

The Englishman grunted and eventually smiled. 'Of course.'

'How are ye all the day?' The voice took them by surprise. Jessie came feeting from the house and bade them all welcome. Dougie noticed that she had removed her apron.

'Fine,' grunted Magnus.

'Canna complain,' said Jocky.

'What's this ye've gien us now?' asked Jessie.

Dougie indicated the newcomer. 'This is Mr Nicholl, mither, o the Redriver mining company. They want permission to make test drills on our land for uranium.'

He watched carefully to see how she would take this all in.

'Fancy,' she breathed cheerfully. 'Well, we'll no be in your road. Will it take a whilie? Dougie'll show ye where to go.'

'It's no as simple as that, mither,' explained Dougie. 'They want me to sign papers for permission.'

Jessie kept looking at Mr Nicholl and her eyes showed an elusive quality. 'I would sign nothing,' she said firmly. 'Whatever they want, they can ask.'

'This is legal business, Jessie,' proclaimed Magnus in his councillor's voice. 'We're dealing wi professionals now.'

'I would sign nothing, professionals or no.'

— My God, who would've credited it.

Dougie suppressed the grin. 'Well, there ye are, boys. Gie me a twa days to look at this.'

'I can pop up on Monday and collect the paper fae ye,' said Jocky.

'Och, I'm nearer hand. I can run up,' said Magnus.

'Monday it is,' sighed Mr Nicholl. 'Well, it's been a pleasure meeting you, Mr Bayne. I'm sure your decision will be the wise one. Now, if you'll excuse us.'

The other two bade their farewells on the move. All three tumbled quickly into the car and Dougie and his mother watched them drive off.

'Na, na, we're no gieing our land to anybody,' muttered Jessie.

'Let's find oot a little more aboot the whole business first,' said Dougie. 'Will Auld has signed his ower.'

Jessie's face twisted in scorn. 'Will Auld was aye a trosk as lang as I can mind.'

Dougie realised the envelope was still in his hand and he took it in and opened it in the kitchen. There was a single sheet inside. At the top were the words REDRIVER (UK) INC. and the address and suchlike. The rest of the document comprised closely printed paragraphs, numbered, with a space at the bottom for a signature and a date.

'It'll take a lawyer to figure this oot,' said Dougie, and he read it slowly and with effort. When he thought he had made sense of it, he gave a summary to his mother.

'If I sign this, it will gie them permission to drill test bores to look for uranium. They will drill where they want but will gie us compensation if there's any damage, and I promise to cooperate wi them. If they dinna find anything, they'll make good any damage and that'll be the end o it. If they do find something, I gie them the richt to buy the land for mining.'

Jessie thought but said nothing.

'I dinna like that last bit,' continued Dougie. 'Doing tests is one thing. I dinna mind that but...och I dinna ken. I'm going off to see Will Auld to see if his paper's the same as mine.'

Will Auld's croft was a marackless bit of a place on the edge of the moor. Will no longer worked his land and weeds were growing thick along the gapped flag dykes. Pairs of harrows and a plough and what looked like an electric cooker stuck up, rusting, from the nettles. Part of the roof of the old byre was missing and the stones of the gable stood like the teeth of a saw against the sky.

Will heard the noise of Dougie's van and came to the door of the house. He watched his younger neighbour park and come towards the porch. Will's old bick, her belly almost trailing on the road, hirpled to meet the visitor.

'Hello, Glen,' said Dougie, and the collie wagged her tail with an effort.

— Done on the legs, like your maister.

'Aye Dougie,' said Will.

'Aye, aye.'

'What brings ye up this way?'

'Did ye have Magnus Gunn and them all here the day?'

Will scratched his chin and pushed his bonnet up a bit on his brow.

'Aye, the buggers,' he said. 'They came when I was watching the horse racing. Jocky Shearer was there too and an Englishman. He said his name but I canna mind what it was now.'

'Nicholl.'

'Aye, I think that was it. They said they were going doon to ye. So they came, then?'

'Aye,' said Dougie.

Will leaned against the jamb of the door. Dougie thought he looked tired.

'They wanted me to sign a paper for permission to drill test bores on the land. They said that ye'd signed.'

'Aye, I signed it. It was a long screed o a thing.'

'Ye didna read it first?'

'No. I didna bother. It was just permission they wanted. I said that they could do what they wanted for the asking, but no, says Magnus, it has to be legal.'

'They said the same to me but I didna sign anything.'

'Oh.' Will continued to gaze across the nettles and the dockans to the countryside beyond.

'If they find uranium, they'll buy your land off ye,' said Dougie, trying to hide a growing impatience. He was beginning to regard the old man as a traitor.

'Aye, I thocht that micht be in it,' said Will quietly.

Dougie looked sharply at him.

'If they're keen for this uranium stuff, they'll pay a big price for it, too.' Will paused. 'I dinna work this place. I'd sell it tomorrow and get a council hoose in the village. I bought the croft at the same time as your faither bought yours, about the time o the War. But there never was any money in this place and there never will be. It's no fit for anything. Soor, soor ground.'

'Ye're ready to sell your ground.'

'Surely,' cried Will. 'Micht as well get some good oot o it when I'm still alive.'

'I'm no ready to sell mine,' said Dougie.

Will laughed. 'So ye're saying, boy. Wait til ye see what they offer. Ye micht change your mind.'

Chapter Six

His boots, looked down at, seemed out of place at the graveside and the bright blades of grass raged against them like waves attacking a coast. It was quiet — the high walls kept out the wind and there was only faint birdsong to break the silence.

IN LOVING MEMORY OF
DANIEL GEORGE BAYNE

— Faither, what would ye do? Sell oot to them, like Will Auld, or tell them to go to hell? This ground was good enough for my faither and it's good enough for me, ye would say. They'll no work, this young shither nowadays, ye would say, wanting money for nothing. The greed o the deil's on them, ye would rant. Och they're foolish, witless craiturs, ye would rave. When I was a young chiel I had to work for my living, ye would storm. Well I've worked, faither. What think ye o your son now? Proud o me, are ye? I dinna think ye would sell. I winna.

The stone was a flat, black rectangle of granite and the letters were resplendent in gold paint. Twice that summer, Dougie had driven his mother here to plant flowers on the grave — pansies and Livingstone daisies.

IN LOVING MEMORY OF
DANIEL GEORGE BAYNE
I sleep but my heart waketh

He had been surprised when his mother had chosen that text for the stone. It hinted at a knowledge and a religiosity he had not suspected. There was poetry in it.

— Would ye have selt, faither? Of course, it michtna

179

come to that, they michtna find what they're seeking. Would ye have put yourself in thrall, though, hoping that they found nothing? Or would ye think o the money, like Will Auld, and a council hoose and twa drills o tatties to dig in the spring, until the box was ready? Forgie me, faither. I dinna ken what to do. Can I stand up to them? Lord kens what powers they have. If they find uranium, they'll shift me if they want it. Should I clear oot now when there's cash in it? I could buy another place. Better, bigger, more sheep. Would ye say then, faither, that I was a lazy chiel that didna ken how to work? Better ground. Fine, black loam wi a good depth to it. But that wouldna be playing the game, would it? No, I've got to make it work on the same ground, I've got to play ye on the same ground. I'll show ye, I dinna need handicaps or headstarts. The croft is mine and I'll make more o it yet. Ye'll see.

— How long have ye been here now? Nine years? It was this time ye died — the hay time. The place has changed in nine years. I changed it — me, your son. And it's up to me whether or no it changes more in the next year. It'll no take long for the diggers to do their work. It would frichen your faither and your grandfaither delling wi their spades. It frichens me.

— I'm going now, faither. I canna stop here glowering at that stone above ye. I'm no even sure why I came. I kent ye wouldna speak. Am I daft that I thocht I micht find some kind o answer here? Why my land? Why me?

'Why me?'

He was surprised by the sound of his own question in the stillness of the cemetery, among the stones. He looked around but there was no one there to hear.

Saturday night in the bar of the hotel, the lounge bar, and our host, Tom Manson, dispenses glass by glass and tankard by tankard many brews. Young lads are tanking up before departing on the spree, joking in the conspiracy of youth. Tom has his sleeves rolled up and is careful not to stain his tie, the blue one with small fishing flies embroidered on it diagonally, as befits the landlord of an hotel in the Scottish countryside. Two men from the south, up for the fishing, watch the ice cubes melt in their malts and compare the produce of Strathspey with the darker, peatier Hebridean offerings. The stool at the bar where Jonah always sat is empty, whaling and Antarctica forgotten, for poor Jonah is dead and buried a year since. John Campbell has not yet arrived. Margaret Manson is in the kitchen, stirring the broth shortly to be put before the two southern fishermen. Dougie, with a pint and a packet of peanuts, sits near a window, watching nothing.

— I wonder do they all ken. Nobody's said a word yet.

'Hi!'

Alison sat down at the table. She held a glass with a clear liquid and a slice of lemon.

'Hello,' said Dougie. 'I didna see ye come in.'

'No. You were gazing at the fireplace.'

'What's that ye're drinking?'

'Vodka and tonic.' She sipped and looked around the bar. 'Quiet, isn't it?'

'There'll be a few folk in before long,' he said.

'What have you been doing with yourself?'

'Nothing much.'

'Same here.'

Dougie glanced towards the door and saw come in a thin, youngish man who went up to the bar and ordered a drink.

— It's that reporter chiel.

'You're looking very worried,' said Alison.

He blushed. 'Och, I was just thinking.'

— I wonder what she would say... will I tell... that chiel's coming ower this way.

'Dougie Bayne, isn't it?' said the reporter.

'Aye.'

'I'm Alec Munro. We've met before. That day last week.'

'Aye, I mind fine,' said Dougie in a tired voice.

Munro sat down and smiled at Alison.

'Hi,' he said. 'Pleased to meet you. Eh...I didna catch your name?'

'Alison.'

'Alec,' said the reporter. Then he spoke to Dougie. 'It's been quite a week. I expect ye saw the piece in the paper.'

'Aye,' grunted Dougie.

'What's this?' asked Alison.

'Ye're a stranger here? I see. Well, some prospectors have found commercial mineral deposits in the county. Lots o excitement. There have been stories like this before but this time it looks as if it's for certain.'

'Is that good news?' queried Alison.

The tone in her question caught Dougie's attention and he regarded her eagerly.

'You bet,' went on Munro. He fiddled nervously with his tie and took a mouthful of beer. 'This place has aye been on the fringe o things. Unemployment is high here, you know, lot o men oot o work, folk leaving and going south, folk emigrating. Talented folk, brain drain, ye ken the sort o thing. This might stop it, give men a future at home. Oh aye, it's a big chance, a chance we've been waiting for for a long time, a chance we canna miss.'

'What kind of mining is it?' asked Alison.

But Munro was involved in his thesis and ignored the question. 'This county has had a long history o ups and doons. Being a stranger here, ye'll no know all this. We've always been on the fringe and our fortunes have risen and fallen often. When we get a chance like this, we canna afford to let it slip by. It injects a bit o hope into the place.'

— Hope for who? It's my land. What hope is there for me?

'Uranium,' said Dougie.

'Eh?' said Munro, blinking at the interruption.

'Uranium,' repeated Dougie to Alison. 'It's uranium they're for mining.'

She stared at him. 'Here?'

'Aye,' cried Munro. 'Who would have believed it? In canny, couthy auld Caithness. Uranium. Next to oil, what could ye have wished for?'

'What about the pollution?' asked Alison. 'And the radioactivity?'

'We've been a centre o nuclear power for years,' said the reporter. 'We ken how to live wi it up here.'

'It doesn't appeal to me,' said Alison quietly and she took some more vodka and tonic.

'They want some o my ground,' said Dougie.

'Aye, I ken,' said Munro. 'That's one reason why I came ower to talk to ye. Wait a minute.' He fished a notebook from his pocket and opened it. 'What was your first reaction to the news?'

Dougie stared at the poised pen. 'Are ye interviewing me?'

'Just a few questions. In case I can use it in a story. I'll tell ye if I do.'

— Me. In the papers. Better watch my words, especially if it's the neighbours... Funny how ye can never think o the richt thing...

'I'll give you a quote,' said Alison firmly. 'I don't like it at all. Have you any idea what mining will do to your countryside?'

Munro blushed and fiddled with his tie again, and said in a smart-alecky voice, 'Ye canna eat scenery.'

'My God,' breathed Alison.

'What d'ye think, Mr Bayne?' went on Munro.

'It came as a surprise to me,' said Dougie, and the pen moved. 'And to tell ye the truth — dinna write this — I dinna ken richt what to make o it. There's no doubt that it would be o benefit to a lot o folk...'

'Is that all?' urged the pen wielder.

'Well...'

— Damn and blast me, I'm scared to tell him what I really think. Why can they no just all go away and leave me in peace?

'Are ye going to sell your land?' asked Munro.

'It hasna come to that yet,' replied Dougie.

'What's this about your land?' asked Alison.

'Mr Bayne's farm is one of the sites the company want to test,' explained Munro. 'There are certain legalities that have to be gone through.'

'It's a croft,' interrupted Dougie. 'They want to make test drillings on my land and they've given me a paper to sign to gie them permission to go ahead.'

Alison looked concerned.

'Are ye going to sign?' asked Munro, turning to a fresh page in his notebook.

'Are ye writing all this doon?' cried Dougie in alarm. 'No, I havena signed yet. It needs a bit o studying.'

'Don't,' said Alison firmly. 'Don't sign anything until you've seen a solicitor.'

'Do you think that's necessary?' asked the reporter.

'I most certainly do,' said Alison.

— A solicitor. Christ, I never thocht o that.

'Ye seem opposed to this whole idea,' said Munro mildly to Alison. 'Do you know the background — what kind of mine it is, what kind of work it will be, how it may affect the village? Man, it's something for the whole county, this. We've been waiting on something like this for years.'

'I know what you've got already and I think it's very fragile, something to be cherished, and I'm afraid for it,' said Alison.

Munro glanced at Dougie and smiled as if to say 'incomers'.

John Campbell appeared.

'What's this Magnus was telling me, boy?' he cried to Dougie. 'Ye're sitting on a gold mine by all accounts.'

Dougie girned in agony. 'First I've heard aboot it,' he muttered peevishly.

But John was not to be diverted from his quarry. 'I think ye ken fine,' he said over his pint. 'But I suppose we'll have to wait to find out.'

'I must be going up the road,' said Dougie, setting his empty glass on the   table and reaching for the cigarettes in his dungaree pocket.

Munro regarded him carefully but Dougie did not look at him. 'Thank ye for talking to me, Mr Bayne,' he said, always careful to exercise the etiquette of his profession.

'Good nicht to ye, boys,' said Dougie and he went out.

It was not dark yet but the shadows were deepening under the pink and grey-blue brightness.

'Dougie.'

He turned and discovered that Alison had followed him. She came across the tarmac to the van, her face serious.

'Are you all right?' she asked urgently.

'Aye. Why?'

'You left in a hurry. Is all this true about the uranium on your land?'

'I dinna ken,' he said feebly. 'All I know is that an American firm want to prospect and that they've asked me to give them permission in writing, and I havena done it yet.'

'Don't!'

'What d'ye mean don't? It's no as simple as that.'

'It is.'

'No, it's no. There's my neighbours I've got to think o. Ye're a stranger here — I dinna mean to insult ye by saying that, it's just a fact — but ye are...and ye dinna understand, ye canna, it's no your fault.'

Alison remained silent.

'Och, lassie, can ye no see what I mean? Ye're just new here. Ye can...ye may be leaving again soon...'

'No,' she said. 'No. I had intended to stay and I'm not running this time. Have you thought this thing through?'

Dougie shook his head and then checked himself. 'I'm thinking aboot it. I havena seen a solicitor yet but...I havena just myself to think o. The reporter was richt. There's a lot o chiels wi no work...'

'Work,' cried Alison. 'I keep hearing this about people wanting work. Will people never get rid of this notion that to live they need to be given work? All this I work therefore I am bullshit. I am. I am. I am, whether I work or not. People are conditioned to have work given to them so that they're incapable of creating their own work which they would enjoy doing. They are encouraged to stand in assembly lines and clock in and clock off, and they've forgotten how to do anything for themselves. Are you going to give up what you've got for that kind of work? Has nobody here got enough imagination to think of how to earn a living? Do you always have to rush to lick the backsides of outsiders and wag your tails and roll over to have your bellies scratched?'

'What the hell are ye on aboot?' His anger rose from a deep pit of perplexity. 'I dinna understand all that nonsense. It's alricht for ye to talk. Ye've got some money. Some folk have none and maun work. We canna all make stupid, fancy pots.'

Alison stared at him angrily and strode past without another word. He watched for a moment and then got into the van, slamming the door after him.

The darkness around him is almost total. A deep, blue-black Stygian gloom with neither glimmer nor spark to warm the spirit, a musty, fusty jet darkness with neither top nor bottom nor left nor right to it. And then a lightening, only a fraction but enough to reveal a cavern with the walls curved like ribs so that floor and ceiling are joined in a great sweep. The floor is firm enough. And strangely, the air is warm. Dougie advances through the mirk and as he goes forward the walls of the tunnel close ahint him and he cannot turn back but only go on, on into the opening gloom.

And there is a door. Richt in front o him, a great, muckle wooden yett, oak, dark-varnished, wi rows and rows o six-sided heids o coachbolts and broad straps o iron, painted black, stretched across the timmers. On either side the tunnel walls lower and glower, and he keeks up, but there is no top to the door. It soars up and up, oot o sicht intil the black lift.

What do I dae noo? There's a knocker wi a face on it, the face o a bird, a maa, its twa een narrow set and watching me, and hinging fae its beak, a beak wi sic a kype on it ye never did see, a ring. Well, what else to dae but knock.

Clang! Clang! Klangggg! The bells ring and echo as Dougie gies a dunt to the maa's neb. And the door swings open. But does he see a horrible sicht, some twisted, deformed craitur wi green een and slevvers running fae a bloody jaw, some further depth o Hades as black as the Earl o Hell's waistcoat, is Auld Nick there himself hotching on the pipes wi maybe a wee tam o'shanter on his heid atween the twa horns? No. For this isna your eighteenth-century elves and goblins on their annual outing to Alloway for the communion. As the yett swings back, Dougie is blinned by a flood o licht, pink and primrose and orange and purple and white. He raises his hand to shield his dark-weakened een fae the glare. And instead o the foosim Caliban? A large, cheery gentleman in a white suit, that glistens and gleams like armour, coming forward, and a smile on his face like to split it, teeth gold crowned, bootlace tie, a stetson snowdrop white, and a proffered hand. What's this? A riverboat gambler on the Styx?

'Hi, Doug,' cries the man. 'Glad to see yah. Welcome to the mine. Let me take your coat. How's your mother, the dear old lady? It was real nice of you to drop by.'

And the big hand, like a raw hamburger, grips his shoulders in a friendly way and bears him forward as if he is on castors. They are in a great hall, the floor spotless linoleum, the walls a pale pink plastic, now changing to a delicate mauve, syne to a gentle crimson and then again to the faintest of creamy browns. All is light. It oozes from the floor, it beams from above and glances off the furniture. Oh aye, there's a desk and a counter and twa-three chairs — upholstery scarlet. And music. Guitars.

'This is my mine?' he asks incredulously.

'Changed a bit, huh?'

They pass on through doors that slide apart at their approach with a soothing hiss. The colours change and the music changes but not so far as to disturb the senses.

'This is where it all comes fae?' he whispers in disbelief.

'This is where it's at,' says his guide.

In his oily dungarees, he feels out of place, scared lest his tackety boots mark the waxcloth, but when he looks down he finds that mysteriously his garments have changed. Now he wears spotless, seamless, silkily smooth raiment of a kind he has not seen before.

'My claes?'

But his guide ignores the question and ushers him on through another set of hissing doors. 'This is the mine,' says the stetson.

He sees a long gallery, filled with a greenish light, though not a deep, unpleasant cold green but a warm, yellowish shade, such as you might see looking up into the canopy of a tree on a sunny day. But the main thing about the gallery is that it's full o folk. As far as the eye can see, along both sides, a row of men and women. They do not react to the visitors but continue working. Everyone has a pair of gyangs and they are shearing from the walls white ropes of material that fall around their feet like lurks o cloth. Click click click go the gyangs. And the white stuff falls softly, silently to the floor, where others come and pull it away and fold it up and place it in untidy bales on a conveyor belt running the length of the gallery and bearing it away in a never-ending stream.

'This mine produces ten billion, five million and sixty-eight thousand tons of uranium per diem,' announces his guide. 'Prime grade.'

They go through a door to another room, where there is another conveyor belt, and on it long strings of bright pink sausages. At the end of the belt women in overalls and delicate little hats gather the sausages and pack them nimbly into striped paper boxes, six at a time. Their fingers never stop, always gleaning sausages half a dozen at a clasp and neatly folding them into the boxes.

'We have six hundred and forty-one belts carrying the processed uranium to the packers, of whom there are five thousand three hundred and two employed full-time,' described the guide. 'If you look closely you'll probably know some of them.'

Wi a start, Dougie recognises Will Auld, Jean fae the shop, Jim Sinclair the joiner, Pogo the tink, Helen and her man, Alec Munro, John Knox in his cassock, the Hieland laddie, Flora MacDonald, Betty the nurse, Rob Roy, Harry Lauder (Sir), oor Wullie, Davie Sutherland and Isobel, auld Macdonald fresh fae Glencoe in his sark, Jonah, the Soutars o Selkirk, twa dugs, the Secretary o State, Drs Livingstone and Finlay, the shadow Secretary o State, Jimmy Shand withoot his accordion, Annie Laurie, Red Rory of the Eagles, Mr Bremner the minister aa in black, Moira Anderson, the auld man o Hoy, the wee cooper o Fife, Mrs Macpherson o Inveran, Tom and Margaret Manson, the Moderator o the General Assembly, Kenneth McKellar, Jocky Shearer, aa Jock Tamson's bairns, Andy Stewart — aa the shither o this day and mony anither ane. They're aa at it wi the gyangs or putting sausages o uranium intil peedie boxes, six in each ane, neat as ye could want. Sic a scene o industry ye would hardly credit, no, though ye'd downed a gallon o heavy.

'So that's how ye do it,' says Dougie. 'I'm impressed.'

'That's the way it is,' says the guide cheerily. 'Our production is the highest in the world, our earnings touched a record last week — fifteen-x bracket three minus y to the power n bracket squared billion dollars. We love the skill and hardworking integrity of the people of the Highlands. Would ye believe that we wear out six hundred and nineteen pairs of gyangs a day?'

'D'ye tell me that now?' says Dougie.

But what's this? More surprises for our intrepid explorer of dreams. Forward comes a black and white collie, who ignores him and goes at once to the guide and jumps up and licks his face and wags her tail like a whirlwind.

'Sit down, Bess,' says the guide.

'Would ye like a cup o tea?'

Behold his mother pushing a trolley with a giant urn on it, hissing and bubbling. Jings, they're aa working here.

'No thanks,' he says, 'I've just had a pie and chips.'

'Now come through here,' says the guide, and on again they go, more doors sliding away to admit them.

This inner chamber has no one in it apart from themselves. But there is a table, a long, polished, oaken brute o a thing, flanked by rows o chairs, and in the middle a decanter wi thistles on it and filled wi a clear liquid. On the further wall there hang two portraits. The guide pushes forward and regards them wi reverent een. They are very familiar.

'This is a portrait of Sir Magnus Gunn,' declares the guide. 'He used to be village headman here, a man of great foresight. He knew where it was at. He died Lord Provost. And this...' turning to the other picture '...is the man we owe it all to. He is the pioneer, hard-working, dogged, but with it all, a simple farmer.'

'My father,' breathes Dougie with a start.

For it is he. Daniel George Bayne. The face stares straight down at the watchers, the mouth slightly open, the lips parted, the whole expression vacant as if uncomprehending.

'What's he doing here?' gasps Dougie.

'It's all due to him,' says the guide in quiet awe. 'He worked this land before we came. He gave it to us in a gift of such generosity.'

'No!' Dougie's cry echoes in the room.

The eyes in the picture take on life, the lips crease up at the edges and Daniel George Bayne smiles. 'Aye, boy,' he says. 'Ye ken it all noo. D'ye see this?' And the thick, peasant's finger points down to a small plaque.

'Hero worker,' reads Dougie.

'Yup,' cries the guide. 'Good ol' Dan. He's our kinda fella. Come on, I'll show you some more but first some refreshment. Coffee?'

Dougie nods dumbly. The guide rings a little bell that is standing on the table and in the wall beside the portraits a door flips up, revealing two plastic cups, steaming. The guide presses buttons and sugar and milk spurt. Suddenly beside them appears a woman, excited, her hair dishevelled, panting, her eyes flashing. It is Alison. Her clothes are rags and her skin is dirty.

'Take me away from here,' she gasps. 'I am a slave. Rescue me. Dougie, save me.'

And now he is running, with Alison faint in his arms. She is not heavy and his tackety boots speed like noisy lightning over the shinging floors. The colours of the wall flash by in a blurred kaleidoscope — orange, mauve, purple, green, crimson, tangerine, emerald, indigo. And the faces turn and fingers point and the tongues chatter. The enemies are closing in on every side and the door, the portal to safety, is inching inexorably shut.

'Dinna look back,' he shouts.

'Save me. Save me. Take me away from here,' pleads his burden.

The walls close in, the lights dim. His feet sink into soft, wet peat and he lifts them and thrusts them forward with wrenching effort.

'Douglas Bayne,' booms the deep voice. 'You have interfered in matters that do not concern you. You have impeded the course of science. You have been selfish and stubborn and you have broken the laws of your community. You are condemned to death. Have you anything to say before sentence is carried out?'

'I didna ken, your honour,' says Dougie weakly, afraid to look at the eagle face with the flowing white curls.

A great weight pushes down on his head, forcing it low, almost between his knees. His hands are gripped and tied behind his back. Someone turns his shirt collar in so that his neck is bared...

CHAPTER SEVEN

When Dougie woke, his neck was stiff. The pillow had slipped sideways.

The details of the dream began to fade rapidly from his memory until all that remained was the image of a row of faces turned in his direction, familiar neighbourly faces with expectant eyes.

The rest of the day passed uneventfully, as most Sundays did, and on Monday he went to see the solicitor.

Hector Robertson and his office had aged together. For decades he had sat at his desk at the window overlooking the street and the folk passing, executing wills, arranging the sale of houses, writing character references for delinquents, writing contracts and organising the renting of shops. As the paint cracked on the walls, so deep lines etched the solicitor's face. As the stoor gathered on the bookcase, so did the drifts of fluff and ash and detritus in the creases and pockets of the solicitor's waistcoat. As the bundles of files yellowed in the presses, so did their owner's liver before the onslaught of malts. What could this aging practitioner of the anciaunt and noble laws of Scotia do for Dougie?

'This is a difficult business,' said Robertson, holding the Redriver paper at arm's length. Pride would not admit to long sight. 'A difficult business.'

Dougie shifted on his chair, a greyish, plush contraption that creaked as he moved.

'It's true what you say,' went on Robertson. 'If you signed this and they found uranium, you'd have to sell the land to them.' He let the paper fall to the desk and moved his eyes upward to stare at the ceiling.

'So...so what d'ye advise?' asked Dougie hesitantly.

The eyes dropped quickly to look at the crofter and blinked.

'Advise? Aye, well. You'll need to make up your mind. I can tell you what's likely to happen if you sign...but it's for you to sign or not. If you sign there might be money in it for you.' The eyes swivelled ceilingward again. 'Is it seven year now since your father passed away?'

'Nine,' growled Dougie.

'Nine, did you say? Well, well, time surely flies. I would hardly have credited it was that long. It seems like just the other day that he was in here...aye, well, we're all getting older.'

And that was all the advice Dougie got from the solicitor, but at least it had been confirmed that the contract was, as Dougie saw it, a bad one. Maybe he could ask them to change it so that they could go ahead with their tests and if they found anything they could draw up another agreement. That would give every chiel time to think, especially himself.

Magnus Gunn was not pleased that he had not signed, when the councillor came as he thought to collect the document that would ensure prosperity. In fact, Magnus was very displeased and showed it. After all, he had driven two miles out of his way.

'Ye canna be so deugend on this, Dougie,' he said. 'Ye're holding up the progress o the place, wi ye and your didoes.'

'It's my land,' said Dougie firmly. 'There's a lot o things to be considered.'

'Well, I'll ask them if they'll draw up another agreement,' girned Magnus. 'There's a meeting o the council on Thursday when we'll be discussing this, and I think Nicholl will be attending when we speak. I'll ask him.'

Tuesday morning came, rich with dew. The forecast

promised grand drying weather for the rest of the week, and Dougie decided to cut some hay. He hitched the old mower to the tractor and started into the first park, where the clover and the thistles, the vetches, speedwell and the grasses lushly waited. The blades sliced and the vegetation fell cleanly before them, and the scent of freed sap rose from the land. Many a moosag lost his home that day.

On the top of the day, Dougie ran out of fags and drove down to the hotel. The public bar was empty when he went in but Margaret soon appeared.

'Fine day,' she said. 'Pint?'

'Aye.'

'What's doing wi ye?'

'Hay.'

Then Jim Sinclair the joiner came in, his hair like a bird's nest. He ordered a pint of lager and proceeded to clean his pipe. He glanced at Dougie.

'Big things afoot nowadays, by all accounts,' he said.

'So it seems,' muttered Dougie.

'Magnus is buzzing around like a red-arsed bee. Thinks he's back in the army.'

'What way?'

The joiner took his time before answering, poking in his pipe with a knife and blowing out loose shreds of tobacco.

'This mining business,' he said. 'They're after your land, too, I heard.'

'Aye, they are. But they havena got it yet.'

'No, no, they havena got it yet,' said the joiner. He filled the bowl of his pipe and then took a mouthful of lager. 'It's warm the day. I was needing that.'

A match was struck and grey clouds of smoke were born.

'I dinna ken what to make o this business,' he went on. 'Hardly a month passes but some chiel comes up fae the south and tells us o the great things that can be done.'

'Ye dinna think they micht be richt this time?' Dougie always found it hard to ascertain what was running through the joiner's mind. Jim Sinclair gave little away.

'Will Auld has signed a piece o paper,' he continued, between sucks on the pipe. 'This time it may be the real thing. But I dinna hold wi all this fuss. I've seen it too often afore. News like a new balloon, and soon all the wind escapes and all ye've got is a flipe o useless rubber. Magnus is like a bairn wi a new toy.'

Dougie laughed and felt the warmth of comradeship.

'They asked me to sign the same paper Will Auld signed. Magnus was keen to get me to sign.'

'Dinna be in a hurry to put your name to the end of such a thing,' said the joiner.

'Mining isna like anything else,' said Dougie.

Jim Sinclair grunted and drank.

'There's the pollution side o it, too,' went on the crofter.

'They're no thinking o that,' said the other. 'They're thinking o the jobs and the new money. But they micht be disappointed there too. I canna see more than twenty men working at any mine. If it was that big, it would have been opened up years ago. And it micht run oot after a dozen years. Where would we be then? Left wi a muckle hole in the ground and damn all else.'

'Micht be handy for a dump,' grinned Dougie.

They drank.

Dougie left the bar a happier man. He grabbed Bess who all the while had been asleep in the front seat of the van and gromished her lugs with such delighted vigour that the poor bick groaned in annoyance.

— There are others who think as I do. I didna expect Jim Sinclair to be on my side. Wi Alison, that's two. There's maybe more. I micht win oot yet. Now, who's all this crowd ootside the shop, waiting for the bread van? There's Donald's Jamie, face like a lichthoose; and Donnie; and that's Peggy Gunn — I wonder what she's thinking, now that Magnus is heid-bummer. Is she looking at me wi daggers? There's Catriona too — the Gunns are oot in force the day. Gunn — gun — cannon — bazooka —

Magnus Bazooka, President and Minister of Defence of the
Caithness banana republic. I wonder what they're saying
about me. I'm getting paranoid. All een are on me. That
was a funny dream the other nicht. I wonder what the
council will do. Compulsory purchase? Magnus the bailiff,
wi big bobby's feet — Corporal Magnus — 'On wi ye, lads,
take no prisoners' — torches arching onto the scroos,
flaming arches, rainbows o lowes. The trial o Magnus
Sellar. Och, poor Magnus, he's only doing his job.

— I'll soon get the hay done at this rate. Lucky so far.
No stones to take the teeth oot o the blade, and a good
crop o clover to keep the skittering army happy in the
winter. What was that? That cry? Heard it above the noise
o the tractor. There it is again. A corncrake — that's what
it is. God, that's rare nowadays. Very few left, I was
reading. What a lonely, eldritch kind o a sound it is. Krekk!
Krekk! What's it saying? Go back, go back, calls the grouse.
Krekk? Maybe it's swearing at me, damning me for de-
stroying its habitat. Dinna fash, corncrake, away ye go into
the barley and bide there for a few months. I'll no hurt
ye. They want to drive me oot, too — I ken how ye feel.
It's a haunted voice, ye've got. Will ye still be here when
I'm gone? Ye'll be like a minister wi no congregation, a
shepherd wi no flock. Ye can stand alane and lay off ye a
langersome krekk to naebody. Naething between ye and
the lift, but the radioactive efterwal o us. Does fall-oot
look like fanns o snow against the dykes? Or like a fine,
white stoor, like icing sugar? And us? Burnt tae cinders,
fit for the aisehole, fertiliser for gykes and thirsles, and
shelter for the corncrake. Your krekk micht be a laugh,
birdy. Are ye laughing because ye can see what's coming?
I'll be damned if I sell this land. There are others who'll
stick up for me, now. Alison. I must tell her I've decided.
They can take their piece o paper and stick it up their
banana-uranium republic.

About tea-time, English holidaymakers — a retired
couple from Durham — arrived with a caravan. They

asked if they could camp anywhere and Dougie showed them a corner of a field where they could stay. He thought they were nice folk, the man a cheery, jaunty fellow with a pipe and a tartan bonnet, the woman a scrawny sort o a craitur with blue-rinsed hair.

'It's bonny here,' said the man. 'I think we'll stay for ever.'

'He's been saying that everywhere we've stopped,' giggled his wife.

Dougie smiled indulgently.

'It's been the grandest holiday,' continued the man. 'It's lucky folk who live in the country. There's no pub for sale in this area?'

'Aye, Jamie,' said Dougie as he wound down the window of the van.

The old man bent and filled the opening with his red face. 'Ho, ho, boy, off tae the pub again? Ye was there at dinner time.'

'This hay is thirsty work.'

'And good weather for it, too.'

'Coming doon for a glass?'

'No. No me. Donnie and me are for the fishing again. We got some grand coddies last nicht.'

'The old man and the sea.'

Donald's Jamie laughed until he began to cough, and he straightened, taking a hankie from his anorak pocket and blowing his nose loudly.

'D'ye want a run doon to the pier?' asked Dougie.

'Can we go to the hoose first and get Donnie?'

'Peggy Gunn hadna many good words to say for ye the day, when ye gied past at dinner time.' Donald's Jamie was grinning maliciously as he spoke.

'Oh,' grunted Dougie as if he didn't care.

'Ye're a greedy, grasping so-and-so, according to her,' went on the passenger.

Dougie turned the van off the road and came to a stop at the pierhead. A tide of gulls ebbed from a clump of fishboxes. He watched them wing into the grey sky.

'We can talk aboot that anither time,' said Donald's Jamie. 'Come on, young chiel. The fish are waiting wi their mooths open.'

Grandfather and grandson ambled down the pier with their fishing rods, set them upright against some creels and disappeared in search of limpets.

— Whose side is he on?

Dougie got out and regarded the slates of the Shore Cottage roof. He found the path through the marram and slowly made his way towards the cottage. Behind him the benty hills rose and cut off the world of the pier.

The door was closed. He knocked and waited. 'Hello,' he cried. No answer. He tried the latch but it would not move.

He stepped back from the door and scratched his head, and felt lonely.

'So that's the way o it. There's to be a public meeting in two weeks' time.'

The councillor's voice was heavy with sadness. Dougie almost felt sorry for him.

'What about my idea that we should have separate agreements for tests?' asked the crofter.

Magnus had not bothered to get out of his car, a hint that he did not intend to stay for long. He studied the dashboard before answering. Dougie stood bent at the open window.

'No use at all,' sighed the councillor. 'It's no worth their while to fiddle aboot like that. They said the cost o this kind o survey is such that it's either all or nothing. They need agreement on all the sites they want. Otherwise, it's no use taking the equipment up fae the south.'

'Oh,' said Dougie slowly.

'Ye've put the kibosh on the whole scheme wi your deugendness,' said Magnus. 'My God, it's no too late for ye to think again.' And he looked pleadingly at Dougie.

'Ach,' said the young man, 'I'll wait for the meeting now that they've called it.'

— Say goodbye to your OBE, Magnus.

'Mind, it's no just ye,' said the councillor. 'There's a gey few against it.'

'Is that right?'

'Bloody incomers, the lot o them. Retired up here. They've nae need to work, or else they've got jobs already. They're no thinking o others.'

— Dinna cown, Magnus. This is democracy in action.

'There's a few folk in this village who'll no thank ye for what ye've done, Dougie. I widna count myself among them, mind. I've tried to understand ye, but ye're making it gey hard.'

'Aye,' said Dougie slowly.

'Ye havena won yet though.' Defiance rang in Magnus's voice. 'Just wait for the meeting. Ye micht have to change your mind.'

And with that, they parted.

The good weather held and Dougie began to bale his hay crop. The tractor lugged the baler around the parks, the tines gripping and stuffing the grass into the mechanical maw, solid rectangles of bound and knotted fodder dropping from the extended metallic anus. It was steady but pleasant work and, as he hurled up and down the length of his land, he felt proud of it and pleased with himself. But in the evenings, anxiety crept back.

One day there was a thunderstorm. His mother rushed to put towels over the mirror and bade him not to stand near the window, lest lightning coming down the lum needed an exit. He did not bother to argue or point out the absurdity of such superstitions but took a book and read until the weather cleared. As the rain drummed on the windowpane he thought again of the black rain falling on Hiroshima and Nagasaki, and the little thuds on the glass were like drumbeats in his heart, tocsins in the night.

EXTERIOR. STILL OF DOUNREAY ATOMIC POWER STATION.

SOUND FX. WIND AND CURLEW.

VOICE OVER   Here on the bleak, remote northern coast of Scotland sits this great metal ball which has become a symbol of the modern progressive Highlands.

CAMERA PANS LEFT TO SHOW

REPORTER STANDING ON SHORE.

REPORTER   Dounreay Nuclear Power Development Establishment has been here for many years and since 1962 has been pumping electricity into the National Grid.

JUMPCUT. HELICOPTER

OVERFLYING MOORLAND.

REPORTER   Soon, however, Dounreay may not be the only aspect of the nuclear industry to be found here. Or that is the hope of the Redriver mining giant. Beneath this blanket of peat

CAMERA PANS FROM

MOORLAND TO FARMLAND

REPORTER   and this farmland there may be reserves of uranium which the Redriver Corporation wishes to mine. I say may because as yet the prospectors are uncertain how large the reserves are, and whether or not they are commercial. To find that out, test bores have to be made.

JUMPCUT. REPORTER STANDING EXTERIOR.

SOUND FX. SHEEP BLEATING.

REPORTER   And that's the rub. For many years the communities along these northern shores have welcomed the nuclear industry, when their southern neighbours have put obstacle after obstacle in the path of development. Redriver perhaps expected no problems.

JUMPCUT. OFFICE INTERIOR.

ROGER NICHOLL, REDRIVER INC.   There are always problems. In this case, we have had very few. In fact I want to state publicly that we have had full cooperation from the local authorities and the media. The people have taken a very responsible attitude to the prospect of a local mining industry.

REPORTER   But there has been local opposition.

NICHOLL   There is always some opposition. And the people
      have a right to know what we intend to do. Once
      they have been given the facts I feel sure there will
      be no more problems. After all, they are being
      presented with new concepts, new ideas, very quick-
      ly. If I were a crofter, I would ask questions myself.
      Redriver appreciates this concern.

JUMPCUT. FIELDS.

REPORTER   Last week, a number of the crofters in the area
      was asked to give their permission for test drilling
      on their land. Mr Will Auld is one. Mr Auld, you do
      not object to these tests?

CAMERA PANS RIGHT
TO WILL AULD.

WILL AULD, CROFTER   No, no, I dinna object.

REPORTER   You are not concerned about adverse envi-
      ronmental effects?

ZOOM FOR CLOSE-UP
OF CROFTER.

WILL AULD   No. No.

REPORTER   Some of your neighbours have refused to
      sign.

WILL AULD   Some have, aye, but...

JUMPCUT. REPORTER WALKING
ACROSS MOOR WITH ALEC
MUNRO. TRACKING SHOT.

REPORTER   What Mr Auld did not say was that the
      agreement to permit test drilling contained a clause
      that would give Redriver the right to buy any land
      that has commercial deposits of ore. Is this why there
      has been some objection to the scheme?

ZOOM TO HEAD AND SHOULDERS
SHOT OF ALEC MUNRO.

ALEC MUNRO, LOCAL JOURNALIST   In a word, yes. Some
      farmers are concerned by that clause and would like
      to see it changed. However, I think that you should
      see this as a minor obstacle, which we hope can be
      sorted out.

ZOOM OUT TO TRACKING
SHOT OF REPORTER
AND ALEC MUNRO.

ALEC MUNRO   We have very high unemployment here. We've not been able to enjoy the benefits of developments further south.

REPORTER   The environmental question does not concern you?

ALEC MUNRO   Dounreay has been here since 1955. Caithness has welcomed the nuclear industry and has benefited greatly from it. If Dounreay were to close, it would be an economic disaster and although we are naturally concerned about our scenery and so on, which we think is unique, and we have a tourist industry, we hope that a way forward can be found. This is a chance we cannot afford to turn away.

JUMPCUT. OFFICE INTERIOR.

JOHN MOODY, LOCAL COUNCILLOR   We have over six hundred square miles of splendid moorland scenery and some of the most spectacular coastal scenery in the whole of Scotland, if not Europe. I think we can afford to give up a little for economic reasons. The folk have got to work. We dinna get paid for looking at heather. *(laughs)*

JUMPCUT. EXTERIOR. REPORTER
OUTSIDE VILLAGE HALL.

REPORTER   But not all welcome this possible development that could lead to the prosperity promised by Redriver. At a planning meeting last week, several councillors expressed concern at the way Redriver is pushing for a quick decision. The Highland sense of time is not given to pleasing American businessmen. The extent of the opposition is as yet unclear. No one is willing to talk openly to us.

CAMERA PANS RIGHT
TO FOCUS ON HALL.

REPORTER   Tonight in the hall behind me, these canny villagers are meeting to hear the corporation's plans for their village. It is being held here at the special request of Redriver. Normally such meetings take place in Wick or Thurso, the two towns in the county. But the question is...after so many years of contented marriage to nuclear power, is this the first step towards divorce?

Dougie leaned back in his chair and considered the programme. First the papers, then the television. And Will Auld on it, too. Wi his muckle face, it was a wonder they didna have to turn the camera sideways to get it all in. He remembered passing the post office the day before and the temptation that entered his mind to let the air out of the tyres of the old man's bike when he saw it propped against the wall. The childish idea had pleased him, and he wished again that he had done it. Would the TV crowd be at the meeting tonight? He had seen the helicopter going over but had not known its errand. They had not come to interview him — likely Alec Munro or Redriver had seen to it that no one came near him. But if others were opposed to the scheme, it was no longer up to him alone.

'Are ye coming doon to the meeting?'

'Och, no,' said his mother. 'What would I be doing at a meeting? Ye can go. Dinna spend too muckle in the pub afterwards. The bobbies'll be on the go.'

As he drove to the village, he thought of Alison. He had not seen her for near on two weeks. Neither had Donald's Jamie, when he had cautiously speired after her whereabouts, and the two men had concluded that she must have gone off south again.

Her words had, however, stayed with him. The anger with which she had spoken that night outside the hotel was a dim memory but he was still intrigued by the ideas she had. He wanted very much to see her and to ask her what she had meant.

He arrived at the hall just five minutes or so before the appointed time. The ground around the building was packed with cars and he had to search for a parking space. Once inside, he slipped into a seat near the back. A few heads turned in his directon and nodded, but most of the crowd were too busy blethering among themselves to notice his arrival. On the platform at the far end of the hall stood a table, a row of chairs and a blackboard. It was still bright outside and the hall curtains had been left open. This atmosphere of dusty, wan sunlight and the blackboard made Dougie think of being back at school.

A door opened beside the platform and a hush descended on the throng. Alistair the teacher came out and went up the short flight of steps to the table. After a few seconds he was followed by Magnus Gunn, Jocky Shearer, John Moody, Roger Nicholl and a tall, thin man whom Dougie did not recognise. The platform party chatted and smiled to each other as they took their places.

'Hello,' said Alison in an eager whisper, sitting down beside Dougie.

'I thocht I would never see ye again.'

'I've been away. I just got back this evening and found this meeting on. What's been happening?'

'Nothing,' he murmured. 'But we micht find oot tonight.'

'There's a big crowd,' she said.

They looked across the rows of heads — hats, hair of all colours, bonnets, bald patches, head scarves.

'I dinna ken half o them,' confessed Dougie.

On the platform, Alistair rose and announced that he was to be the chairman for the evening. He welcomed everybody and thanked them all for coming to what could be an historic assembly. He said that each member of the 'panel', as he called it, would speak for a few minutes and then would answer questions, 'if there are any'.

Magnus spoke first and urged his fellow citizens to listen carefully to what Redriver had to offer, because here was an opportunity that would not come their way again. Apart from that, he said little that was either new or exciting. No one had any questions. Nicholl spoke next, describing the work that Redriver carried out elsewhere in the world and referring from time to time to a flipchart that he produced and hung over the blackboard. Jocky Shearer conveyed the feelings of the council on the matter and hinted at grants and subsidies. Then, the stranger was introduced as Mr Williams, a nuclear scientist, and he gave a spiel about uranium mining and industrial safety. Finally

John Moody got up and more or less repeated the
exhortations delivered by Magnus.

This sermon in five voices lasted for a good forty
minutes and was received virtually in silence.

'Now I can throw the meeting open to questions from
the floor,' said Alistair. 'Please keep your questions brief
and to the point.'

Alec Munro stood up first and asked how many men
could expect to find work through this new project.
Nicholl was unable to give a precise figure but he thought
it likely that several dozen would find permanent employment. Someone asked how long it would take to establish
a mine. As if waiting for a cue, Nicholl stated that it would
depend to a large degree on the villagers themselves.
Redriver was keen to start but unless the local authority
and the landowners made up their minds about the
scheme the Corporation 'naturally' would have to consider the wisdom of their investment.

Then a young man stood up and half-turned to the
audience before putting his question. 'Are the folk here,'
he said, 'aware that during the mining of uranium a gas
called radon is released that when inhaled by the miners
causes an unusually high incidence of lung cancer?'

Heads jerked up. Who was this chiel? His tongue was
Highland, not Caithness. Bonnets and headscarves becked
and bowed to each other and a murmur of excitement
filled the hall.

'Mr Nicholl, can you deal with that?' asked Alistair.

'Yes. The questioner is perfectly right but he is forgetting that in a modern mine safety is paramount and
ventilation equipment would ensure a perfectly safe level
of any contaminant in the atmosphere of the mine.' And
he added with a knowing smile, 'You must remember of
course that we would not be creating anything new and
terrible. The uranium is there already, as is the radon, and
for centuries our ancestors have been walking over it
without apparent harm.'

The councillors smiled and nodded to each other.

'I have another question,' said the stranger.

'Yes,' said Alistair uncertainly.

'Would the representative of Redriver care to comment on the fact that the incidence of lung cancer in miners in the company's mines in South Africa is thirty-five per cent above the national average in that country?'

Nicholl rose to his feet, his face set. 'I fail to see what that has to do with the issue facing us,' he declared.

Alison touched Dougie's arm and grinned, as if to say this was fun. Some of the villagers obviously did not agree with her and there were shouts of 'Here, here!' and 'This isna Africa' and 'Sit doon'.

'May I ask who you are, sir?' went on Nicholl. Magnus, Jocky and John levelled their machine-gun eyes on the front row, where the stranger was standing.

'I represent BANISH News.'

This caused bewilderment and silence.

'BANISH stands for Ban Nuclear Industry in the Scottish Highlands,' explained the man. 'My name is Tom Sneckie and we publish a newsletter. Copies will be on sale outside the hall...'

'We'll banish ye,' cried someone in the audience, and the hall filled with laughter. When it subsided, Alec Munro got up again.

'I want to point out,' he said, 'that Mr Sneckie's point is a serious one but I don't think it central to this meeting, which is called mainly to inform us about Redriver's proposals.'

'Thank you, Alec,' said Alistair, trying to regain his authority as chairman. 'Any more? Yes...Helen.'

– Helen?

Dougie sat up. Yes, it was Helen. He had not seen her for a while but across the assembled heads she appeared as beautiful as ever.

'How does Redriver propose to dispose of the tailings, the waste from any mine, and is this waste material not itself radioactive? And how long will the mine be operative? And what happens to the mess after it closes down?'

Helen sat down quickly. The audience were once again

hushed. After all, she was a local lassie, one o their ain. Sensible and clever. Let's see what they say now.

Nicholl answered by outlining Redriver's commitment to landscape architecture, tree planting and proper waste disposal, and he emphasised that there would be minimal disturbance to the 'beautiful, magnificent, wild scenery' of the region. Local bodies concerned with conservation and the environment would be fully involved in the decision-making process, he added.

Another man stood up and waved his hand to attract the attention of the chairman. 'We're getting off the track here a bit,' he said in a firm, loud voice. 'They want to open a mine here that would give us boys some work and there are two or three wi well-paying, comfy jobs already — and I mean farmers as well as others — that are worried aboot birds and scenery and...There are no trees here anyway.' This provoked laughter and a round of applause. 'Go on, tell them, Geordie,' called a supporter. Emboldened, he did just that.

'Dounreay's been here for years,' he cried. 'When that opened I mind folk saying that if it blew up we'd be wiped off the map. It hasna exploded yet. There are just as many maas now as there were then. Dinna let us lose the place altogether, boys. If a mine means less lads on the broo, I say let's start a mine.'

Through the laughter and shouts that followed, the man from BANISH tried to make himself heard. Dougie caught only snatches of it. 'My friend...Dounreay's safety record...we know nothing about what goes on...'

Alistair, hammerless, chapped on the platform table with his knuckles until the noise subsided. 'Ladies and gentlemen,' he cried. 'Order please, or we'll get nowhere.'

A woman stood up and received the chair's permission to speak.

'I would like to support what Geordie has just said,' she declared. 'It's all very well for them wi work already to talk but my bairns have left the school and what prospects have they got?'

'What prospects would they get from radiation?' Dougie thought it was Helen who called but he could not be sure.

After that the proceedings settled into a tedious routine of question and answer. The spleen had been vented, it seemed, at least for the time being. Towards the end, one of the speakers, John Moody it was, made reference to those who were holding the community's future to ransom because of their reluctance to part with 'certain permissions'. Dougie's brows went down and he felt stubborn anger pulsing. It was finally resolved that there be set up a committee to look into all aspects of the scheme, taking into consideration the views of every sector.

Magnus Gunn nominated Alistair to be chairman of the committee, and it was hard to tell whether the teacher was pleased or annoyed by this new responsibility, but all approved and he accepted the role. Someone from the floor then nominated Magnus himself, and Mr Bremner the minister found himself elected by acclamation, and John Moody, and a few others. Alec Munro declined to accept, saying that it would interfere with his impartiality as a journalist.

Alison stood up and Dougie was suddenly overcome by blind panic.

'I nominate Dougie Bayne for the committee,' she said.

That did it. All eyes turned to the back of the hall. Dougie, face red like a partan, stared at a knothole in the floor and the brown, hard pupil stared back at him.

'No,' he hissed and tugged Alison back into her chair.

'I think...I think the committee's big enough,' said Alistair hesitantly. 'Mr Ure can represent the farmers.'

— What do I do now? There's only one thing for it...

'Thank you,' Dougie found himself on his feet, speaking. 'But I dinna think I want to be...eh...on the committee. Thank you all the same.'

And he sagged like an empty pock into his chair.

'What did ye do that for?' he whispered.

'I'll tell you later,' said Alison cryptically.

After a few minutes the meeting broke up and the folk began to disperse in a cloud of conversation. Donald's Jamie made his way through the mob.

'Ye nearly got yourself a position,' he said gleefully to Dougie.

'Och, husht,' pleaded the crofter.

'Hard luck,' said the old man to Alison. 'That was a good move. It's aye the same crowd on them committees.'

'That's what I thought,' she agreed blithely.

John Campbell went past and put in his twopence worth. 'Ye'll be standing for parliament next, boy.'

'Come on,' said Dougie. 'Let's get oot o here.'

In the crowd funnelling through the entrance, Helen came up and grabbed his arm. 'Ye should have taken your place,' she urged.

He thought of sand-dunes. 'They didna want me on it anyway,' he muttered. 'They ken where I stand.'

Helen put her hand on his wrist and squeezed it. 'Dinna gie up,' she whispered. 'Sandy and me are behind ye.' The mention of her husband's name and the appearance of that husband at her shoulder scattered his memory of the dunes.

Outside the evening had grown cool and a pink tinge was in the sky.

'Fancy a refreshment?' he said to Alsion.

'That's a good idea,' she said, 'but not in the hotel. It'll be packed. Come down to the cottage.'

CHAPTER EIGHT

Shore Cottage was a cavern of fading brightness when they arrived. Its windows faced west and were catching the last retreating light, but it was growing chilly inside and Alison told him to put on the fire. An old fishing basket by the hearth sat full of sea-drift.

'Coffee?' she asked.

He grunted his agreement with this as he arranged the kindling. A few minutes later the salt-soaked wood began to spit little sparks onto the hearth. They sat and drank and ate oatcakes smeared with butter and crowdie. Since his last visit, a battered couch had arrived and the potter's wheel had been pushed further from the fire to make room for it.

'I've a better idea,' she said and went to the press and brought out a bottle. 'Wine. Fancy some?'

He couldn't remember having had any and accepted a glass out of curiosity. It was dark red and had a bitter-sweet taste.

'Bew joless,' he read from the label on the bottle.

'Beaujolais,' she corrected.

He repeated the word clumsily. 'It tastes good whatever.'

'Don't drink it so fast.'

'Is it strong?'

'Not too bad.'

'Why did ye put me up for the committee?' he asked at length.

'It's your land they're after. You've a right to be on it.'

'I'm glad I'm no on it. I was in the running once for being the treasurer o the Young Farmers but I wasna keen. Anyway, Magnus wouldna be wanting me on a committee wi him.'

'He's your enemy, isn't he?'

'Och no, no an enemy.' He was silent for a moment and then smiled. 'I hit him once. Oh aye. I didna hurt him. I didna hit him richt.'

He saw that this amused her and told the story in more detail.

'But you're not enemies now?' she asked.

'In a small place like this? That would be ridiculous. It doesna do to harbour grudges against a neighbour. Anyway I was drunk, blazing.'

The fireglow faded and he bent to put on more sticks. The wine lay in his stomach with the warmth of a cat. He felt very relaxed. Alison rose and put on a cassette player.

'What kind o music's that?' he asked.

'Rachmaninov,' she said. 'Piano concerto.'

They listened in silence. He had never bothered with classical music but, with the wine and the fire and the comfortable proximity of this English girl, the notes seemed to fit exactly the way he was feeling. There was a savage kind of melancholy in it, an impresssion of opening vastnesses, land stretching for miles and miles and becoming or not becoming heaving wastes of sea.

'Thinking?' asked Alison.

'Aye,' he replied dreamily. And then he did something which when he recalled it surprised him. He described his thoughts, or tried to. 'I was thinking aboot my mother,' he said. 'She's a poetic kind o a soul and I've only just realised it. D'ye ken what she put on my father's gravestone — he's been dead for some years — I sleep but my heart waketh. I've never really understood why.'

Alison smiled at him and he felt no embarrassment.

'I used to write poetry myself,' he went on. 'Och it was just rubbish. D'ye like poetry?'

'Sometimes. But tell me more about your family.'

'There's nothing to tell. We're just ordinary folk. Ordinary gaun-aboot bodies.'

'I don't understand you half the time.'

The wine was good.

'I dinna ken myself either sometimes. Here I am making a fuss aboot a bit o ground. But I canna gie it up. It's part o me. When I was a young chiel, I hated it. I would have left but my faither made me stop. Now I dinna want to go.'

'I understand.'

'D'ye?' He looked at her suspiciously. 'Ye've never said how ye came to be here.'

'I used to stay in London but...well, I had a row with the man I stayed with. No, it wasn't a row, it was a complete break. He left me and I...One day I nearly broke a window in Oxford Stret. I saw my reflection in it and I hated myself so much that I almost swung my bag at it. To destroy that image of myself. I remember the window. There were two plastic ducks on springs that kept bobbing up and down. That's me, I thought, like a bloody yo-yo. I went and got drunk, completely pissed, and then I was sick on the bus. Even then, people ignored me. I could have poured petrol over myself and struck a match and no one would have cared.'

She paused and he thought she was going to cry.

'Funny now, looking back on it,' she said. 'Anyway I decided I'd had enough of the great, stinking metropolis. I decided I should try to make a go of it as a potter somewhere in the country. So I packed everything in the car and drove and drove. I got this far because it was the furthest I could go without putting the car on a ferry. And suddenly everybody was so friendly and strangers spoke to me...and, well, that's it. Here I am.'

He did not know what to say. They sat and listened to the spitting sea-drift for a few moments.

'Let's open this other bottle,' she said.

His glass recharged, Dougie ventured a question. 'What did ye mean that time aboot work?'

'What time?'

'When we focht — had a fight — ootside the hotel? D'ye mind?'

'Oh I don't know,' she laughed. 'I just had this notion that life here might be idyllic. Stupid idea, a dream, but I thought that people would have some kind of communal spirit, working for each other, not for wage packets.'

'Kind o idealistic, would ye say?'

'Very.'

'There's some sense in it, though,' he mused. 'There's a lot o things that could be done here wi some imagination and some determination. I've thocht that.'

'Here's to us,' she cried, raising her glass and slopping some wine onto the couch. 'Damn the uranium miners.'

'Here's to us,' he echoed. 'No bad stuff, that wine.'

They drank some more.

'I'm glad ye came here, whatever,' he said tenderly.

She leaned against him and snuggled into his oxter, and he felt at peace. Then he put down his glass and cupping her chin in his hand he kissed her.

'Aye, I'm glad ye came,' he whispered.

'Don't speak.'

And they said little, until the sky began to grow pale in the east and the fire had long since turned to grey ashes. Then, with the oyster catchers strutting and piping in the new day, he remembered he had a home to go to.

CHAPTER NINE

Dougie lived in a dwaum of love for all that day. His feet took him around the croft but his mind was fixed on Alison's face and lips. The cow, when he milked her sleepily, stared at him with eyes like brown saucers and he did not swear when she scutched him with her sharny tail. Bess lay in the grass and watched him warily. The yowes glanced in alarm when he leaned over the fence and cried, 'How are ye all the day, my bonnie craiturs'. His mother just thought he had taken one of his stoons and paid him no heed.

He sought out a little anthology of poetry and looked up all the love poems, from King James I onwards:

Gif ye a goddess be, and that ye lik
To do me pain, I may it naught astert;

he agreed with William Dunbar:

Sweet rose of virtue and of gentleness,
Delightsome lily of every lustiness,

thought that Alexander Scott had something:

There is no man, I say that can
Both love and to be wise;

and:

Whattan ane glaikit fool am I
To slay myself with melancholy;

sighed over the anonymous:

O gin my love were yon red rose,
That grows upon the castle wa'
And I mysell a drap of dew,
Into her bonny breast to fa'!

He stuck out his tongue at Andrew Lang:
 Oh, happier he who gains not
 The love some seem to gain.

He climbed the hill and looked out over the land and stared for ages at the distant roof of Shore Cottage.

— Is she sleeping? Her een closed, dreaming o me? Her hands folded across her breists? Her knees drawn up, like a bairnie in a wame? Her sumptuous hurdies and her cream-white thighs? Is she dreaming o me?

— How did ye do your courting, faither? Somehow the thocht o ye...Did ye take your boots off, and your drawers that ye used to change once a fortnicht? Were ye ever slim? Was my mither ever young? Did ye long to see her and take her in your arms and kiss her? Was I begotten in a nicht o steamy passion, the caff-seck rustling and snug? Damn ye, faither, ye've been through it all, long before me. Were ye aye dour?

— I canna understand ye, mither. Ye shuffle aboot the place, sometimes like ye were dottled, sometimes like an ambling fount o wisdom. I sleep, but my heart waketh. Is that yourself? How can ye keep all that poetry in ye? Would I have signed that paper and gien away the croft if ye hadna stormed into the close. 'I would sign naething. Whatever they want, they can ask.' Ye love this place as much as I do myself. It's in your blood, the very stoor o the place thumps in your veins and birls in your brain. Ye've seen it all, every last etchal that can happen to a person. If only ye would tell me...but I'm condemned to live in ignorance and feel my way like a mole, grubbing in the netherways o the world.

So taken up, he was moved to try his own poetry again and dug out the jotter where he had written years before. With a pencil, he scribbled 'Ane litanie anent the pouer o atoms' but could think of nothing more to put down.

He went back to Alison. She was making pots and clarted with clay, but she greeted him and they drank coffee together. His tongue could not find the power to speak and his thoughts rattled in his head.

She offered to help bring in the hay and laughed at his

half-hearted warnings about the weight of bales and thistle purrs. For two days, she lifted and heaved with him until the gilt was complete and sat foursquare in the yard. He was surprised by her strength and amused by the childlike enthusiasm of the city-born. She sweated until her shirt was stained by dark circles and her hair stuck to her brow, and he had to tell her to take it easy. Donald's Jamie came up on his bicycle and blethered; when he left, Dougie told funny stories about him and made her laugh. His mother seemed to like her and they took their half-yokings in the house in a snowfall of scones, bannocks and butter.

He was the feudal baron, lording it over his patrimony, surveying his estate from the high east tower (the top of the hay gilt), dispensing justice to his serfs ('That's too heavy for ye!'), defending his women from marauding reivers ('Here's Jamie again!'), the leader of his clan, judge and decision-maker ('That'll do for now — it's time for our tea.'), the driver of evil spirits and the healer of the sick ('Damn thistles!'), master of the earth and gleaner of its fruits ('Fancy a can o lager?').

And the sun shone and beat upon the ground.

— Green. The colour o life. Every leaf, every blade, every stalk. Hotching wi sap and peedie chloroplasts, aa sooking in water and air and belching oot carbohydrates — sweet sugar o life, gallons and gallons o it, appearing in every park, heather buss, shrub, tree, ditch, strang, puddle and garden. Food for ilka manner o creeping thing — worm, klock, flech, bluebottle, dragonfly, shonnag, shitey-flee. For the whaup on the brae, the hare and the fox on the hill, the grilse in the burn, the sellag and the whale in the sea. All this was his to protect. He was the steward of the whole stramash and resolved to defend it.

But he felt less sure when letters from foes and allies began to appear in the papers, and he was suddenly reminded of the fragile hold he had on his acres.

One read: Redriver might well help in tidying up the environment. Their assistance could be enlisted to remove the hulks of rusting cars which scar our fine landscape and which deter tourists.

Another: How long is this tedious committee going to delay the prosperity of their fellow citizens?

And again: Redriver should be asked to give a firm undertaking on how many unemployed men are suitable for their requirements, and how long the employment is likely to last.

More: The disincentives for the scheme are the adverse effects on amenity, notably visual and the noise pollution likely to result.

But: The possibility of a large industrial development is a matter of the gravest concern. The importance of fostering employment is fully appreciated but the price here would be altogether more than we could bear.

And: Uranium mining is an unacceptable threat to the environment. Caithness people should be prepared to go to jail to defend their county.

Murdoch Ure took his duty on the committee seriously and came to visit Dougie one evening. A farmer with several hundred acres of hill ground to his name, he was a gaunt, tall man who habitually wore plus fours and a tweed jacket. He said that the committee was too slow for the Americans' liking and they were threatening to pull out altogether unless a decision was reached soon. Most folk seemed to be for it but the few against the scheme were making more noise than their numbers warranted, and were trying to open a proper public inquiry which would take months. Dougie commiserated with Murdoch, because he seemed so bowed under the pressures of office, but was secretly glad. A number of other crofters and farmers had been approached about tests on their ground but no more had signed anything, said Murdoch with a hint in his voice that they were following Dougie's lead.

The crofter relayed it all to Alison later that same night when he took her home, and they danced a makeshift jig beside the potter's wheel.

'Ye're doon a heap at the shore these days,' said Donald's Jamie. 'Or should I say nichts?'

They had met outside the post office, where Dougie had headed to collect his mother's pension.

'Tak it canny, boy,' whispered Donald's Jamie. 'No every chiel in this place is on your side.' Then he chuckled and added, 'I would take a few precautions, that's all.'

'I'm doing nothing that's any chiel's business except my own,' protested Dougie.

'Have ye thocht o a bike?'

Dougie thought this daft and said so, but Donald's Jamie just laughed at him.

Inside the post office, he met Jean, buxom among the postal orders and the stamps. She let her eye rove all over him when he set the little bell above the door tinkling, and kept a steady frown as she counted out the banknotes of his mother's pension. Then the coins rattled on the plastic countertop.

'Ye're keeping well?' she said.

'Aye.'

'Is that all ye want?'

The post office doubled as a shop.

'I've messages,' he said, taking a paper from his pocket on which his mother had listed provisions. 'Matches, strawberry jam, Orkney biscuits, cough pastilles, a pair o broon laces, baking soda, a sixty-watt bulb and a packet o fags.'

The plunder grew on the counter and was transferred in silence to a leather message-bag. Then he noticed the bright boxes near the door. 'I'll take a box o chocolates, too,' he said.

Jean's mind filed this departure from custom. 'Oh aye,' she said.

He met Peggy Gunn in the street.

'I havena seen ye for a whilie,' she said. 'Have ye thrown in your lot wi incomers?'

He met Mr Bremner, the minister, who enquired after his mother's health.

'Fine,' said the crofter.

'She's a hardy soul,' observed the man in black. 'Be a good son to her. Render unto Caesar that which is Caesar's.' And he passed on.

He met Mairi, Alistair the teacher's wife.

'How's Alison?' she asked brightly.

'Eh? Oh, she's fine,' he stammered, 'last time I saw her.' And with a smile, Mairi passed on.

He met Jim Sinclair who did not refer to anything.

He met Davie Sutherland who said they had received a letter from Rob and Tammy in America. 'They're all fine,' concluded Davie.

'Tell him I was asking for him,' said Dougie.

'Aye, I will. I hear that ye're courting strong.'

'Who told ye that?'

'I canna mind,' lied Davie. 'It's no afore time, a young chiel like ye.'

And he passed on.

— It's hard in Caithness to go where no chiel kens ye. Een watching ye fae every corner, fae every bush and dyke. I wonder how many pairs o binoculars swivel on Shore Cottage to see if the van's ootside. Telescopes o the astronomers o clash. Jean's face was as plain as a headline when I bocht the chocolates. I'd better warn Alison. But she probably wouldna care. Neither do I, tae hell wi them. That auld gowk, Donald's Jamie, saying I should take to the bike and hide it in the bent...ye're as bad. 'There's no muckle doing the nicht, Kathie. Is that handlebars I see abeen the brae?' Jean and Peggy Gunn in the post office, muckle paps meeting across the counter. 'He's bocht her chocolates. There's no other body they're for but her.' 'He'll get a fricht when she starts getting sick in the mornings. Ye can only play that game so long.' I wish I could take ye away somewhere, Alison. I wonder what they say aboot ye. 'It's her that's putting him up to it. No selling the land — does he think he's a laird?'

Guilt, shame and defiance hung about Dougie like a cloud and followed him to the town. Even in the library, when he changed his books, he read the assistant's look as one of disapproval.

— But how could she know?

Another week or two went by. The committee continued to meet and the news spread that they would come to a decision in favour of the mining project. There were more letters in the papers and, once, the whole affair was mentioned on the national news. No one came from either the local authorities or Redriver to visit Dougie again.

One day, when he happened to be passing the railway station in town, he was stopped by a group of young folk who asked him where the village was.

'I live there myself,' said Dougie.

'Do you?' said the man who had done the asking. He was dressed in a khaki anorak with 'U.S. ARMY' sewn above the pocket and wore on his head a striped ski-hat. 'We want to camp there.'

'Ye can camp there alricht.'

'Great,' came the reply. 'Is it far?'

Dougie explained how they could catch a bus and apologised for not being able to give them a lift as the van was full, what with his mother and some sacks of poultry feed.

'They haven't started yet, have they?' asked another young chap, his face blotched with pimples.

'What?' said Dougie.

'Mining,' explained a girl in a gleaming yellow anorak. 'Uranium mining. We've come to help the people defend themselves.'

Like a roving tribe of neolithic hunters, they came and pitched their tents near the shore along the sand dunes, and alarmed tourists by staking their territory with banners on poles. Some read BANISH, some had cryptic signs that the villagers did not understand. Folk had seen nothing like this in the place before.

'Where are they fae?'

'The south. All parts o the south. Some o them have English tongues. One is Irish, they say.'

'Have they no work to do at home?'

'Lord kens. Damn crowd o students, I think. They'll neither work nor want.'

'Their folk are worse than they are.'

'Just say it.'

'How old are they?'

'I'll swear there's hardly a one ower twenty.'

'Where are they getting money fae?'

'Ye and me, where else? The government's paying for craiturs like that no to work. That's where your taxes and mine are going.'

'Ach, they'll no be here long. The wind'll shift them.'

Not everyone looked with scorn and suspicion at the newcomers. Jean's till clattered with joy all day and gathered a rich harvest into its metallic innards. Schoolbairns spent the last days of their summer holidays in and around the braes and found new sources of entertainment.

Alison took Dougie along to the camp one evening. He was reluctant but curious, and ended up enjoying himself. Alison seemed particularly carefree as they went from the cottage to the tents; perhaps this is the kind of company she's used to, he thought, and he felt pangs of jealousy like notes being plucked on some deep, inner cord.

The campers had built a fire from driftwood and they sat around it in the darkening, some with blankets around their shoulders to keep out the chill, others in thick anoraks and jerkins, both men and women. It looked like a guerrilla camp on the edge of some fearful war. But they were a jolly crowd and welcomed the visitors. When Alison explained who Dougie was, they turned to him as if to a martyr and a hero. He felt embarrassed, especially when a girl with long blonde hair embraced him and told him not to worry. What did these people know?

Another chiel took a guitar and sang, after mentioning that he had written the words himself. The others joined in the chorus.

Ye cooncillors by name, lend an ear, lend an ear,
Ye cooncillors by name, listen here;
Ye cooncillors by name, oh ye are aa the same.
We wish ye wid bide hame and no come here.

We gied ye aa oor votes, in guid faith, in guid faith,
We gied ye aa oor votes, in guid faith;
We gied ye aa oor votes, we didna think ye's goats,
But noo ye're aa turncoats, we've nae faith.

Ye're weel in wi the Yanks, d'ye hear, d'ye hear?
Ye're weel in wi the Yanks; up tae here;
But we dinna want their cash, or their radioactive
trash,
And if ye'd sense, ye'd wish they were no here.

We'll fecht tae keep oor land, lend an ear, lend an
ear,
We'll fecht tae keep oor land, hae nae fear.
We'll stand up tae the Yanks, and aa the southron
banks;
We ken aa their pranks. They've bocht ower dear.

Cans of beer appeared, and they drank and chatted and sang more songs, until a mellowness crept over Dougie

and he felt at home among these youngsters. Shither wi
the richt ideas, he thought to himself. In the dancing
firelight, Alison's face appeared warm , orange and invit-
ing. Her eyes sparkled as she sang and he put his arm
around her and belted out the verses when he knew them.
Some of the campers asked him questions about his croft
and seemed to listen in awe to what he had to say. Beer,
a bonny lowe, singing — he sensed something primeval
and satisfying and he abandoned himself wholly to it.

The next morning, his throat was dry and sore and he
could feel a cold coming on. The first cigarette with the
breakfast tea set him a-coughing.

'Have ye catched the cold?' asked his mother.

'No,' he grunted.

'Oot at nicht withoot a jacket,' went on Jessie. 'Oot to
all hours. Where was ye last nicht?'

'I gied doon to see the campers.' The tea was soothing
on the thrapple.

'That crowd at the sands? Donald's Jamie was saying
they're like a mob o tinklers. Men wi hair doon to here.'

'They're no tinklers. They're students mostly. On their
holidays.'

'Well, I dinna ken,' mused Jessie.

'A fine crowd,' went on Dougie.

'Was Alison doon wi ye?'

'Aye. She was there.'

'Likely she kens some o them.'

'No, she doesna ken them anymore than I do,' said
Dougie angrily.

'Ohh.' His mother nodded her head and gazed through
the window.

No one knew exactly how many had come to camp near
the beach. Some said a dozen, some thirty, some forgot
numbers altogether and spoke about brigades and regi-
ments. Most of the time there were probably no more

than twenty, Dougie knew, but every day a few left and others came.

The singer and the girl with blonde hair walked around by the fields and visited him. They came from Glasgow, they said, and were both students, he of biology and she of politics, and they were concerned with what was happening in Scotland. Dougie listened to them and answered their queries about the croft.

'Ye were born here?' said the girl, whose name was Elaine.

Dougie nodded.

'Great. I wish I had been born here. My dad was a miner, but I think my great-grandfather came frae Skye. It's bonny here, is it no, Ian?'

Ian stroked his beard and nodded sagely. 'Worth fighting for. We've got to protect our environment. We depend on the food web for our survival and the world around us, intact, for our sanity. It's no just our feathered friends we're fighting for. They have their place in a whole. It's that whole and the right to decide the course of our own lives as part of the pattern.' And he grinned, a bit sheepishly, at his attempt to put such important convictions into words.

Dougie decided that to remain silent would be the wiser course. Some feelings should not be betrayed by words. He rather liked the role in which they had cast him, and this was no time for questions. Besides, talking too much hurt his throat.

He offered them tea and they accepted, taking their places in the kitchen with beaming faces. Elaine talked loudly and slowly to Jessie, who was not a bit deaf but who was too polite to point this out to her visitors. Dougie took in with some amusement the wry glances his mother cast at Ian, who was dressed in a tattered pair of dungarees and a jersey with holes at the elbows.

'If they're students and fae the toon,' she said later, 'ye'd think they would be ashamed to gang aboot like yon. Anyway, I gave some eggs. She was a poor, thin-like craitur. No enough clothes on her, summer though it be.'

Chapter Ten

That same afternoon, the postman brought a letter from Rob in California.

'Dear Dougie,' it began, 'How are you getting on these days? Tammy sends her love. Likely you know that we have a son now — Robbie Junior. I think he has a good look of a chuchter about him but of course no one understands that here. I heard from the old couple about this uranium business and how you refused to give up your land. Hang in there and keep the old spread together. The thought of a mine in the parks where we roved after shochads' eggs — do you mind the night we took Sannag's cart? — fills me with horror. I hope you don't sell or let them push you into it. If ever you have the time, drop us a line. I don't know when we'll get back to Scotland next but if ever you feel like crossing the pond there's a bed for you in California. Aye the best, Rob.'

— Aye, Rob, it was good o ye to write. But it's easy for ye, sitting on your patio in California below your palm trees, to offer encouragement. What would ye say if ye were here, in the face o it? Still, we're thinking the same way, though maybe no for the same reasons. If it's your granny's hieland hame ye're fashed aboot, it'll be safe in my hands. It would be grand though if ye came home and stood up and said what ye've just written.

Some did begin to stand up — and march. To the amazement of ordinary, gaun-aboot citizens, a demonstration filled the streets of the town on the afternoon when the council met to decide what to do to keep Redriver keen. There were women wi bairns in prams, loons and lassies trowing fae the school, a puckle o teachers and retired men o worth, and in the van the campers. There were placards that read 'No uranium', 'Only one earth', 'Go home Redriver', 'Banish uranium mining', 'Radioactivity kills', and other sic-like epithets, calculated to sway the minds of the populace.

Such a curriewumple had never been experienced before in the town, John Campbell told Dougie. The bobbies had been scutching back and fore, like to shite themselves, and the traffic had been held up for an hour, and horns were blaring, and folk were shouting and shaking their fists.

'The maist o them werena local shither at all,' said John, 'but a crowd o incomers. They were handing oot leaflets. One gied up to Peggy Gunn but she wouldna take the paper. 'We're all fellow workers,' says this chiel, a waadrap o a student, 'Unite against the forces o capitalism.' 'Get oot o here,' says Peggy, mad. 'Ye've never done a day's work in your life.' And then some o them gied for coffee but nobody would serve them. A fecht broke oot. The bobbies lifted one chiel.'

Dougie was horrified by this. He went to Alison and tried to express his concern but she shrugged and said that the people were standing up for their rights.

'It'll do no good at all,' he moaned. 'I canna see it stopping them mining.'

'It might help,' she insisted. 'It'll let the authorities know that we feel so strongly about the affair that we're prepared to challenge them.'

'Ye werena there?' he asked in dismay.

'Of course I was,' she replied. 'You should have marched too. You've more to lose than most.'

He waved his hands in meaningless circles. 'Ye dinna understand. I couldna do a thing like that. I belong here. I would lose every last bit o sympathy. It's no our way.'

But he saw that his case was hopeless, and lapsed into a dark silence. Alison pumped strongly at the wheel and drew a pot from the spinning lump of clay.

The next thing that happened was that the local garage-owners refused to sell petrol to those whom they suspected of having come north to cause trouble. Young lads with energy but no work began to haunt the fringes of the camp at the beach, looking for an excuse for a fight. The campers let it be known that they were ready, but the police turned up in two patrol cars and everybody sat glowering at each other. Ever ready, Pogo the tink arrived with a hastily repaired set of bagpipes and entertained the watchers. As he knew only three tunes, he did not collect much for his efforts but the campers welcomed him to their fireside and plied him with drink and drugs, folk said, until he did not know daylight from darkness.

Many of the campers left, Ian and Elaine among them, until only four hardy souls remained. They had transport of their own and were not worried about being stranded. Gradually folk lost interest in them and the bobbies drove back to the town.

All four were in the hotel bar one day when Dougie went in. Throughout the fuss Tom Manson and Jean had supplied food and drink as long as the campers had had siller to pay. 'Ye canna let folk starve,' Jean had said.

Dougie was still in a disgruntled mood. The future seemed nothing but a great, shimmering question mark, and he stravaiged about in a dwaum of uncertainty. He was angry at Alison and at himself.

— She's shown me up. I was too scared to take part in a demonstration. I wish the whole damn business would end. Take the bloody land. Take every last blade o grass, for all I care, only get it ower wi. If ye want it, ye'll take it, so why wait for me to sign a bittie o paper. I'm no a lawyer, or a radical, or a fechter. Soon the whole village'll be against me. They're saying already that it's all my own fault. They'll be calling me a warlock next. If milk goes sour, or blue mould grows on cheese, or a bairn catches measles, or a coo comes a-bulling, or a car battery goes flat, they'll blame me. No like his faither, they'll say. Must be an awful trial and worry to his mither, they'll say.

So, in the bar, he asked Margaret for a pint of heavy and did not look at the four campers in the corner.

'Fine day again,' said Margaret.

'Aye,' he said in a flat voice. 'Gies a packet o fags, too.'

The door opened and the owlish form of Jim Sinclair came in.

'Aye, aye the noo,' he said. 'A half-pint o lager, Margaret, when ye're ready. What's doing wi ye, Dougie?'

'Damn all,' grunted the crofter.

The joiner looked at the campers but said nothing. He took a mouthful of lager and began to clean his pipe.

One of the four in the corner, a bearded chiel of medium height, came up to the counter and asked for a packet of crisps. He turned to Dougie.

'Have you heard anything yet?' he asked in a soft, friendly voice.

'Heard what?'

'Redriver. You know, we're very proud of you. And we just want you to know that.'

Dougie girned inwardly and stared straight at the well-wisher. The face was young and pink above the shaggy fuzz on the chin, the eyes wide and blue.

— He's only a bairn. A grand loon, most likely. I enjoyed that night around the campfire. But...

'For God's sake, go,' said Dougie softly, and he saw the blue eyes widen and blink. 'Go home. Pack your bags and go home. Ye've done all ye can and I'm grateful. But this nonsense has gone on long enough. So, take your tent and your belongings and go. Leave us to sort oot our own affairs.'

'I didn't mean...' began the young man.

The other three were sitting up, their mouths open.

'I ken, I ken,' went on Dougie. 'Ye didna mean any hairm. Maybe ye did some good. And I'm sorry but... please go.'

Margaret put the bag of crisps on the counter and stared at the crofter.

'Aye,' muttered the young man. 'I think I understand.'

— Do ye?

'We were thinking about leaving. Term starts soon. But we'll be watching out for news. It's our land too.'

The four shambled slowly from the bar, murmuring quiet cheerios to Jim Sinclair and Margaret. When the door had closed behind them, Margaret took a cloth and began to mop up spilled beer from the counter. She polished around the ashtrays.

'Well, it's no afore time some chiel said that,' observed Jim Sinclair.

'No, maybe no,' muttered Dougie.

'They were no a bad crowd,' said Margaret. 'Just the ringleaders that caused the bother. We had no trouble wi them in here.'

Larksong — distant and faint. Dougie's boots made tiny thuds as he walked out from the hotel. His mind was cobwebbed with strings of thought — words, phrases, ideas, feelings, a labyrinth heading him now in one direction, now another, doubling back on itself and branching off to nowhere.

— Like being drunk. Alcohol's no the only thing that can make ye lose your wits. My feet are moving by themselves. Direction-finders in my toes. A horse coming home by itself — or a chicken without a head rushing in circles. No guiding principle. It's a lovely day. Bricht — warm. The barley is starting to turn. I dinna ken...I'm just here and the world is whirling aboot me. First one thing happens. I do nothing. Then another thing — still I do nothing. But it seems as if I've acted, as if I've worked oot my destiny, withoot moving a finger, withoot opening my mouth, withoot even kenning what I've done. Ye called me a professor once, Jonah. I was proud o that. I had become a sage, a learned man — but I was nothing o the sort, just a gowk who didna ken a thing he was doing. Is

this how heroes are made? Just being in the richt place at
the richt time. Why should I care aboot a few acres o
ground? Or uranium? Or pollution? We all have to die
sometime, but we act as if we're going to live for ever.
I've nothing coming after me. No bairns, no seed. Ye had
me, faither. I could understand ye saying 'Stop — this'll
no do — this winna be'. But ye wouldna have understood
either. Ye would have sold oot like Will Auld. Aye, like ye,
Will, wi your dreams o a council hoose, but ye'll no get
your loot either, if I dinna agree to sell mine. We'll rise
together, and we'll go doon as one. That's what's called
community.

A distant rumbling penetrated his thoughts and brought
his eyes to the road. There, coming towards him, still small
but rapidly growing nearer and bigger, was a leviathan of
a lorry. Its exhaust pipes curled up behind the cab like
the horns on a bull, snorting clouds of stinking diesel
fumes into the air, as it snarled along.

He watched it pass. Four wheels, six, eight...then, a
bobby on a motorbike, the headlamp a brilliant eye, used
the width of the hotel carpark to overtake the monster
and slip into place before it, like a remora before a shark.

The ground rumbled under Dougie's feet. A loose
window pane in the hotel tinkled gently.

But his attention was held by the load the lorry was
carrying. It was a great yellow tractor — only it wasn't a
tractor, not just a tractor. From the front, two huge arms
sprouted to grip a giant hod — for lifting earth, he
surmised — and on its back an intricate gallimaufry of
pipes, levers and nozzles stuck up into the sky. On each
side were pillars with broad plates of iron...

— A digger! It canna be. They canna start yet...

He decided to follow the metallic moby dick and made
for his van. As he opened the door and slipped into the
driver's seat, a police car, the purple light revolving
officiously on its roof, slid past. He started the engine and
cursed the clutch for not engaging more smoothly. But
now he was mobile, his eyes fixed on the convoy and
grimly determined.

The object of his pursuit passed through the village. Betty the nurse, coming in the opposite direction in her car, was waved to one side and left to gape. Bairns and dogs stared.

Dougie kept asking himself where it could be going. His worst suspicions were confirmed when they neared the side road that led up to Will Auld's croft. The convoy slowed. Brake lights came on. The police car edged up onto the grass verge and doors opened. Dougie slowed. One of the bobbies saw him and signalled to him to stop. He wound down the window and heard the crack of police boot-leather on the tarmac.

'Ye canna get past just now,' said the bobby, leaning on the van window and having a good glower at the interior while he was at it.

'Will ye be long?' asked Dougie.

'He's going to turn up the road there. The gate's no very wide.'

'Is it the Forestry Commission?' asked Dougie innocent-ly.

'No, man,' said the bobby. 'What would they be doing wi a thing like that?'

'Och aye,' agreed Dougie. He paused before speaking again. 'What is it for then?'

'It's a drill.' The bobby was unable to resist showing off. 'It can go doon six hundred feet in half an hour.'

'Never?'

'I'm telling ye.' Then he went off about his business. Another car beyond the lorry hooted impatiently, and the leather boots marched into action.

— The sneaky buggers. Will, ye're no canny. The committee hasna reported yet but they're moving in to be ready. It must have cost a fine penny to take that monstrosity all the way up here. And there ye are your-self...

And there was Will Auld, standing at the end of his road with his bike. The lone crofter, the downtrodden salt of the earth, with a grin like you'd think he'd won the football pools, and holes in his gansey the width of his face. He was gesticulating to the driver of the lorry, who was attempting to turn his charge into the road.

— I canna let him see me here.

Dougie angrily rammed the van into reverse gear and began a three-point turn.

CHAPTER ELEVEN

Four days later. Four days that saw Dougie moving about his business and the village with a tight-lipped, set expression, saying little, keeping himself to himself.

'Ye're awful quiet,' said Margaret, pulling him a pint of heavy.

Dougie shrugged.

'Is your mother fine?' There was a note of concern in the voice.

'Aye.'

'What are ye in a stoon for, then? God kens but I see enough long faces aboot here already.'

'Ach, it's this uranium business. I'm fed up wi it.'

Margaret leaned on the bar, claiming a substantial part of its area for her elbows. 'We're all sick to death o that.'

'Aha! But have ye heard the latest?' John Campbell piped up. 'Will Auld had a digger in. Redriver sent it up to make some preliminary trials, while the committee was considering its verdict, ye ken. There's a rumour that it was Will's idea, so that he could get some o the green chiels anyway, but I dinna ken if that's true or no.'

Dougie set his lips and studied the little whorls of froth on his pint.

'I saw the digger going by,' said Jim Sinclair. 'It's still up at Will's.'

'Aye, and it'll be there for a while yet,' laughed John.

Jim Sinclair's eyes narrowed, as he waited.

'What happened?' asked Dougie.

'They had a devil o a job getting it into one o Will's

parks. They had to knock oot two strainers and roll back the fence...'

'He'll be after compensation for that,' grinned Dougie suddenly.

'But that's no the main thing,' went on John, his round cheeks like to burst with the treasures he was about to impart. 'When they came back the following day to start the digger, ye'll never guess what happened.' He paused for effect and smirked teasingly at his listeners. 'They got the digger doon off the lorry and got it across the grass to the first spot. And it birled away for a whilie but then it stopped and they couldna get it started again.'

'It broke doon,' said Jim Sinclair.

John got down off his stool and began to act out his story. 'They reeted and guttered in the engine.' He bent and twiddled his fingers as if he, too, was delving into the guts of a motor. 'They checked the diesel in the tank.' He unscrewed an imaginary tank cap and peered into its dark, invisible depths. 'Full. It's no that. They looked at the ignition. It wasna that. The thing was in perfect working order. But it just wouldna start. They scratched their heads, had a fag, pulled at some wires and pipes, had anither fag. Nothing doing...'

Dougie drank his beer with great concentration.

'Will was fair popped,' laughed John, even trying to imitate the old man. 'He started offering advice. Check the oil, boys, try the starter, maybe she's just cold.' But he kent nothing. Then...' John held up his finger '...one o them noticed something. Wi all their glowering and peering it was a wonder they hadna seen it before. But there it was. In the grease around the diesel tank, what d'ye think they found? Sand! Specks o sand. Some bugger had put sand in the tank.'

'Good heavens,' said Jim Sinclair. 'No wonder it stopped.'

'Is it bad for engines?' asked Margaret.

John Campbell suddenly assumed the mien of a Free Presbyterian minister hearing an elder swear. 'Bad? The engine will have to be stripped and cleaned completely.

The filters are all clogged, the pumps blocked. And they had it running for a whilie. Every piston and bearing'll be scored.'

'Where did ye hear all this?' asked Dougie.

'One o the mechanics is staying in Thurso. I was yarning wi him in the pub.'

'Well, well,' said Margaret, signalling an end to the suspense by gathering empty glasses into the sink under the bar.

'So there'll be no drilling for a while,' said Jim Sinclair.

'That'll please some folk,' said Margaret.

'Nobody kens who did it,' said John. 'The bobbies were oot. They had a tracker dog wi them, but he was more interested in Will's auld bitch.'

'Was it some o the demonstrators, d'ye think?'

'That's what the bobbies think anyway. But if it was them, they've cleared off.' At this point, the mechanic's love of sweetly turning gears reasserted itself and John shook his head. 'Putting sand in an engine. A hell o a thing to do.'

Dougie finished his pint. 'Well, I must away,' he announced. 'I must shift some sheep.'

He sighed with relief when he found himself alone in the carpark. No more drilling. He smiled and found himself wanting to share this little victory, and set off down the road towards the sea and Shore Cottage.

He had not gone far when a car slowed and drew up beside him.

'Dougie!'

Magnus Gunn was winding down the window, peching with the effort of leaning across the empty passenger seat.

'Dougie, have ye heard?'

'Heard what?' Dougie felt his face redden and hoped that Magnus would not notice.

'They've pulled oot. The Yanks. Redriver. They've said that they've no more time to wait for a decision up here and they've withdrawn their scheme.'

Dougie stood and stared at the moustached face.

'Are ye alricht?' the face asked.

'Aye, aye. Ye mean that they dinna want the land anymore?'

'That's what it means,' said Magnus.

The larksong suddenly seemed to grow louder and a smile appeared on the crofter's face. Magnus noted it grimly.

'Aye,' he said slowly. 'Ye've won this time. But there'll be anither day. The stuff's still there. And they'll come back.'

'I heard that somebody interfered wi the machine they took up to Will Auld's,' said Dougie.

'Them bloody demonstrators fae the sooth,' exploded Magnus. He let in the clutch and drove off with a roar.

Dougie stuck his hands deep into the pockets of his dungarees and straightened his back, turned his face up to the sky and whirled in a circle on the road, like a bairn lost in his own magic. As his fingers felt the rough texture and the angular fragments of shell, grit and sea-sand still lurking in the folds of the denim, his smile grew wider and wider until he began to laugh. And he started to run.

There was the pier, and the benty hills and, beyond them, the roof of Shore Cottage. He ran up the path, kicking the sand in joyful clouds, like the boy who had taken Sannag's cart one dark night years before; and as he went he gathered within himself the force for a great yell. He opened his mouth and flung back his head and shouted 'Alison!', and the breeze picked up the triumphant shout and carried it to the corners of the nation.

GLOSSARY

aime	heat haze
ain	one, a woman
aise	ashes
aisehole	ashpit
barm	to talk nonsense
beise	cattle
bent	marram grass
bick	bitch
birl	to rotate rapidly
blackjock	blackbird
boags	scrotum
bo'man	a supernatural being
bool	boulder
broo	forehead, also unemployment exchange
caff-seck	traditional mattress, stuffed with chaff
chap	to knock
chiel	man
chuchter	yokel
cown	to weep
curriewumple	melee
daud	dollop
deugend	stubborn
didoes	antics
doadles	testicles
dwannie	delicate
efterwal	aftermath
eisewaas	eaves
etchal	iota
fae	from
fann	snowdrift
fleag	housefly
flech	flea
flipe	a limp slice of material
fowggy	dry and crumbly
fusim	dirty
gilt	hayrick
glumph	to bolt food
gromish	to rub vigorously
gyangs	sheep shears
gykes	weeds
half-yoking	mid-morning or mid-afternoon break
heid-bummer	chief
hirple	to limp
hullup	to limp or to walk with a rolling motion
hurl	to run about in a vehicle
klock	beetle

laim	earthernware
laiteran	pulpit
langersome	lonely
leean	mendacious
linie	shopping list
liv	palm of the hand
loon	boy
lowe	flame
lurk	fold in cloth
maa	seagull
maitter	mucus
marackless	untidy
meint	remembered
moosag	a small mouse
nether	adder
partan	crab
peedie	small
pelly	covered in pellets of hard dung
preeg	to plead
purr	thorn, to prick
rive	to pull with force
scroo	cornstack
sellag	fingerling of the coalfish
shither	people
shitey-flea	a fly that frequents cowpats
shochad	lapwing
shonnag	ant
skint	a drop of liquid
skittering	army cattle
skook	to lurk
sneck	door latch
soarn	to search
sooked fish	sun-dried fish
stab	fencepost
strainer	large fencepost
strang	the drainage channel in a byre
swacken	to make supple
tant	hard, severe
traipse	to walk heavily
trock	rubbish
trosk	fool
trow	to play truant
tursh	bundle, wisp
tuskar	peat spade
waadrap	a worthless fellow
wice	wise, sensible